TAKE
A BOOK FOR
MURDER

MILLIE MACK

ISBN: 978-1-7346234-4-4
Library of Congress Control Number: 2024915521

Publisher: Dark and Stormy Night Mysteries
Darkandstormynightmysteries.com

Other Books in the Faraday Murder Series

Take a Dive for Murder

Take Stock in Murder

Take a Byte Out of Murder

Take the Spirit of Murder

DEDICATION

I dedicate this book to the loyal readers of the
Faraday Murder Series.

ACKNOWLEDGMENT

Thank you to members of my critique group, Eileen and Janis, for their unique abilities of honesty and wisdom in helping make the book a better tale of murder. And a special thank you to Janis for her legal advice.

My grateful appreciation goes to Mark, a fellow author and friend, for proofreading the final manuscript. His eagle eyes catch what I miss, and then he offers sound advice for plot enhancements.

A big thank you to Beth Martin (Beth Martin Books), who provided all the skills necessary to format this book for publication.

1

"Congratulations, Carrie, I'm so proud of you," Charles said as he brushed her curly brown hair aside and kissed his wife. "Are you excited about your first book signing?"

"I bet you never thought I would finish my mystery," Carrie responded.

"Not true. I've always had complete faith in you," Charles said. "I knew all the real murder cases we solved kept you from finishing your fictional book."

Charles referred to the several cases they helped solve, starting with the murder of his brother and their most recent adventure that involved ghostly sightings and murder at Milford Manor. Charles held the car door for Carrie.

"Weren't you going to sell copies of your book at the event?" Charles asked as he looked at the empty cargo area of their SUV.

"I asked Marge and Madge from the Tri-County bookstore to handle the sales. This way, they get credit for the purchases, and I don't have to cart boxes of books to the party."

"Then off we go to your signing," Charles said. "May it be the first of many."

The hosts for the party, Joanne and Dan Quinn, lived a few blocks away. It was only minutes before Charles parked their car in the circular driveway and rang the doorbell.

"Well, here are my famous friends," Joanne Quinn said as she opened the front door.

Joanne and Carrie had known each other in high school, and when Carrie moved back to Tri-City, they renewed their friendship. The two were the perfect example of how opposites could be friends. Joanne was outgoing, an active member of the country club set, and stylish in manner and dress. Carrie was reserved, avoided social events, and constantly worried about wearing the right outfit.

"You must have a tiny circle of friends if you're classifying us as famous," Carrie laughed.

"You are famous. Many people talk about writing a book, but you're the first person I know who did it." Then Joanne looked at Charles. "Not to mention all the real-life murders you've solved." Joanne stepped back from the door. "Come in, come in. Some of your guests are already here."

"Thank heaven. I can breathe a sigh of relief," Carrie said. "Part of me worried that no one would show up."

"Sounds like my friend is suffering from a case of nerves," Joanne said. "Everyone I've talked to can't wait to read your book, especially the ladies from the country club." Joanne lowered her voice, "Most want a copy of your book to ensure they don't appear as one of the characters."

Joanne had no sooner mentioned the ladies of the Tri-County Country Club when Marilyn Armstrong rushed over to Carrie. Marilyn was tall, had perfect salon blonde hair, and dressed in the latest fashions. She was also the president of the ladies' guild for the country club.

Marilyn said, "Carrie, I'm so excited for you. And, of course, you're forgiven."

Carrie wondered why she needed forgiveness.

"This explains why you missed several club meetings," Marilyn said, holding up her mystery. "You were completing this wonderful book. I can't wait to read it. Well done, my dear."

"That's very kind. Thank you, Marilyn," Carrie said.

"When I heard it was about a mystery, I was afraid it might be a true crime book of your involvement with Todd Barrington's murder. But Joanne assured me the book was completely fiction," Marilyn said.

Carrie closed her eyes momentarily as she remembered her arrest for Todd's murder. Only with the support of Charles and diligent sleuthing did they prove her innocence. "Believe me, the Barrington murder is one part of my life I want to put behind me, not write about it." Carrie glanced around the room, hoping Marilyn would take the hint and find other guests to greet, but she continued talking.

"I understand. Have you heard about Mrs. Barrington? With her oldest son, Brad, in jail for murder, she wanted to get away and has retired to Florida," Marilyn said, gently touching Carrie's arm.

"But putting gossip aside, Joanne also mentioned that authors often use people they know as characters in their books."

Joanne gave Carrie a wink, acknowledging her part in spreading the rumor. Carrie played along with what Joanne had started. "Joanne is correct. Authors use their experiences and the people they meet to create fictional characters."

Marilyn raised an eyebrow as she stared at Carrie. "If you'll excuse me, there are several other folks I want to greet before the program starts."

Marilyn dashed away as Joanne returned to where Carries was standing.

"That was naughty to tell her that I might base my characters on real people, like the ladies from the country club," Carrie said.

"Hey, a little intrigue was a great way to drum up business for this event and increase sales of your book," Joanne said. "Now go mingle with your adoring public."

Carrie followed her friend's advice and spent time chatting with guests. Thanks to Joanne's rumor, she fielded several more questions about how she created characters.

During a moment between socializing with the guests, Charles pulled Carrie aside. "Everyone seems excited about your book."

"And you helped to generate that excitement. I heard you chatting about my book in glowing terms," Carrie said.

Carrie was five-foot-nine but still had to stretch to kiss Charles. Charles was a good-looking guy, six-foot-two, with thick silver hair and soft blue-gray eyes. He was easygoing, and people loved him, especially the ladies.

"While I prefer to stand here kissing you, we should probably take a minute and grab something to eat. Joanne is getting ready to introduce you," Charles said.

Joanne had a wonderful assortment of finger foods. The selections made it easy for the guests to grab a plate and continue chatting with other attendees. To go with the food were various wines, and Dan played bartender for people who wanted a mixed drink. As Charles predicted, it wasn't long before Joanne tapped on her wine glass to get everyone's attention.

"Ladies and gentlemen, this is your two-minute warning. You have time to refresh your drinks and fill your plates for the second time and for some of you the third time," she laughed. "Carrie is about to read from her exciting new mystery."

Soon, the guests gathered in Quinn's large open living room. Carrie stood at the front of the room and could see beyond the guests through the open French door into the gardens.

Carrie finished reading a selection from her mystery. "Now I have a fun activity. I've renamed several streets from Tri-City in the book," she said. "I'm going to read a description of these streets I fictionalized. Let's see how many actual locations you can identify."

Once the audience identified the streets, Carrie answered questions about how she developed her plot, her writing process, and still more questions about how she created her characters.

Carrie was distracted by a woman standing beyond the patio talking to someone hidden behind a garden shrub. Carrie judged the woman to be in her mid-thirties, blonde, and about five-foot-five. She shook her hand, indicating she disagreed with something the unseen person said or did.

Carrie continued to look out the window and didn't hear Marilyn's question. Marilyn cleared her throat.

"I'm sorry, Marilyn. Could you repeat your question?" Carrie asked. She noticed Charles followed her gaze, but the woman had moved away.

After her talk, Carrie spent the remaining time signing copies of her book. She didn't have time to think about the woman in the garden. Later, when the guests were leaving, Charles joined her at the table.

"Everyone enjoyed your reading," Charles said. Then, he added, "Did the questions bother you? I noticed you lost focus for a minute."

"No, the questions were fine. A woman in the garden was having an animated discussion with someone, which distracted me."

"Did you know her?" Charles asked.

"Never saw her before that moment, and I haven't seen her since. She must have left," Carrie said. "I asked Joanne who she was, but without seeing the woman, she had no idea."

They ended their discussion as Maddy and Marge joined Carrie at the signing table.

"I meant to tell you earlier, Maddy, I love your new haircut," Carrie said.

Maddy had always worn her curly gray hair piled in an unruly bun on top of her head. The new shorter cut made her look much younger.

"Thank you. It's time to join this century. Easier to manage," Maddy said. "But enough about my hair. We sold out. The books, all gone."

Maddy Luther tended to talk in short and sometimes incoherent sentences.

"What my younger sister is trying to tell you is everyone who attended bought one of your books. Many folks bought multiple copies to give as gifts," Marge Millford clarified.

"It means we need more. Won't have enough," Maddy said.

Marge shook her head. "Tomorrow, we'll have to order more books, so we have enough when you do your book signing next week at our store."

"That's wonderful news. Thank you for handling the sales," Carrie said and hugged both the sisters.

"I guess you and Charles are glad you are dealing with a different type of mystery," Marge said.

"A different type of mystery?" Charles questioned.

Marge responded, "A fictional mystery book that doesn't involve a real murder."

2

Although Carrie was exhausted from the book signing the night before, she was up early, dressed, and fixed Charles's breakfast before he left for the office. She could have opted for more sleep. Instead, Carrie worked on her article about covered bridges. She became interested in the old-fashioned bridges when she and Charles stayed at Milford Manor while solving their last case.

It was hard to focus on her story because she kept thinking about the woman she saw in the garden. Who was she? Why hadn't she seen her after the reading? Carrie leaned back in her chair and dozed off before she knew it. She wasn't sure how long she had slept but jolted awake when the phone rang.

"Carrie, you need to get over here right away."

She heard the urgency in the voice but wasn't awake enough to identify the caller.

"I'm sorry, who is this?" Carrie asked.

"It's the person who threw you that fabulous party yesterday."

"Joanne, is that you? What's the matter?" Carrie sat up fully awake.

"Do you remember the woman you saw in the garden?" Joanne asked.

"I do. Did you figure out who she was?" Carrie asked.

"No, but we should know shortly," Joanne said. "I think it's her body I found in my garden."

"Body. She's dead! Where? How?" Carrie blasted the words out like bullets.

"Beyond the patio, close to where you saw the woman standing yesterday. There's a gun next to her body, and I can see what looks like a bullet hole near her heart."

"Shot! Is that what the police said?" Carrie asked as she started to pace back and forth.

"I haven't called them."

"What? Joanne, you need to call the police. What are you waiting for?"

"You. I wanted to give you a chance to check out the scene. I need someone who has experience with these matters. Someone to protect me," Joanne said. "As soon as you get here, I'll call the police."

"Joanne, wait!" Carrie yelled, but Joanne hung up.

Carrie was glad she had dressed earlier, so it only took her a few minutes to grab her bag and car keys and hit the road.

***

When Carrie arrived at Joanne's, she parked on the side street. She wanted to be out of the way once the police activity started.

Carrie rang the doorbell, but no one came. Then she heard someone calling her name from the side of the house.

"Over here," Joanne waved for Carrie to join her.

Carrie moved quickly to where her friend was standing.

"There's no sense wasting time inside when the body is out here," Joanne said as she led Carrie to the back garden.

Carrie looked at the victim and identified her as the woman she saw in the garden. She lay on her side next to a small pistol. Carrie wondered why the killer had left the gun.

Carrie didn't want to get too close for fear of contaminating the crime scene, but she could see the bullet hole above her heart. There was no blood at the scene. Except for the pistol and the bullet hole, the body seemed peaceful as it rested in the grass.

"Joanne, did you look at the location of the body?" Carrie asked.

"I looked when I discovered her. I'd rather not look again."

"Don't focus on her face or the bullet hole. Look at the body's position."

"You mean the fact she's on her side," Joanne said.

"Exactly. A body doesn't fall on its side with its hands neatly tucked under its face after being shot."

"Yes, I get what you mean. You think the killer staged the scene," Joanne said. "But why leave the gun? Were they trying to make it look like suicide?"

"If I had to guess, I would bet the gun belonged to the victim. The murderer didn't want to deal with its disposal," Carrie said,

"Now you understand why I wanted you to survey the scene before the police arrived," Joanne said. "You have fantastic insights when it comes to ..."

"You were about to say murder," Carrie said.

Joanne changed the subject. "One more thing. Look over at the bush near the victim's head."

Carrie followed the direction Joanne's hand pointed. Then, a look of shock showed on her face. "Is that my book?" The book was almost invisible, hidden by several branches.

"That's the other reason I called you," Joanne said. "Neither of us saw her purchase a book yesterday. Where did she get it?"

"I'll ask Maddy and Marge if they remembered the victim purchasing a book and if they remembered anything else about her," Carrie said.

Did the victim toss her book in the bush before confronting her murderer? Did she leave it as a message? While Carrie pondered these questions, she took a small digital camera from her handbag and began snapping photos of the body and surrounding area. Photos were the best way to capture and share the scene with Charles.

"Did you hear anything last night? Like a gunshot." Carrie said.

"No, nothing. After everyone left, the neighborhood was quiet," Joanne said. "Our master bedroom is on the opposite side of the house from the garden, and our neighbor, the Collins, are away."

"I'll be interested to see if the police think her murder occurred at this spot. There are no signs of a struggle, no blood, and no matted grass," Carrie said. "Speaking of the police, you better make that call. I'll take a few more shots and leave."

"Don't go. I don't want to be here alone with the police," Joanne said.

"Why are you so nervous? Did you murder her?" Carrie asked, trying to lighten Joanne's mood.

"Don't be ridiculous. But the body is in my backyard," Joanne said. "Look how the police wrongly accused you of the Barrington murder with nothing but circumstantial evidence."

Carrie nodded as Joanne's words reminded her again of a past situation she wanted to forget.

Joanne finished calling the police as Carrie entered the kitchen, "What should I tell the police when they get here?" Joanne asked.

"The truth. Mention the book signing and how many people wandered in and out of the house," Carrie said. "They are bound to ask you if you knew the victim, so have your answer ready."

"Okay, I get that part. What do I tell the police about you?" Joanne asked.

"I came over to help with the cleanup from yesterday's party. Don't volunteer that you called me. You saw the body when you went onto the patio to clear off the outside tables."

"That's exactly how I found her body. Good, I'm glad we have a plan because I hear sirens," Joanne said.

3

When the police arrived, Carrie remained in the kitchen while Joanne showed the officers the victim's location. It was only a few minutes before she joined Carrie in the kitchen.

"They told me to stay in the house until the detectives arrive," Joanne said. "While waiting, let's see if I can figure out our victim's name. You fix coffee, and I'll get my laptop."

As Carrie prepared the coffee, she watched the police activities outside the French doors. The first officer taped off the crime scene. Then, the forensic team arrived decked out in protective gear and started gathering evidence.

Joanne returned with her laptop and began taping the keys. Carrie brought the coffee cups and fixings to the table.

"Do you have a list of attendees?" Carrie asked.

"The signing wasn't an "invitation-only" event, but I kept an informal list of who responded. Mostly to ensure I had enough food and drink."

"The food, by the way, was delicious," Carrie said. "It was smart to have all finger foods so people could munch and mingle."

"Thanks," Joanne said as she continued looking at the screen. "Now I remember. Terry Conan asked if she could bring a guest since her husband couldn't come."

"You think her guest might be the victim?" Carrie asked. "Was she a member of the country club? You know everyone who belongs."

"I know lots of folks who belong to the club, but I don't know everyone," Joanne said, amused at Carrie's compliment. "Maybe she recently joined. That would make sense since Terry is on the club's welcoming committee."

Within a few seconds, Joanne said, "Ah."

"Do you have a name?" Carrie asked.

"Next to Terry's name, I typed Gwen Smith,"

"You've got to be kidding. The woman's name was Smith. Do you think that's her real name?" Carrie asked.

"Don't know, but I remembered something else. Terry said her guest wanted to meet you," Joanne said as she closed the lid on her computer and reached for her coffee.

"I need to catch up with Terry and learn more about Gwen Smith."

"Does that mean you and Charles will investigate?" Joanne asked.

"Not sure about a full investigation. Police don't like amateurs interfering in their cases," Carrie said. "But I'm curious why this woman wanted to meet me."

They continued watching the yard activity as they drank their coffee.

"I'm going to text Charles and update him on what's happening," Carrie said,

"I called Dan right after I called you," Joanne said. "He wanted to come home, but I told him he should stay away in case I needed bail money."

"Why? Did you think you might need someone to break you out of jail?" Carrie said, laughing.

"It's no joking matter. I wasn't sure what might happen," Joanne said. "I mean, I held the party, the body was in my backyard, and I discovered her."

"That doesn't mean you killed her," Carrie said. "There's nothing to indicate you were involved. Is it your gun?"

"No. But remember the Barrington's murder? The gun that murdered Todd wasn't yours."

Carrie felt a cold chill as she remembered the details. "Yes, but I fought with him earlier in the evening," Carrie said. "You didn't even know this Gwen person."

Carrie thought about Joanne's words when a knock on the French doors startled her. Joanne jumped at the sound. She opened the door and ushered two detectives into the kitchen. Carrie couldn't hide her surprise when she saw Detectives Jenco and McCall. These were the same two detectives who handled the Barrington case. Maybe Joanne should be worried about a murder charge.

Detective Jenco didn't address Joanne. Instead, he looked at Carrie. "Mrs. Faraday, what are you doing here?"

Carrie could tell by his tone that he wasn't pleased to see her. She tried to keep her voice even. She said, "Joanne, Mrs. Quinn held a book signing for me yesterday."

"We found a book near the body," Jenco said. Jenco held up an evidence bag with Carrie's book sealed in plastic. "I didn't realize you were the author until I saw your name on the book."

"The party was to launch my book. Copies were available for sale," Carrie said. "I came over to help with the cleanup. Joanne discovered the body in her garden." Carrie hoped her short Maddy-like sentences didn't reveal how nervous she felt.

Carrie avoided mentioning when Joanne discovered the body and hoped the detectives would assume it was after Carrie arrived.

"I hope your cleanup didn't include the area around the body," Jenco said.

"Absolutely not, Detective Jenco. Except for Joanne showing the officers where she discovered the body, we've been sitting in the kitchen," Carrie said, annoyed at the implication.

Jenco was tall, with the first traces of gray showing at the temples of his black hair and intense brown eyes. Carrie remembered how intimidating his eyes were when being questioned. His fashionable dark suit looked tight as if he had gained weight, but perhaps it was the cut of the new two-button suits men wore.

Behind him, his associate, Sergeant McCall, stood poised to record the events. However, a computer tablet replaced the pen and notebook he had used in the past. McCall was smaller than his boss and didn't seem to have aged. He wore gray slacks with a navy blue sports coat. He saw Carrie staring at him and quickly ran his hand through his buzzed, cut, sandy hair.

"Mrs. Quinn, can you tell me how you discovered the body?" Jenco asked.

Carrie wondered how Joanne would describe the events. She looked at her friend. Despite all her earlier fears about dealing with the police, she seemed relaxed and unphased as she told her story.

"As Carrie mentioned, I had a book signing for her yesterday. By the time everyone left, I was tired and decided to wait until today to finish the cleanup," Joanne said. "I saw a couple of wine glasses sitting on the patio table and went to get them."

"And you could see the body while clearing the table?" McCall asked.

"Not the full body. Just a pair of shoes sticking out from under a bush. I went over and discovered the body," Joanne said. "Carrie arrived shortly after my discovery, and I called the police."

Listening to Joanne's neatly woven story so impressed Carrie that she didn't hear Detective Jenco's question.

"Mrs. Faraday, are you paying attention? Did you hear my question?" Detective Jenco asked.

"I'm sorry, this has been a bit of a shock. What did you say?"

"Did you go into the garden and look at the body?" Jenco repeated.

"I looked briefly at the scene while Joanne called the police."

"Mrs. Faraday, come now. You don't expect me to believe this incredibly abridged version of events explains everything."

Carrie hoped the panic she was feeling didn't show on her face. She figured the game was up, and Jenco figured out Joanne called her after she discovered the body.

Jenco continued, "Surely, with your passion for detecting, you noticed other things."

Thank heaven Jenco wasn't questioning the timeline. Carrie composed herself. "There were a few things I noticed. I can summarize them all by saying the crime scene looked staged," Carrie said. "I'm sure you noticed the body didn't die in the place or position we found her."

Jenco said nothing.

"The lack of blood at the murder scene also supports my theory," Carrie added.

Jenco raised an eyebrow and continued, "Mrs. Quinn, did you know the murdered woman?"

"No. I never met the victim," Joanne said.

"How about you, Mrs. Faraday?"

"I never met her, but I saw her in the garden when I read the selection from my book. She was having what appeared to be a heated conversation with someone," Carrie said. Carrie hoped that mentioning this conversation would provide Jenco with a suspect to investigate other than Joanne.

"And the other person..." Jenco waited.

"I don't know. I couldn't see the second person. Several shrubs concealed them," Carrie said.

"You two don't know the dead woman. You don't know who was with her in the garden. Is there anything you do know?" Jenco asked.

"We believe Gwen Smith might be the victim's name based on the invitation list. But neither of us knew her," Joanne said for the second time.

"If neither of you knew her, how did she get invited to the party?" McCall asked.

"This was a casual event. I sent invitations to individuals I knew, with the understanding they could bring a friend." Joanne said. Anticipating his next question, "I believe another guest, Terry Conan, brought the victim as her plus one."

"I'll need Terry Conan's contact information," McCall said. "I would also like your list of attendees."

For the second time, Joanne opened her laptop and retrieved the information. "Here is Terry's information." She said, pointing to the screen.

McCall stood behind Joanne and captured the information on his tablet. Then Joanne hit the print button to produce the attendee list. As Joanne stood to retrieve the printed document, she paused. The group watched the attendants wheel the stretcher with Gwen's body past the French doors.

Detective Jenco broke the silence, "Mrs. Faraday, you're free to leave."

Carrie would have preferred to stay to support Joanne, but she knew Jenco would not allow this. She gathered her handbag and said to Joanne, "I'll call you later."

As Carrie headed for the front door, Jenco said, "Mrs. Faraday, you and your husband consider yourselves amateur detectives, but I want to clarify that you and Charles are not to get involved."

Carrie said nothing as she grabbed her things and left Joanne to deal with the police.

4

"I'm beginning to think that dead bodies seek us out," Carrie said to Charles when he returned home from the office.

Charles gave her a lovely hug and a glass of her favorite wine, a crisp white riesling.

"Are we cursed?" Carrie asked, swirling the wine in the glass before taking a sip.

"We've helped friends and family find solutions and closure to terrible events. That's not a curse. That's a blessing," Charles said. "How is Joanne handling the situation?"

"She was afraid that she would automatically be the prime suspect since it was her party, her garden, and she found the body. When Jenco and McCall showed up, I was worried her concerns might be legitimate."

Charles didn't want to get into a discussion about Jenco and McCall. "Dan called me and said he was standing by in case she needed a lawyer," Charles said. "He called later and said the police were gone, and he was going home to be with Joanne. I assume all went well."

Carrie reviewed the details from when she arrived until Jenco told her to leave. Then she showed Charles the photos she had taken of the crime scene.

"You're right. The body's position looks staged. Someone must have killed Gwen in a different spot and then moved the body," Charles said. "Returning the body to the Quinn's garden takes nerve."

"I'm not sure one person could have moved the body. We might be looking for two people," Carrie said.

"What's our next step?" Charles asked.

"Jenco told us not to get involved."

"Yes, but I know my wife," Charles said, refilling her wine glass. "At the very least, you'll want to find out why the murder victim asked to meet you."

Carrie took comfort, knowing Charles understood the way she thought. She grabbed her phone. "I'll call Terry Conan and see what she can tell us about the woman she invited to the party."

When Carrie finished talking to Terry, she turned to Charles and said, "All set. We're going to meet Terry at the Tri-City Pub for drinks."

***

The Tri-City pub was a cavernous old warehouse with high ceilings. While the vast space accommodated a large crowd, it also meant the noise factor was a problem for patrons trying to hold conversations. The owners tried to deal with the noise by creating different sections, lowering the ceiling, and adding soundproof panels to help dampen the sound. Charles couldn't imagine the noise level on nights when they featured local bands.

In the main room, three bars formed a U-shape. At the back was a glass-enclosed restaurant area that gave diners a sense of privacy and relief from the bar noise.

When Carrie and Charles arrived, they searched for Terry Conan. Terry was a petite woman who wore unremarkable clothing and had a way of blending into a crowd. She barely raised her hand from the far-left bar to attract their attention.

"Hello, Terry. Long time no see," Carrie said. "Did you enjoy the book signing yesterday?"

"I'd never been to one before. It was fun." Terry paused. "That was until the police contacted me this morning, and I learned someone murdered my guest. What's the latest?"

"We don't know much. Someone shot Gwen Smith, and Joanne discovered her body this morning while cleaning the patio area," Carrie answered.

"That's more than the police told me. Joanne must be beside herself, having found the body," Terry said as she sipped her drink. "After they questioned me, I felt like I was a suspect. All I did was get her an invitation to attend your book signing."

"We hate to bother you with more questions. How did you know Gwen Smith, and why did she want to meet Carrie?" Charles asked as he signaled the bartender and ordered drinks for him and Carrie and a refill for Terry.

"I didn't know her. I mean, I didn't know her that well," Terry said. "I'm on the welcoming committee at the country club. Whenever there's a new member, I find out their interests. Do they want to join the investment club, learn to golf, play tennis, or do something else? Then I introduce them to other members who enjoy the same activity."

"What were her interests?" Charles asked.

"Her biggest concern was if, by becoming a member, she would have access to the club's library," Terry said. "She was a history professor at Tri-City University, researching the city and the club's founding."

"Sounds like access to the library was why she joined the club and not for physical activities," Charles said.

"Do you know why Gwen wanted to meet with me?" Carrie asked, repeating Charles's question.

"During my introduction to the club, I mentioned several of our prominent members, including you, Carrie," Terry said. "Gwen asked if you were the same person who solved crimes and had recently published a mystery."

"Is that how the book signing got mentioned?" Carrie asked.

"She read the announcement about your book in the newspaper and hoped she could meet you," Terry said. "I called Joanne and asked if I could bring a guest since Bill had to work. That's as much as I can tell you."

Charles and Carrie paused, trying to think of any other questions. "Did she contact any members about the club's history?" Charles asked.

"I gave her Jim Albright's name, but I don't know if she contacted him." Terry spotted Bill and enthusiastically waved for him to join them. "Here's Bill now. We're going out for a celebratory dinner. He got a new big architectural contract."

"That's wonderful," Charles said. "He's worked so hard to grow his business."

"And you helped," Terry said.

"Me?" Charles questioned.

"Yes, you. When you featured Bill's company as an up-and-coming business in the Tri-County magazine, he got several new clients," Terry said.

"Thanks for the compliment, but I'm sure his business is doing well because he's a good architect," Charles said.

Bill looked sharp in a dark blue suit and a multicolored silk tie. After getting Bill a drink, the group chatted for a few minutes about topics other than the murder. Bill looked at his watch. "I'm sorry to end our conversation, but we have a dinner reservation at Gourmet, and if you're late, you lose your spot," Bill said. "We should meet again when we have more time. I'll leave it to our wives to set up a date."

"Sounds like a plan," Charles said. "And congratulations on your new project."

As Terry was about to leave, she turned to Carrie and Charles. "There's one thing I can add. Gwen's sister, Gloria, runs the Train Stop restaurant," Terry said. "It's a wonderful restaurant with family meals."

"The food is good and a lot less expensive than other restaurants, especially if you're feeding a bunch of hungry kids like us," Bill added.

"I've never heard of it. Where is it?" Charles asked.

"By the rail yards but far enough away that you're not bothered by all the train movements. Originally, it was a diner housed in an old railroad car, and then the owners enlarged it as their business grew," Terry said.

"You can't miss it if you go down Railroad Avenue. The original train car sits at the front of the restaurant," Bill said as he and Terry left the Tri-City pub.

Charles smiled at Carrie, knowing what she thought. "I assume we're going to eat dinner at the Train Stop?"

***

The Train Stop was just as Terry described. The couple quickly found the restaurant because the owners painted the original railroad car in distinctive colors of red, black, and gold. The couple entered the restaurant through the door of the original rail car and found a booth.

At the top of each booth was a bar with green checked gingham curtains that provided a sense of privacy for the diners. The individual tables also sported gingham tablecloths, giving the Train Stop an old-fashioned feel.

After looking at the menu, it was only moments before Carrie said, "Assuming the food is as good as the descriptions, we've found a new place to eat. This menu has all your favorites from hot turkey platters, meatloaf, roast chicken, and a wonderful selection of soups, sandwiches, and salads for me."

According to her name tag, their waitress, Bea, was a well-endowed woman in her mid-fifties. "Welcome to the Train Stop," she said with a welcoming voice as she placed glasses of water on the table. "Are you ready to order?"

"I'm ready. I'll have the meatloaf special and coffee," Charles said. "How about you, Carrie?"

"I'll have the turkey club with coffee," Carrie said. "I'd like to keep the menu for a few more minutes. This is our first visit, and I want to see what to order the next time we come."

"No problem. Let me put your food order in, and I'll be back with your coffee," Bea said.

Terry was right about the Train Stop. Their food wasn't fancy, but they had large portions, and the food tasted delicious. They enjoyed the homemade quality. When Bea returned, Carrie and Charles debated ordering a slice of homemade pie.

"How was everything?" Bea asked as she cleared the plates.

"Wonderful. We never heard of this restaurant until a friend recommended it. What's its history?" Charles asked.

"The current owner, Gloria Smith, took it over from her grandparents, who had started and operated the place for decades. It was originally a small diner, mostly for the workers in the rail yards," Bea said.

"They're certainly attracting more than local rail workers," Charles said as he gazed around a room filled with families.

"Her grandmother was a terrific cook. Word spread, and they added extensions to the original train car," Bea said.

"We would like to tell Gloria how much we enjoyed the meal. Is she around?" Carrie asked.

"There's been a tragedy in the family." Bea lowered her voice, "Gloria learned today that someone murdered her sister."

"That's awful," Charles said, not wanting to reveal they already knew about Gloria's sister.

"She isn't here tonight. She's making the arrangements for her sister's funeral," Bea said. "You'll soon see an announcement about a memorial service in the paper. Her sister's name was Gwen Smith."

Charles and Carrie thanked the waitress for the information and left a generous tip.

"A great meal, but no luck meeting the sister," Charles said as he unlocked the car. "What's next."

"We need to attend Gwen's memorial service," Carrie said.

Several days after the murder, Carrie and Joanne were in the car heading to the Railroad Avenue Community Center near the Train Stop restaurant.

"Carrie, you hate funerals, so I appreciate your coming with me. I felt I needed to pay my respects since I discovered Gwen in my yard," Joanne said.

"You're right. I hate funerals, but this is a memorial service to honor Gwen," Carrie said. "And I feel the same way that you do. It's something we have to do. After all, Gwen came to the book signing to meet me."

"I'm surprised Charles didn't offer to come with us," Joanne said as she waited at a light.

"He wanted to, but the Tri-County Monthly magazine goes to press today. It's a bad time for him to be away from the office since last-minute editorial issues always occur."

Faraday Press, owned by Charles's family, published this popular magazine and several others. While Charles wasn't at the service, Carrie would share all the information from the event with him later. Aside from paying her respects, Carrie had another purpose in attending. She wanted to learn more about Gwen by meeting the people she knew. She also wondered if the murderer would attend.

"We should try to meet as many people as possible to learn more about Gwen," Carrie said. "I'm telling you this because you are much more of a social butterfly than I am."

"I'll do my best, but I'll rely on you to help me ask the right questions," Joanne said. "This is exciting. I'm helping my detective friend gather clues to keep me from being charged with murder."

Before Carrie could remind Joanne that she wasn't investigating but was only curious about why Gwen wanted to talk with her, Joanne pulled into the parking lot at the community center. They joined a large group walking toward the entrance, where a woman stood greeting people.

Carrie suddenly grabbed Joanne's arm. "Look!" Carrie stammered.

When Joanne focused on what Carrie saw, her jaw dropped. "I don't believe it. It's the dead woman," Joanne raised her hand to her mouth, realizing what she said could have been overheard by others.

The woman at the door heard the comment and laughed as she extended her hand, "Hello, I'm Gloria Smith."

Carrie stated the obvious, "You and Gwen are twins."

"Yes, since birth," Gloria said with a smile. "I'm sorry I shouldn't make light, especially considering the circumstances. But Gwen and I always enjoyed catching people off guard who didn't know we were twins. I don't believe I've met you before. How did you know my sister?"

"I'm Joanne Quinn. I held the book party this past Saturday for Carrie Faraday," Joanne said, extending her hand toward Carrie. "Gwen attended this event. Unfortunately, the next morning, I was the one who discovered your sister in my garden."

"That must have been awful discovering my sister's body at your home," Gloria said, taking Joanne's hand. "And you're the writer Gwen wanted to meet. I'm glad you came. I wanted to talk to both of you."

"I never had the chance to talk with your sister. Do you know why Gwen wanted to meet me?" Carrie asked.

"Let's talk after the service. It will be a short, friendly gathering of people from her workplace and other associates who will share memories of Gwen's life. After the buffet, I'll join you, and we can share information," Gloria said.

Carrie noticed the line was growing larger, so she and Joanne proceeded inside. They were surprised that the seating was not typical of a church service. Instead, around the room were round tables covered in navy blue cloths. They found a table on the far side of the room near the back since they were not close friends or family. On the opposite side of the room was the buffet table for the reception after the service.

"Good heavens, will you look at who just arrived," Joanne said. "Mrs. Henrietta Brighton-Stanford and company."

Carrie thought for a minute and then said out loud, "Brighton. Isn't that the name of one of the men who founded Tri-City?"

"Yes. Before Tri-City was incorporated, there was a crossroad where the farmers from the villages of Allwin, Dorchester, and

Saint Thomas traded and sold goods," Joanne said. "Henrietta's grandfather, Henry Brighton, convinced the three villages to unite and form one town. Because of his hard work, he was named the first mayor of Tri-City, and ever since, the family remained prominent."

"And our main street, Brighton Boulevard, is named for the family," Carrie said.

Joanne nodded. "The granddaughter, Henrietta, married Evan Stanford, but many still call her Mrs. Brighton."

Across the room, Carrie saw a woman in her early seventies walking toward one of the tables near the front. She was spry and maneuvered independently. A man in his late teens, maybe a grandson, and a woman in her thirties accompanied her.

"She doesn't look like she's from one of the wealthiest families in the community," Carrie said. "I would expect more fashionable attire."

"Don't be fooled, Carrie. That basic black outfit she's wearing is a designer suit costing several hundred dollars."

"Interesting. I wonder what brings one of the first families of Tri-City to a funeral for a college teacher," Carrie said. "Perhaps someone in the family took classes with Gwen. We need to ask her sister how the Brighton-Stanford family knew Gwen."

They were the only two at the table when they took their seats, but now the tables were filling.

"Are you holding seats for others, or may we join you?" asked a young woman in her late 20s with cropped blonde hair and thick tortoise shell glasses.

"We would love to have the company," Joanne said. "I'm Joanne Quinn, and this is Carrie Faraday."

"Hi. I'm Penny Stevens, and this is Brian Amberson." Brian was much younger, maybe only nineteen or twenty. Thin with long hair. He was not in a suit but a nicely creased dark blue slacks and shirt.

"How did you know Gwen Smith?" Carrie asked.

"I was her administrative assistant," said Penny. "I helped her with schedules and research."

"I'm a grad student and her intern for the semester," Brian said.

"What did she teach?" Joanne asked.

Brian looked at Joanne in disbelief. "She was a Ph.D. professor of history at Tri-City University and a great teacher," Brian said.

Pretending something was in his eye, Carrie was sure Brian wiped a tear.

"It doesn't sound like you knew Gwen was a teacher?" Penny asked. "How did you meet her?"

Carrie and Joanne attended the university when it was a two-year institution and then transferred to other schools to complete their degrees. Now, the college was a four-year university attracting professors like Gwen Smith.

Carrie wondered why a history professor at Tri-City University wanted to speak with her. Charles knew more about the city's history than she did.

As was her style, Joanne explained how they met Gwen. "Carrie recently published a book. I threw a book signing party for her that Gwen attended."

"Wait. Didn't I read in the paper that you discovered Gwen's body in your yard?" asked Penny.

"Yes, I found her in my backyard the morning after the signing," Joanne said.

Before the conversation continued, another young woman approached the table. "Hi, Brian. Do you mind if I join you?"

"Yup, plenty of room." Brian turned to Carrie and Joanne. "This is Cindy Russell. She also attends the university, which is how we met."

Joanne and Carrie introduced themselves to Cindy.

"I remember Gwen mentioning that she wanted to attend a book signing. Did you know Gwen before the book signing?" Penny asked.

"No. I learned from another attendee that she wanted to meet me," Carrie said. "Do either of you know why she wanted to contact me?"

"Gwen recently completed a family history for a client. Perhaps she wanted to discuss methodology for writing the report with you," said Penny.

Carrie thought that answer didn't make sense because she knew there were plenty of journalists Gwen could have consulted at the college. Before she could respond, the minister from the local Lutheran Church approached the podium and called the group to order. The minister gave an opening prayer and a brief eulogy. Then, several college associates and friends told humorous stories about Gwen and how enriching their lives were by knowing her.

The last speech was from her sister, Gloria. She talked about their wonderful upbringing and how they continuously played jokes on people who didn't know they were twins. The girls were never apart until they went off to college. Gloria went to a culinary school to follow in her grandparents' footsteps and run the family restaurant. Gwen went to college to study history and continued until she earned her doctorate.

The saddest part of the service was when Gloria announced that, as a twin, she knew inside when her sister passed. She hoped that with the help of everyone attending the service, she could find a way to continue now that her sister and best friend wasn't there for her.

Carrie and Joanne wiped tears from their eyes as the minister gave the closing prayer. Gloria's words convinced Carrie that she and Charles needed to find the murderer of Gwen Smith.

6

After the service, the wait staff opened the buffet. Carrie's stomach reminded her that her cup of coffee and toast for breakfast was long gone. Carrie wished she and Joanne had selected a table closer to the buffet because their table would be one of the last called.

Joanne excused herself to go to the ladies' room. Instead of returning to their table, Joanne got in line right behind Mrs. Brighton-Stanford. Carrie saw she was talking with her as they proceeded through the line.

When it was Carrie's turn for the buffet, she exchanged words with Joanne as she returned to the table with her food.

"I've never known you to jump a food line," Carrie said. "But I believe I understand the reason."

"It was a good opportunity to get information from Mrs. Brighton-Stanford," Joanne said. "You told me to ask questions."

"And did you find out anything?" Carrie asked.

"I did. The young man with Mrs. Brighton-Stanford is her grandson, Hansen Stanford. The woman is her companion and secretary, Rachel Pembroke. Mrs. Brighton-Stanford hired Gwen to do a project about her family's history," Joanne said.

"That explains why the Brighton-Stanford family is here," Carrie said. "I better get in the buffet line before the others wonder what I'm doing."

Other than polite conversation with their table mates, Carrie and Joanne spent their time enjoying the buffet. Carrie was sure the Train Stop had provided the food since she spotted Bea, the waitress who had served Charles and her at the restaurant.

Gloria visited each table and thanked people for attending the service. After her visit, most people quietly left, and the hall began to empty.

When Gloria reached their table, she kissed Cindy on the cheek and said, "I'm so glad you came. I wasn't sure you could make it in the middle of exams," Gloria said.

"Professor Springer was one of the speakers, so he postponed his exam until tomorrow. It wouldn't have mattered. I wanted to be here," Cindy said. "You and Gwen are my family, and I'll miss her."

Cindy teared up, and Gloria hugged her. Cindy composed herself. Joanne and Carrie must have looked confused.

"Cindy is my cousin. Our mothers were sisters, but both are gone now. Gwen and I were delighted when Cindy got accepted at the Tri-City University."

"No other family?" Joanne asked.

"Cindy's father died in her first year at college. Cindy and her brother Joe are the last of our relatives. Or at least the only ones we know about," Gloria said as she touched Cindy's shoulder.

Carrie wondered about Gloria's reference to the only relatives they knew. Was Gwen also researching the Smith family history?

"Gwen and Gloria made sure I had everything I needed at school. And Gloria gave me a job at the restaurant to earn spending money," Cindy said. "Joe sends his regrets. He's traveling for his firm in Europe and couldn't get back for the service."

"I understand. The three of us will get together when Joe returns," Gloria said.

Gloria realized she had ignored the others at the table and turned to Penny. "It's good to see you, Penny, but I don't know this young man."

"I'm Brian Amberson," he said, extending her hand. "I'm your... I mean, I was your sister's student intern."

"Oh yes, she mentioned she had a terrific intern," Gloria said. "Thanks for coming. Carrie and Joanne, can you stay a few more minutes? I need to say goodbye to a few more people, and then we will have time to chat."

After Gloria moved away, Penny said. "It was nice to meet you, even under these sad circumstances. But Brian and I need to get back to work."

"Me too," added Cindy. "I had no exams scheduled today, but I need to study for tomorrow's tests."

When Gloria returned to their table, she placed two sizeable white bakery boxes on the table and sat beside Carrie.

"People certainly enjoyed the food but didn't eat many desserts. We have lots of desserts left," Gloria said. "I've brought you each a box of desserts to take home."

"That's very kind of you," Carrie said.

"Both our husbands have a sweet tooth. They will enjoy these treats," Joanne said.

"Aside from the young people from the university who sat with us, was anyone else close to Gwen at the college?" Carrie asked.

"Gwen often spoke about a fellow professor, Emily Hopkins," Gloria said. "She joined me for the funeral but wasn't able to attend today."

"Emily Hopkins," Carrie exclaimed. Fortunately, most of the tables near them were now empty. "I'm sorry, it's just that Professor Hopkins was my faculty advisor when I attended the school. I'll have to give her a call."

After Carrie reminisced about Emily Hopkins for a few seconds, Joanne changed focus. "When I chatted with Mrs. Brighton-Stanford, she told me your sister was researching her family's history."

"That's true. Because of Gwen's love of history, researching family genealogy seemed the next logical step," Gloria said. "She wanted to study the history of families from the towns that formed Tri-City."

"Did Mrs. Brighton-Stanford contact her about doing the research?" Carrie asked.

"I'm not sure. Gwen was an expert on Tri-City's history and gave several lectures at various community centers, including this one. Since Henry Brighton was a founder, perhaps one of the family attended her lecture," Gloria said. "Now, I want to hear how you two knew Gwen."

"Joanne held a book signing party which your sister attended. Neither of us knew of your sister before this event," Carrie said.

"Gwen asked Terry Conan if she could attend the book signing party with her. Do you know Terry Conan from the country club?" Joanne asked.

"Gwen mentioned she had joined the club, but I can't imagine why. Our family was never part of the country club set."

"Apparently, she joined to get access to the club's historical records," Carrie said.

"That makes sense. Gwen constantly looked for new sources of historical information," Gloria said.

"Do you know why your sister wanted to come to my book signing?" Carrie said.

"The last time Gwen and I met for our weekly dinner, she said she had read your book. The police told me they found a copy of your book next to the body and asked if I knew you," Gloria said. "Gwen said doing historical research and writing a mystery had much in common. You gather clues and then write the results."

"That sheds light on why she wanted to meet Carrie," Joanne said. "Sounds like she wanted to share her findings with you."

"Gwen also mentioned that you and your husband solved several murders," Gloria paused. "I want to hire you to investigate my sister's murder. At least if I hire you, I'll get some answers that the police aren't providing."

"We're not professional detectives, and we're not available for hire," Carrie said.

The disappointment on Gloria's face was evident. Before Carrie could explain, Joanne jumped in. "Don't worry. I've already asked them to investigate, and they've agreed. And they don't charge a dime for their expertise."

"Even though Joanne is your official client, will you keep me informed of your progress?" Gloria asked.

Carrie nodded and added, "The police don't like interference from amateurs in their cases. Therefore, we must be discreet. Please don't mention that my husband and I are quietly investigating your sister's murder."

"I promise. If you think of anything I can do, please let me know. I need to find out who murdered my sister and why."

7

Carrie made an appointment with Professor Hopkin's administrative assistant, and the couple headed to Tri-City University.

When Charles turned onto Campus Drive, a lifetime of memories came flooding back to Carrie. Carrie and Charles's brother Jamie attended the college for two years. Jamie and Carrie dated through college until their careers pulled them in different directions.

Carrie saw the campus green and the tree where she and Jamie spent many hours studying and enjoying college life. She loved Charles and knew she had made the right choice when they married. But Carrie couldn't help but feel a heart tug as she dealt with her memories of Jamie.

"Is everything okay, Dear?" Charles asked as he noticed Carrie did not attempt to leave the vehicle.

"This is the first time I've returned to the school since Jamie and I attended classes here all those years ago. Coming here is like walking into the past," Carrie said.

Carrie returned to the Tri-City to help solve Jamie's murder. Initially, Charles was a suspect, but once she realized they were on the same side, they worked together to find the killer. Soon after solving the case, they married.

"I understand. Coming here has probably stirred unpleasant memories," Charles said.

Discussing Jamie's murder was still a difficult topic for them.

"Far from it," Carrie said as she opened the car door. "His murder can't eliminate the happy memories. Your brother and our friends enjoyed good times while we were here."

Charles and Carrie walked into the main classroom building and got instructions on where to find Professor Hopkin's office.

"Amazingly, Professor Hopkins is still here and in her same office," Carrie said. "She was one of my journalism professors and one of the youngest teachers on campus. Closer to her student's age than the other professors."

Charles laughed, "As students, we automatically assume our teachers are much older than they often are."

They walked down the clean, sanitized hallways painted a light beige and passed only a few students. Since it was exam time, most students were somewhere studying or celebrating the start of spring break. Carrie tapped lightly on the door of Professor Hopkins's office. A booming voice yelled, "Come in."

They found the professor sitting at a standard-issue oak desk with scuff marks showing age. The professor, now in her late fifties, had streaks of gray creeping into her fading brown hair. Her glasses sat perched on the end of her nose, and her warm smile was just as Carrie remembered.

"Hello, Professor Hopkins. Nice to see you again after all these years," Carrie said. "This is my husband, Charles Faraday."

"Mr. Faraday, nice to meet you," she said, standing and extending her hand.

Charles shook hands and said, "Please call me Charles."

"Then you must also call me Emily. Carrie, you can drop the professor and call me Emily, too, since you're no longer my student."

Carrie laughed as the professor led them to a round table near her desk.

Once seated, Emily said, "Gwen was a talented teacher and my good friend. Her death was a total shock."

Carrie noticed Emily avoided the word murder.

"Did you ever discuss the research work Gwen was doing for Henrietta Brighton-Stanford?" Charles asked.

"How did you know about that?" Emily asked, showing concern.

"I learned at Gwen's memorial that Mrs. Brighton-Stanford hired her to create a document about her family's history and the founding of Tri-City," Carrie said.

"I missed the memorial service because of exams, but Gloria asked me to join her at the burial, and I said goodbye there," Emily said softly. "I didn't realize Gwen's work for the family was common knowledge."

"Mrs. Brighton-Stanford mentioned it briefly to one of Carrie's friends at the service," Charles said.

"Did Gwen indicate anything that concerned her from her work on this project?" Carrie asked.

Emily shifted uncomfortably in her seat. "Gwen was always protective of any information she uncovered for her clients and kept her files secure. She never discussed anything specific concerning a particular project," Emily said. "However, recently, we had several conversations about the ethics in presenting the information she discovered."

"Ethics. That seems like an unusual conversation since most historical information is in the public domain," Charles said.

"Gwen wanted to know if the information she discovered was like doctor-patient or lawyer-client confidentiality or if she could share her findings with others," Emily said. "Before her death, she seemed to be, I don't know, I guess, worried about some of the information she found."

"What did you tell her?" Charles asked.

"It wasn't easy to answer because she didn't share details. I suggested she talk with the client who hired her," Emily said. She said nothing for a few moments as if she was remembering the conversation. "It won't hurt to tell you. Gwen wanted to write a book based on her findings, but that won't happen now."

"A book. I would think a book would need a compelling discovery to attract a publisher," Carrie said, looking at Charles. He nodded.

"That I can't answer. Are you interested in Gwen's work or helping the police with the case?" Emily asked.

Carrie ignored the part about helping the police and said, "Gwen came to my book signing and told several people she wanted to meet me."

"I heard you finished a mystery," Emily asked. "I understand you two are quite the amateur detectives. Is your book based on some of the cases you and Charles solved?"

"No, this book is fictional," Carrie said.

"And your previous cases didn't influence your writing," Emily suggested,

Carrie preferred to avoid any discussion about their previous cases. "Of course, they helped. Those experiences provided knowledge about police procedures and how clues help find a solution," Carrie said.

"I'm sure as a journalist, you'll appreciate that a mystery is like writing an article," Charles added. "You get a piece of information, and then you follow it. You gather more pieces and soon have a complete story."

Carrie nodded and smiled at Charles to thank him for reinforcing that she didn't base her book on one of their cases. "Did Gwen tell you why she wanted to talk to me?"

"Your name came up in one of our discussions. Gwen saw an article in the paper announcing you'd written a mystery and attended the university," Emily said. "I told her you were one of my former students and an excellent writer. I also mentioned that you and Charles had solved several crimes."

Carrie felt her face color rising at Emily's praise about her writing. "I doubt it had to do with our mystery-solving. It would make sense if she planned on writing a book. She might want to chat with someone who recently published."

"I hope I didn't speak out of turn telling Gwen about the cases you and Charles solved. She was looking for answers, and I thought meeting you might help with her dilemma," Emily said.

"You said she faced a dilemma. Do you know what it was?" Charles asked.

"Without being specific, she hinted others might be interested in what she had discovered about Tri-City's history because it could have a financial impact. Then Gwen laughed and said she wasn't worried because she took precautions for her safety," Emily said. "Maybe I should have pressed her for more information."

Emily's eyes started to fill with tears.

"Emily, you did nothing wrong. Writers often face the challenge of who and how to share their writing. I'm sure Gwen wanted to meet a fellow writer and ask questions about publishing," Carrie said. "Unfortunately, we never had the opportunity to talk."

Emily nodded, but Carrie was sure she still felt guilty. Fortunately, Charles changed the subject.

"Do you think we could look at Gwen's office?" Charles asked.

"I don't see why not. The police searched the office but didn't seal it off," Emily said. She pulled a key out of her desk drawer. "Let's go down and see what we can find."

Carrie thought Emily sounded excited to help them with their investigation and stop thinking about what she might have done differently to save Gwen. She led them down the steps to the second floor and stopped at an office with Gwen Smith on the nameplate.

Emily inserted her key. "That's strange. The door is already unlocked."

Charles put his arm in front of the two ladies, keeping them from entering. "Could the door be unlocked since Gwen is no longer using it?" Charles asked.

"Not at all. We haven't had time to sort everything and return Gwen's personal items to her sister," Emily said. "I locked the door after the police left."

"Let me take a quick look," Charles said.

Charles pushed open the door, making as little noise as possible. The lights were on as he stepped inside and looked around. He was startled when a young woman with cropped blonde hair popped up and faced him.

"Who are you?" She exclaimed, looking frightened.

"I might ask you the same thing," Charles said calmly, not wanting to upset the intruder further.

Emily looked beyond Charles's shoulder, "Penny, what are you doing here? What a mess you've made."

"I didn't do this," Penny said defensively, adjusting her tortoiseshell framed glasses. "I found it this way."

"Did the police create this mess when they searched the office?" Carrie asked.

"I was here when they searched. They checked drawers and files but didn't dump them out," Emily said. "They wanted Gwen's computer and phone, but they weren't here. They took Gwen's calendar book and gave me a receipt, leaving everything else untouched."

"Were you looking for something specific, Penny?" Emily asked.

"The dean asked me to check Gwen's office for student papers. I knew Gwen finished grading them but didn't turn in the grades," Penny said. "When I arrived, I found this mess. I started straightening things as I looked for the papers."

"Could you tell if anything was missing?" Charles asked.

"With the contents of the drawers dumped on the floor, I won't know until everything is back in place. Although, I found the students' grades." Penny held up an envelope.

"You go ahead and get the grades to the dean. We'll see if we can do a little more straightening," Emily said.

After Penny left, Carrie asked, "Should we call the police?"

"I'll notify the campus police. But since there's no actual damage, I'm sure they'll assume it was a disgruntled student," Emily said.

"Did Gwen have disgruntled students?" Charles asked.

"Gwen had an incident where two students came forward after they received failing grades and accused her of using their Tri-City research for her project," Emily said.

"What happened?" Carrie asked.

"Nothing. The campus Ethics Committee investigated, but the materials they accused Gwen of using were publicly available in newspaper articles and documents at the historical society," Emily said. "I know the incident bothered her. That was the first time she mentioned taking precautions to protect herself from future problems."

Charles and Carrie started picking up materials from the floor and stacking folders on the desk. Emily returned the file folders to the proper drawers.

Carrie noticed the differences between Emily and Gwen's offices. Gwen's office was warm and comfortable. She had a cushioned chair beside her desk and similar chairs at her conference table. Light blue paint adorned the walls, which displayed photos depicting Tri-City's past and present.

"There's one thing that's missing," Carrie said.

Both Charles and Emily stopped what they were doing and looked at Carrie.

"I haven't found any materials on Tri-City's history or the Brighton-Stanford family," Carrie said.

Charles finished his examination of the papers on and in Gwen's desk. "Same here," he said. "Nothing on Tri-City or the Brighton name."

The group continued for another 30 minutes, putting everything back in order as best they could.

"I wonder if whoever searched the office found what they wanted," Emily said.

"I have a feeling the answer is no. The mess the intruder created throwing files and papers around was out of frustration because they didn't find what they wanted," Carrie said.

"Would Gwen have kept work anywhere else?" Charles asked, looking at Emily.

"Maybe at her condo, and she always carried a satchel for her books and papers," Emily suggested.

"Thanks. We'll follow up with Gwen's sister," Charles said.

"We better let you get back to work. I'm sure you also have grades to complete," Carrie said.

"Carrie, it was a pleasure seeing you again. And it was nice to meet you, Charles. If there is anything else I can do to help, let me know," Emily said. "I hope you get to the bottom of this tragedy. Gwen was a fine person and a good friend."

As Emily shook Carrie's hand, she noticed her eyes filled with tears. Emily would miss Gwen's company.

wo weeks after Gwen Smith's murder, Carrie attended her second book signing with Maddy and Marge at the Tri-County bookstore.

"Good grief, what's going on at the bookstore tonight?" Carrie asked as Charles pulled into the parking lot." Look at all these cars."

"They have a book signing with a famous author," Charles said.

"You're quite funny," Carrie responded.

When Carrie entered the bookstore, she was pleasantly surprised to see a massive display of her books at the main entrance. Once inside, she realized Charles had been correct. A line of people waited for Carrie to sign a copy of her book.

Marge came rushing up to Carrie. "Can you believe this response? I hate to admit this, but the murder at Joanne's house probably generated this crowd."

"Unfortunately, murder seems to attract people," Carrie said.

"Regardless of why they came, you're going to have a good event," Marge said. "I'm glad my sister tripled our order of your books. As they say, they're going like hotcakes."

"Speaking of selling books. Do you remember selling a book to the murdered woman at Joannes?" Carrie asked. "They found one of my books next to the body."

"I can't answer because I didn't know the woman. She may have purchased one at the party," Marge said. "Or she could have bought it earlier in the week and brought it with her."

"I guess I better get started signing books. I want to keep your customers happy," Carrie said.

Carrie and Charles followed Marge across the store. Carrie could hear a murmur as she passed the people waiting. Her introverted self was overwhelmed, but she smiled and nodded.

"We have you at a table in the center of the room. Maddy is taking care of the book sales," Marge said.

When Carrie was seated, Charles whispered, "Have fun, darling. While you're with your adoring public, I'll see what other books deserve my attention."

"I'm sure Marge and Maddy have a few books that might interest you," Carrie said.

***

Charles visited the newly released book section. He checked several of the latest books. Most choices were romance and self-discovery books that didn't appeal to him. With all the news surrounding Gwen's murder, he headed to the history section, looking for books about Tri-City.

While Maddy and Marge's store offered an extensive historical section, Charles found little on the city's history. At the bottom of one shelf, he spotted a book called *Early Families*. The volume covered hardships the early settlers faced in the villages but didn't focus on any founders. As Charles stood up, he realized someone was next to him.

"Are you Mr. Faraday?" the woman asked.

She was as tall as Carrie, at five foot eight, in her mid-thirties, attractive, with red curly hair.

"I am. And who might you be?" Charles asked, offering a warm smile.

"I'm Rachel Pembroke. "I'm Mrs. Brighton-Stanford, Henrietta's companion," Rachel said, waiting to see if Charles recognized the name.

"Is Mrs. Brighton-Stanford here tonight?" Charles asked as he glanced around the store.

"She's not in the line yet. She has someone holding her place while she sits in a chair. Standing for long periods is taxing for her," Rachel said

"Does she like mysteries?" Charles asked.

"She's interested because Gwen Smith mentioned she read your wife's book and wanted to meet her."

"I understand that Gwen researched the Brighton family history and Tri-City's founding for your employer," Charles said.

"That's true. Many records document the Brighton family history, but there are fewer records about the other founders and how they worked together to form a new city," Rachel said. "That was the focus of Gwen's research."

"Gwen's work would have been a nice addition. There aren't many books about our city," Charles said, pointing to the bookshelves. "Did Gwen share any of her writings with the family?"

"Not a single page," Rachel said. "Although her work must be somewhere, she told Henrietta she was at the end of her research and was finishing her final report."

"Her report is probably with her possessions. Her sister will have access once the police have completed their investigation," Charles offered.

"I hope so. It would be interesting to see what Gwen discovered," Rachel said. "Gotta go. Henrietta is in line."

Charles wondered if Rachel's concern about finding Gwen's research was more than idle curiosity.

***

Once Charles left, Carrie focused on the first customer waiting in line. Before she could utter a greeting, the woman blurted out, "I hope we don't have another murder tonight at this event."

The comment astounded Carrie, but she kept her cool. "The police don't believe the book signing had anything to do with the woman's murder. They are exploring other avenues." Carrie knew that what she said might not be accurate, but she needed to make tonight's attendees feel comfortable. She smiled, signed the woman's book, thanked her for coming, and quickly greeted the next person in line.

Maddy and Marge kept the line moving. Maddy rang up the sales, and Marge opened each book to the title page for Carrie to sign. Even though people were anxious to get their books signed, Carrie spent time with each customer, answered their questions, and even posed for selfies. Many questions concerned Gwen's murder, but Carrie's answer was always the same. "The police are investigating and will find a solution."

Finally, the line started to dwindle. Carrie looked unsuccessfully for Charles but thought she saw Hansen, Mrs. Brighton-Stanford's grandson. The young man darted behind a bookshelf before she could be sure it was him.

"I'm Henrietta Brighton-Stanford," a voice said.

Carrie looked up, startled to see Mrs. Brighton-Stanford standing before her. Tonight, she wore casual black slacks and a magenta sweater. Joanne would probably tell Carrie it was an expensive outfit if she were here.

"Hello. Would you like me to sign the book to you?" Carrie asked.

"No need. Your name and date will be fine." Mrs. Brighton-Stanford smiled pleasantly.

Carrie decided to take advantage of the situation. "I saw you at Gwen Smith's Memorial service, but I didn't have a chance to introduce myself."

"Had I known you were at the memorial service, I would have spoken with you as well," Mrs. Brighton-Stanford said. "I understand your first book signing was at Joanne Quinn's home, where she discovered Gwen Smith's body."

Mrs. Brighton-Stanford didn't waste words. She was direct, and Carrie liked that quality. "Yes, that's correct. Joanne discovered the body the next morning."

"Did Gwen say anything to you about a project she did for me?" Mrs. Brighton-Stanford asked.

"I never spoke with her," Carrie said.

"That's unfortunate," she looked disappointed that Carrie couldn't provide more information. "I was hoping you might have some answers."

Mrs. Brighton-Stanford grasped the arm of the woman behind her. "This is Rachel Pembroke, my companion and secretary."

"Nice to meet you," Rachel said.

"Not that I want Carrie to lose a sale, but you could have borrowed my book when I finished," Mrs. Brighton-Stanford addressed Rachel.

"With all the interest surrounding the book, I don't want to wait to read it." Rachel handed her book to Carrie.

"In that case, would you like me to make it out to you, Rachel?" Carrie asked.

"Oh yes, please," Rachel said.

Carrie signed the book, tilted her head to one side, and saw the remaining customers growing impatient.

Mrs. Brighton-Stanford also saw the waiting customers. "I'm looking forward to reading your book." As she turned to leave, she asked, "Would you join me for tea one afternoon? I have some information about Gwen Smith I want to share."

"Tea would be lovely," Carrie said.

As she signed the last book, Charles reappeared. Carrie leaned back in her chair, and Charles rubbed her neck. She relaxed for the first time that evening but also wondered what information Mrs. Brighton-Stanford wanted to share about Gwen.

"You're probably exhausted, and your hand must hurt from signing all those books. But could you sign a few more for cus-tomers who couldn't make it tonight?" Marge asked.

"You know I will. And if you run out of signed copies, call me. I'll run over and sign more," Carrie said. "This was a wonderful turnout, and I can't thank you enough."

After Carrie signed the extra books, Charles and Carrie gathered their things and left.

"Can I take my famous wife somewhere for a late-night snack?" Charles asked.

"I'm worn out. I would rather go home and enjoy a snack and wine with you." Carrie said.

"Then your chariot awaits," Charles said.

As they walked towards the parking lot, Charles suddenly stopped.

"What's the matter?" Carrie asked.

"There's someone by our car," Charles said, then yelled, "Hey you!" He started to run towards the person. "What do you think you're doing."

"Charles, stop!" Carrie screamed. "He may be armed."

Charles ignored her advice as Carrie ran after him. If he got into a confrontation with this person, she wanted to be by his side to help. The hooded person bolted from the parking lot and headed for the woods on the other side of the boulevard.

"Doesn't look like he damaged the car," Carrie said.

Charles walked around the car. He then checked the tires. "Everything looks okay," he said.

"Wait a minute. There's a note on the windshield," Carrie said. She removed the note, moved under one of the parking lot lights, and read, "Stop investigating, or you'll be sorry."

9

True to her word, Mrs. Brighton-Stanford called to invite Carrie and Charles to join her for tea two days after the signing at the Tri-County bookstore.

On the drive to Mrs. Brighton-Stanford's home, the couple passed Charles's childhood home. He lived there with his mother, Geraldine, and his nephew, Christopher, until he married Carrie. When Christopher selected a Florida university to attend, Geraldine sold the house and moved to Florida to be near her grandson.

"Are you sorry we didn't buy the house from your mother when she offered it for sale?" Carrie asked as she gently touched Charles's arm.

"No, we made the right decision. It was a great house for my brother and me growing up, and it held many wonderful memories," Charles said. "But it was time to create new memories with you. Besides, I love our farmhouse."

After Charles and Carrie married, they purchased an old farmhouse on several acres outside the city. They spent many months renovating and bringing the house up to code and many more months designing the interior to create the home they wanted.

After a couple more streets, Charles pulled into the circular drive of Mrs. Brighton-Stanford's home. It was larger than Charles's boyhood home but of a similar Georgian design. They rang the doorbell, and Rachel appeared.

"Hello, Rachel. It's nice to see you again," Charles said. Charles caught the surprised look on Carrie's face that he knew Rachel. He would have to tell Carrie about their bookstore discussion later. "Did you have the chance to meet my wife at the book signing?" Charles asked, turning towards Carrie.

"I did, and I'm enjoying your book," Rachel said. "Henrietta is waiting for you in her sitting room."

Rachel led them down a long hallway to a room bright with sunlight streaming from large windows, comfortable overstuffed chairs, paintings, and photos adorning every bit of wall space. The logs crackling in the fireplace added to the cozy atmosphere. Charles hoped he might get an opportunity to look at the pictures since they looked like historical shots of Tri-City.

"Come in and make yourselves comfortable. I'm looking forward to our discussion," Mrs. Brighton-Stanford said. "Rachel, perhaps you could check on the tea."

"I'll be happy to," Rachel said, leaving the room.

Then Mrs. Brighton-Stanford turned to Charles. "I should have asked if you would prefer something stronger like whiskey or a glass of wine?"

"We're both fond of afternoon tea, Mrs. Brighton-Stanford," Charles said.

"Please call me Henrietta," she said.

"And we're Charles and Carrie," Charles responded.

Henrietta had been reading when they entered the room. As she placed the book on the table beside her, Charles saw it was Carrie's.

"Are you enjoying my wife's book," Charles said.

"I am," Henrietta said, looking at Carrie. "Your book has a fast-paced plot that keeps the reader turning pages. I hate a book where you get bogged down in the middle."

"Let me know what you think of the ending," Carrie said.

"Wouldn't it be wonderful if life was as simple as reading a book? In the end, you have the solution and know why everything happened," Henrietta said reflectively.

"You might be surprised to learn that's exactly how it worked in the cases we've solved. We help catch the culprit, solve the problem, and life returns to a new normal," Charles said.

Henrietta nodded. "That's another reason I wanted to talk to you. I've heard about the murders you've solved."

Charles was curious why Henrietta wanted to talk to them about murder, but at that moment, Rachel wheeled a tea trolly into the room.

"Would you like me to serve the tea?" Rachel asked.

"We can manage," Henrietta said. "Would you like to join us?"

Charles felt the offer was out of politeness and not meant to be accepted.

"Thank you, no. I want to finish those letters we discussed this morning while the thoughts are still fresh in my mind," Rachel said. "If you need me, just buzz the office."

Henrietta poured the tea, and Charles held the plate of sweet treats while the ladies picked. Then, he selected a lemon bar, one of his favorites.

"As I was saying, I invited you here today," Henrietta paused, then blurted out. "I'm afraid that Gwen's murder was my fault."

Charles looked at Carrie, unsure what Henrietta meant.

"Why do you say that?" Charles asked in a gentle tone since Henrietta was visibly upset.

"I'm sorry. I realize I'm not making much sense," Henrietta said. "Let me start at the beginning. Were you aware I hired Gwen to research our family history?"

"At the memorial service, you told Mrs. Quinn that Gwen was doing family research. How did you select Gwen?" Carrie asked.

"I attended one of her lectures on the founding of Tri-City at a community center. Her lecture focused on the years after the city was established and started to thrive. My grandfather was one of the founders and was instrumental in bringing the three founding families together to form our city," Henrietta said. "I hired her to assemble a history, so there was a permanent record of my father's accomplishments and the other founders."

"I've heard very little about the other families," Charles said. "That would make a great article."

"That was my motivation, and I wanted to share what Gwen found with others," Henrietta said.

"Aside from potentially gathering a family history, how did you plan on using her research?" Carrie asked.

"I wanted her to prepare a document I could pass on to the historical society and leave for future historians. You begin to think about these things as you get older," Mrs. Brighton-Stanford said. "Gwen never finished. When I read that they discovered her body after your book signing, I hoped she may have said something to you about her findings."

"I would think you would have more information than anyone else," Charles said.

"Yes and No. Everyone knows the same general information. My grandfather and several others created a charter to develop the city," Henrietta said. "But there are boxes in the attic with records and photos that no one has reviewed. I hired Gwen to sort them and add more facts to the original story."

"Did Gwen work here in your home?" Charles remembered they found no Brighton-Stanford materials in Gwen's college office.

"She did. I set her up in an empty bedroom on the third floor near the attic and had the boxes and a trunk brought down for her to sort," Henrietta said.

She poured them another round of tea and passed the cookie plate. After Charles took two more cookies, Carrie moved the dish out of his reach.

"Did Gwen remove documents?" Carrie asked.

"She could have, but I don't believe she did," Henrietta said. "She worked with a computer and used her phone to take pictures of documents and photos. I'm sure she captured what she needed without taking the original paper."

"I understood that she finished her research and was writing her final report," Charles asked.

"Almost. Gwen indicated she had a few more details to verify but had started writing her report," Henrietta said. "Unfortunately, I saw no results before she died."

"I wished I had the opportunity to talk with her," Carrie said. "Apparently, she had concerns about how to present the information."

Henrietta sat quietly and then looked directly at Carrie and Charles. "There is something else," she said. "After chatting with you, I believe I can trust you with what I'm about to say."

As Henrietta stood, she knocked Carrie's book on the floor. Charles jumped up to retrieve the book and placed it on the table. Charles saw his opportunity to get a closer look at the photos. "May I look at the pictures and photos on the wall?" Charles asked.

"Yes, help yourself. Those photos capture much of the early history of our city," Henrietta said.

Charles looked at the images while Henrietta crossed the room to a lady's writing desk in the corner. She took a key from her pocket, unlocked the desk, and removed several papers. She handed them to Charles, and they returned to their seats.

Charles took the pages, and as he read them, he realized they were poison pen letters. Before he passed the letters to Carrie, he noticed two things. The words cut out and used to form the sentences were the same fonts he used in the Tri-County magazine. Second, the phrase "stop investigating, or you'll be sorry" appeared in several letters. This wording was the same as the note left on their car.

"You've received letters demanding you to stop Gwen's research?" Carrie asked.

"Yes. Gwen had just started her work when the first one arrived," Henrietta said. Then I received the four additional letters over the next several weeks."

"How did Gwen react? It doesn't sound like she stopped working," Charles said.

"I never told Gwen about them. That's why I feel guilty," Henrietta said, twisting her handkerchief. In a softer voice, she added, "Had I shared them with her, she might have decided not to continue and still be alive."

"You're assuming her research had something to do with the murder. While it's possible, we don't know if that is true," Charles said.

"Even if Gwen's research was a factor in her death, history was her passion. I doubt she would have stopped," Carrie said. "Don't blame yourself for something you couldn't control."

"And there's no reason to assume these letters came from her killer. But you need to notify the police about these letters," Charles said. "Contact Detective Jenco. He's heading the investigation."

"Thank you for your encouragement. I've been bothered since I read of Gwen's death," Henrietta said.

"Before we leave. I have one more request. Could I see the room Gwen used?" Charles asked. "I would like to see some of the documents Gwen found."

"Let me get Rachel to show you the room. The elevator doesn't go to the third floor, and my knees aren't what they used to be." Henrietta picked up the phone next to her chair and pressed a button.

Charles saw Carrie mouthed that she would wait with Henrietta. He was glad Carrie stayed behind. He wanted a one-on-one with Rachel about Henrietta's household and what she thought of Gwen. Charles couldn't believe that researching Tri-City could be a reason for murder.

10

Charles met Rachel in the hallway.

"It's quicker if we take the backstairs," Rachel said as she opened the door to a set of steps.

Charles felt in good shape for his age but had to concentrate on keeping up with Rachel, who bounded up the steps. Finally, they reached the third-floor hallway. Charles caught his breath as Rachel opened the door of a small room.

In the days when the house had a full complement of live-in staff, Charles assumed this was a maid's bedroom. Today, the space housed a table and a chair. Scattered around the rooms were storage boxes in various states of disarray.

"Was Gwen a sloppy worker?" Charles asked. The minute he asked the question, he saw the shocked look on Rachel's face as she scanned the room.

"Not at all. Gwen was very organized," Rachel said. "A couple of times when I checked to see if she needed anything, I witnessed her process. She opened one box at a time, captured the contents on a digital recorder, made notes on her computer, and sometimes took photos with her phone. When she finished with the box, she would place one on top of the other along the far wall."

Charles looked at the wall and saw boxes no longer stacked. Most had lids thrown aside and contents scattered.

"Looks like someone other than Gwen searched the boxes," Charles said. "Who has access to the room?"

"Three of us live on the premises. Henrietta, myself, and Mrs. Lancaster, the housekeeper and cook," Rachel said, "Although I can't imagine Mrs. Lancaster coming up here. Like Henrietta, the steps are difficult for her to navigate, and she would have no interest in the family's historical records."

While Rachel was talking, Charles walked around the room and looked at some of the papers and photos. Most of the documents seemed to represent Henry Brighton's business dealings. The images would need more study to understand the people and events pictured.

"Are there other visitors who would have access to the room?" Charles asked.

"Henrietta's son Henry and her grandson Hansen live in the carriage house at the back of the property. Mr. Henry, when he's not traveling, often stops in for dinner," Rachel said. "He's a hard-working individual who manages the family business. I can't imagine him coming up here, searching the boxes, and leaving this mess."

Charles thought he heard a certain admiration for Henry in Rachel's voice. Was there something more between them?

"Hansen has a room on the second floor and sometimes stays here, especially if his father is traveling," Rachel said. "His grandmother dotes on him."

"Does he work with his father?" Charles asked. Charles had the impression that while Henrietta doted on Hansen, Rachel didn't.

"No. Hansen is a student at the university. And before you ask, he took some courses with Gwen," Rachel said. "He visited with Gwen several times while she worked."

"Anyone else who has access?"

Rachel thought momentarily and then added, "Sometimes, on weekends, Hansen hosts a get-together for friends from school. The food and music are downstairs, but I can't guarantee a guest didn't come up to the third floor."

"How does Henrietta feel about Hansen having parties at the house?" Charles asked.

"She enjoys having the young people around," Rachel said. "We both make appearances so the young people know there are adults in the house, but we aren't watching over them.".

Charles agreed with Henrietta about having young people around. When Christopher, his nephew, visited during vacations and semester breaks, his youthful exuberance filled the rooms of their farmhouse. Charles shifted the conversation back to Gwen's work.

"Without Gwen's final report, there's nothing to indicate what she discovered or what someone else wanted to find," Charles said.

"True. That's why Henrietta wants Gwen's final report found."

Rachel and Charles returned to the sitting room, where they heard Carrie and Henrietta discussing their favorite authors.

Rachel interrupted their conversation. "Henrietta, it looks like someone searched Gwen's work area."

"What do you mean searched?" She looked to Charles for confirmation.

"We discovered boxes opened with papers scattered about the room," Charles said.

"I can't believe someone searched Gwen's workspace!" Henrietta exclaimed. "This is not acceptable. We must take immediate steps."

"You should call the police," Carrie suggested.

"I'm not sure that will serve any purpose since we're not sure when this happened or who did it," Henrietta said. "It's been several weeks since Gwen was in the room."

Charles wondered if Henrietta didn't want to involve the police because she thought the culprit had to be someone with access to the room. Perhaps a family member.

"What would you like me to do?" Rachel asked.

"Call Johnny. That's our handyman," Henrietta explained to Carrie and Charles. "Have him install a padlock on the door."

"Maybe we should also call the security company and have a camera installed in the hallway upstairs," Rachel suggested. "With a large house, we can't know what's happening on every floor."

"Good suggestion." After hesitating, Henrietta turned to Charles and Carrie, "I want to hire you to solve Gwen's murder."

Charles looked at Carrie. He knew what she was thinking. This would be the first time three people wanted to hire them to solve the same crime.

"We're quietly looking into Gwen's death for the Quinns, but we can also keep you informed of our findings," Carrie said.

Charles added, "Please don't mention this to anyone, especially when you share the letters with Detective Jenco. The police don't appreciate interference in their cases."

"I understand," Mrs. Brighton said, then looked at Rachel, who nodded.

"I'm going to get back to work," Rachel said. "Good to see you both."

"We should go, too. Thank you for the tea and the conversation," Carrie said.

As Mrs. Brighton walked them to the door, she said, "I know your mother, Charles. Geraldine and I stay in touch. Geraldine is proud of your accomplishments in maintaining the family business," Mrs. Brighton said. "I'm hoping one of your new accomplishments will be the solution to Gwen's murder and finding the document she created about my family's history."

***

"How was your second meeting with Rachel?" Carrie asked as they were driving away.

Charles laughed, knowing that nothing escaped his wife.

"Once we realized someone searched the room, our conversation focused on possible suspects," Charles said.

"I wondered the same thing," Carrie said. "How can a person enter a room in the house without Henrietta or Rachel knowing about it? There can't be that many people with access."

"There are more people than you might think," Charles said. "Henrietta, Rachel, and the housekeeper, Mrs. Lancaster, live there. I didn't ask if there's any daily help, but there may be others. Her son Henry and grandson Hansen frequently drop in for visits, and Hansen often stays overnight," Charles said. "But the real issue is Hansen, who hosts weekend parties with his college friends at his grandmother's home."

"That's not good. There could be dozens of visitors who could sneak off to the third floor," Carrie said. "Speaking of Hansen. I forgot to mention I saw him at the bookstore the night of the signing."

"Is that so unusual since his grandmother and Rachel were there?" Charles asked.

"It looked like he was avoiding them, and his grandmother didn't mention him," Carrie said. "Also, Hansen is the same size and build as the person who ran after leaving the note on our car."

"What would his purpose be in stopping our investigation or Gwen's research?" Charles asked.

"No idea. And I can't be positive it was Hansen," Carrie said. "Whatever the searcher wanted must be of great importance. They took a chance of getting caught when they searched the room Gwen used."

"Maybe the question is why weren't they caught," Charles said as he waited at a stop light. "Did Henrietta share additional information besides her favorite book when you talked with her?"

"We looked at the pictures on the wall, which included the certificate of incorporation and photos of a ribbon cutting and a Founder's Day picnic," Carrie said.

"I saw that photo. That was quite a crowd," Charles said.

"They were family members of the three founders. Aside from the grandparents and her parents as children, Henrietta couldn't identify the rest," Carrie said. "She said Gwen was also interested in that photo and hoped to identify more of the people."

"We need to find Gwen's research," Charles said as the light changed, and he turned towards their home.

"Maybe I should offer to continue the Henrietta's project?" Carrie offered.

"Absolutely not," Charles said. "We don't know if Gwen's Brighton research was the cause of her death. If it was, I don't want to alert the killer you are following in her footsteps. Let's quietly continue our investigation to find her murderer."

11

Carrie finished her article on covered bridges. She checked for accuracy and then emailed it to the magazine. This article wasn't for Charles's Tri-County Monthly. Instead, she sent it to a publication in the northern part of the state with the most covered bridges.

Once she had verified that the publication accepted her email, she turned her attention to making a list of what she knew about Gwen's murder.

- Someone shot Gwen with a gun. Was it hers?
- Where was she shot? Not in the garden where Joanne discovered the body.
- The police found one of my books near the body. Did Gwen buy the book, or did her murderer place it next to her?
- Gwen came to the book signing to meet me. Did she want to talk to me about previous cases or ask for help with her report for Mrs. Brighton?

- Mrs. Brighton hired Gwen to prepare a family history.
- Gwen reviewed boxes of records at the Brighton home. Were there more records that held secrets?
- Where was Gwen's computer or other electronic devices she used to capture the information?
- Who sent Mrs. Brighton the poison pen letters?
- Who would benefit if the research stopped?
- What did Gwen know that caused her murder?

Carrie looked at her list and realized she had more questions than answers. Before she could decide on her next steps, the phone rang.

"How about meeting me for dinner at the country club?" Charles asked.

"That would be lovely," Carrie said. "I'm frustrated. I've written a list of what we know about Gwen's murder, and I'm afraid we don't know much."

"I have an idea where we might find more information," Charles said. "Before we eat, I want to talk with Jim Albright, who knows the history of the club and Tri-City. Terry gave Gwen Jim's name, and I want to know if he met with her."

"Great idea," Carrie said. "I'll join you."

Charles hesitated. "I believe I should talk to Jim alone. You know he can be a flirt when an attractive lady is present. I want him focused on history and Gwen."

Carrie wanted to participate in the conversation but appreciated Charles's insight into how Jim would react. "Thanks for the compliment," Carrie said. "In that case, I'll be in the bar waiting to hear what gems of wisdom Jim provided."

***

When Charles arrived at the club, he went straight to the bar to find Jake, the bartender. Jake was a pleasant young man with a smile everyone adored, and members felt comfortable confiding their secrets with him. Everyone also appreciated that whatever information they told Jake would be kept private.

"Mr. Faraday," Jake said, smiling. "What brings you to the club this early?"

"I'm meeting Carrie for an early dinner. In the meantime, I wanted to ask Jim Albright a few questions about the club's history," Charles said. "Any idea where he might be?"

"He's in the library," Jake said. "Can I fix you a drink to take with you?"

"No. I'll wait and have something with Carrie." Charles said as he headed to the library.

"I'll take care of Mrs. Faraday until you return," Jake said while polishing a glass.

Charles found Jim Albright stretched out in a chair, reading a book. Due to the hour of the day, he was the only one in the room.

"Hi ho, Charles. What brings you to the library at this hour?" Jim asked and added, "Where is your lovely wife?"

"Carrie will be joining me shortly, but I wanted to talk with you privately," Charles responded.

Charles piqued Jim's interest, and he sat upright.

"I don't know if you heard, but there was a murder after Carrie's book signing at the Quinns."

"Charles. How can you even ask that question," Jim said. "This is the country club where everyone knows everyone and everything that happens in Tri-City."

Charles nodded his head and smiled. "Carrie and I learned that the murder victim, Gwen Smith, recently joined the country club," Charles said. "We also heard she was researching the history of Tri-City."

"Are you and Carrie investigating Gwen's death?" Jim asked.

"No, we're leaving solving the murder to the police. But we learned that Gwen wanted to speak with Carrie, but we don't know why. We're trying to learn more about Gwen's activities," Charles said. "Knowing your historical knowledge about Tri-City and the club, did Gwen contact you?"

"That she did," Jim said. "We had a lovely discussion about the families that founded our fair city."

"What was so good about your discussion?" Charles asked as a subtle way to find out more about Gwen and what she asked.

"She was a very bright young woman and knew her subject," Jim said. "Did you know she was a history professor over at the college?"

Charles nodded. Before they could continue, Jake entered the room.

"You rang the bell, Mr. Albright. Are you ready for another drink?" Jake asked.

"How about you, Charles?" Jim asked.

"Jake, I changed my mind. I will have a drink. Gin and tonic, please," Charles said. "I'm sure Carrie will order some wine when she arrives."

After Jake left, Charles said, "You were impressed by Gwen and her interest in the club's history."

"She started with some general questions about the founding of Tri-City and when they founded the country club," Jim said.

"I didn't know the Tri-City founders started our club," Charles said. "When did this happen?"

"Almost immediately after the founding of Tri-City," Jim said. "People looking at the history may wonder why the founders didn't build schools, hospitals, and other community buildings first, rather than a country club."

"I can't say I disagree with that sentiment," said Charles.

"But there was a good reason," Jim said.

Jake returned with their drinks. Charles charged the drinks to his account, and Jake left.

"Where we were?" Jim asked.

"The beginnings of the country club," Charles prompted.

"Ah, yes. It's more like something that fell into the founders' lap. Dorchester owned the country club land and wanted to get rid of it," Jim said.

"You said Dorchester, not Brighton," Charles said.

"Correct. Dorchester had inherited a farm in the middle of the area Brighton represented. It was too far away from Dorchester's existing farm for him to manage both properties. He thought the new city could put the land to good use," Jim said, taking a long sip of his drink.

"Did he donate the land?" Charles asked.

"There were no tax benefits for a donation back then, and the new city didn't have the money to pay a fair price," Jim said. "Instead, they established a contract whereby the new city would make two payments a year to Dorchester based on a sliding scale for property value and inflation."

"It still sounds like an insider type of deal," Charles said.

"Perhaps. But the new city didn't have to pay a huge sum of money, which they didn't have, and the property was right in the heart of the boundaries for the new city," Jim added.

"Is the contract still in effect today?" Charles asked.

"No. It ended about ten years ago when the last Dorchester family member, a granddaughter, died. They're all gone," Jim said.

"Didn't the state have a claim?" Charles asked.

"It was a private contract that stated payments ended when there were no more heirs," Jim added.

"Doesn't seem right the founders opted for a golf course," Charles said.

"It's not as it appears. You're talking about a brand-new community surrounded by farmland without a single building for running the new city. They used the massive stone farmhouse on the property as the first government building," Jim said. "Since it was a gathering place, they added a community picnic area, cleaned up the lake on the property for swimming, and added a couple of holes of golf for recreation. And from there, it grew."

"Is our stone entrance part of the original farmhouse?" Charles asked.

"It is," Jim said as he sipped his drink.

"I never knew this," Charles said. "This would make an interesting story, and I'll bet Carrie would enjoy writing it."

"Most of our members belong to the club without realizing it has a rich history," Jim said. "And we have archives that capture these early days they can access."

"Are these the records that Gwen wanted to see?" Charles asked. He took a glance at his watch, knowing Carrie would arrive shortly.

"Gwen spent several afternoons with me looking through the files. She was a true historian," Jim said.

"Any particular record you remember that she wanted to see?" Charles asked.

"Her interest was the founders' families and what happened to them. She wasn't as interested in the city's development other than the lease agreement," Jim said.

"Refresh my memory. Henry Brighton, Edwin Allwin and Samuel Dorchester represented the three original villages. Were there others?" Charles asked.

"They were the three members who created the incorporation agreement, but plenty of other players helped," Jim said. "I remember Gwen was particularly interested in the photos that showed the different families."

"How are the photos archived?" Charles asked. "I periodically see historical photos on the club's walls changing,"

Jim smiled and then said, "Come with me." Jim produced a set of keys. He walked to the far end of the room and unlocked the door. He turned on the light inside, revealing a large room with filing cabinets, shelves, and wooden boxes. Jim used another key, unlocked the cabinet, and removed a box. Charles saw photos stored inside protective glassine covers. Jim stood back and allowed Charles to examine the pictures.

"You've numbered the photos chronologically," Charles said as he leafed through the pictures. He stopped and then went through them again. "Are you aware that photo number 14 is missing?"

Jim gently pushed Charles aside and went slowly through the stack again.

"You're right," Jim verified.

"You think Gwen could've taken it?" Charles asked.

"Gwen never had access to this room. I would bring pictures or documents to the table in the main room. When she finished with that group, I would put them back and bring her the next set," Jim said. "Besides, I saw her taking photos with her phone. There was no need for her to steal pictures or documents."

Jim returned the box to the cabinet and locked the room, and the men returned to their seats and drinks.

"Jim, do you remember what the missing photo pictured?"

Jim laughed. "I'm getting up there in age, but my mind is still sharp as a tack."

"It is," Charles said. "That's why I come to you for accurate information."

"It was a Founder's Day Picnic photo? Jim said. "It pictured all the founders and members of their families. There were probably 25 people in the photo, including kids and grandkids."

He saw a photo like Jim described on Henrietta's wall. He wondered if it was the same as the missing photo.

Jim snapped his fingers and said, "I can't believe I forgot this." He went to the archive room and returned with a ledger book. "Here I was touting how sharp I was, and I forgot to check the logbook," he said as he flipped through the pages. "The photo isn't missing. It's hanging in the entrance hallway."

Jake returned to the room. Jim held his glass up, and Charles shook his head.

"Your wife is in the bar," Jake said.

"Then I better go. Put Jim's drink on my tab," Charles said. "It's always a pleasure to talk with you. Thanks for the information."

Charles left Jim sitting comfortably in the library. He went to find Carrie and share the additional puzzle pieces he discovered.

12

When Carrie arrived at the country club, she didn't see Charles. She went to the bar and grabbed a stool to wait for him. It was only seconds before Jake spotted her.

"Hello, Mrs. Faraday. What can I get you?" Jake asked.

"I'll have a glass of that new riesling you're featuring," Carrie said. "Has my husband stopped by?"

"Mr. Faraday arrived about a half hour ago and went to the library to meet with Jim Albright," Jake said. "I can serve your drink there if you want to join them."

Carrie wanted to find out what Jim had to say, but Charles was right. He would get more information if she weren't there. "Thanks, but I'll sit with you and enjoy my drink," she said. "When Charles is hungry, he'll come looking for me."

"He might be awhile. Mr. Faraday wanted to talk about the club's history," Jake lowered his voice. "I don't think there's anything Jim doesn't know about the club and its members. But he can talk on the subject forever."

Carrie checked that no one else was within earshot. "I wanted to talk to you."

Carrie had Jake's undivided attention. Carrie wanted to know the reaction of club members.

"My husband wanted to ask Jim if Gwen Smith contacted him about the club's history. I guess you heard about Gwen Smith's murder," Carrie said. "What are the members saying?"

"Yeah, that was tragic. Most members hadn't met her," Jake said as he opened the bottle of riesling. "She seemed nice. I liked her."

His comment surprised Carrie. "You met Gwen? I mean, she was a new member."

Jake laughed. "The first place new members check out is the bar. She stopped here multiple times, including after meetings with Jim Albright."

"Did she say anything specific about what she discussed with Jim?" Carrie asked.

"She never said much," Jake hesitated. "I guess it won't matter if I tell you now that she is gone. She made an unusual comment on the last day I saw her."

"What was that?" Carrie took her first sip of wine. It was cold and crisp, just the way she liked it.

"I asked her if Jim provided the information she needed. She said his records verified something she had previously discovered. Now she needed to figure out what to do with the information and how to share it." Jake corked the bottle of wine and returned it to the refrigerator behind the bar. "She probably said more than she wanted. After a couple of drinks, she was thinking out loud."

"Anything else?" Carrie prodded.

"Sorry, that's all she said. The bar got busy. The next time I looked, she was gone."

"Thanks for sharing." Carrie paused. "Suppose we keep this conversation between us."

"Are you and Mr. Faraday investigating her murder?" Jake asked.

"We're reviewing Gwen's historical research about the founders. We thought there might be a story for the magazine," Carrie said. "The police are handling the murder."

Jake arched an eyebrow in disbelief but said nothing and left to serve another member.

Carrie was deep in thought. What had Gwen verified with Jim? Was it an item she found in Henrietta's home or someplace else? She was so engrossed in her thoughts that Carrie didn't notice when someone slipped onto the barstool beside her. When the visitor spoke, she discovered Detective Jenco sitting next to her.

"Detective Jenco!" Carrie exclaimed. It was difficult to hide her surprise. "Are you here on a case?"

"No. I'm a country club member and off-duty," he said. "Since I'm a bachelor, it's nice to have a drink and a good dinner," he said. "The chef serves a mean prime rib dinner on Tuesday nights."

"That explains why my husband wanted to have dinner here. I forgot that it's prime rib night," Carrie said.

"Is your husband here?" Jenco asked, scanning the bar.

"We arrived separately, but he's around. Probably checking on our dinner reservation."

There was a moment of silence, and then Jenco said, "I visited Mrs. Brighton-Stanford today. She mentioned you and Charles had visited her."

Carrie knew where the conversation was going. He wanted to ensure that neither Charles nor she had interfered with his investigation. She hesitated about how to respond. Hopefully, Henrietta didn't reveal that she wanted them to solve Gwen's murder.

"Mrs. Brighton-Stanford attended my book signing at the Tri-County bookstore and invited us for tea," Carrie said. "It's always nice when a writer can discuss her book with one of her readers."

"And you want me to believe Gwen's name never came up in the conversation," Jenco said.

"We briefly discussed Gwen. Her murder concerned Henrietta since she was doing work for her," Carrie explained. "She thought I met Gwen at the signing, which I didn't. Even though you found my book near the body, I'm sure you noticed I never signed it." Carrie realized she sounded defensive and was blabbing.

"Not having her book signed doesn't mean you didn't meet her," Jenco said.

"She still would have had to come inside to purchase a book. No one saw her," Carrie said in an even tone. She knew Jenco was always trying to get her to react. "I'm sure you checked with Maddy, Marge, and other attendees whether they saw Gwen inside."

Jenco said nothing and maintained a poker face. "Back to your conversation with Mrs. Brighton-Stanford."

"You knew she hired Gwen to write a family history." Carrie deliberately sounded vague.

"I knew," he said, annoyed at Carrie's inference, that he missed something. "We checked the room Gwen used and found nothing of interest. There were only stacked boxes of family records."

Stacked boxes told Crrie that someone had straightened the room. Jenco's comment meant the police didn't disturb the boxes.

Then, who searched through the boxes of documents? Carrie refocused as Jenco continued.

"Is that all you discussed? Nothing else?" Jenco prodded.

"She showed us some poison pen letters," Carrie said, watching Jenco's reaction. "We advised her to get in touch with you."

"She did, but why didn't you call me?" Jenco asked.

"You met Mrs. Brighton-Stanford. She's quite formidable. We didn't feel it was our place to report something that happened in her home," Carrie said. "I'm glad she took our advice and reported them to you."

Fortunately for Carrie, Charles arrived, which ended Jenco's interrogation. Charles took the stool on the other side of Jenco. "Detective Jenco, it's been a while."

"I was just talking to your wife about Gwen Smith and my visit with Mrs. Brighton-Stanford," Jenco said.

"I heard you mention the poison pen letters. Are you making progress on the case?" Charles asked.

"It's early days. Like Gwen Smith, we're still doing research," Jenco said.

Carrie knew Jenco wouldn't share information, but Charles wanted to be polite.

"Good to know," Charles said. Then he turned to Carrie. "Our table is ready. Detective Jenco, did you know it's prime rib night?"

Jenco nodded as he sipped his drink. Charles took Carrie's arm as she slid off the barstool. "Then let's get you a cut of meat," Carrie said."

Carrie looked back at Jake, and he nodded. She knew what they discussed was safe with him.

In keeping with their practice of not discussing work while eating, they waited until after they devoured their prime rib dinner and finished their crème brûlée before Charles told of his conversation with Jim.

While sipping coffee, Carrie asked, "Did you learn anything new?"

"A few things. Gwen was more interested in the founders and their families than the city's development," Charles said. "She used her cell phone to capture documents she wanted to retain."

"It would be nice if we could look at her phone. I assume the police have it," Carrie said.

"We should check with Gloria and see if the police returned it," Charles suggested. "Did you learn anything from Jenco?"

"Are you kidding? Not a word from Jenco," Carrie said. "But Jake had a tidbit to share. Gwen told him that Jim had verified the information she had found and that she needed to decide how to present it. She said the information had a financial impact."

"Maybe Gwen wanted to talk to you about the best method to present her discoveries," Charles suggested.

"We won't solve it sitting here. Are you ready to go?" Carrie asked.

As they left the restaurant, Carrie waved to Detective Jenco, who sat at a corner table. When they reached the club's entrance, Charles stopped and examined one of the photos on the wall.

"Did you find an interesting photo?" Carrie asked.

"It's the Founder's Day Picnic photo. Jim said this picture interested Gwen, and there's one just like it is hanging on Henrietta's wall," Charles said.

Carrie took the small digital camera she always carried in her handbag and snapped a photo. "Since we don't have any other leads, this photo might be our next clue."

13

Carrie and Charles planned to spend a quiet, leisurely Saturday morning at their farmhouse completing tasks. They designed their study with two desks and two sofas. It allowed them to do simultaneous projects, such as sharing the Sunday paper while stretched out on a sofa.

Today, Charles was doing Faraday Press paperwork at his desk. Charles was an excellent manager and skilled in money and business management.

While Carrie didn't have a head for business, she was a writer who understood electronic devices and software. Their skills worked well together, especially when solving cases.

Baxter, their cat, shared the sofa with Carrie as she used a laptop computer to access Tri-City's history sites. They were engrossed in their work when Carrie's phone rang.

"Joanne, why are you calling so early? You're not a morning person, especially on weekends," Carrie said.

"Have you and Charles made any progress with the case? Your police detectives were here again," Joanne spoke rapidly.

Carrie wanted to say they weren't her police detectives, but she could tell from Joanne's stressed tone her comment wouldn't help. "We're talking to people and gathering information. Why did the police return?"

"They wanted me to review every step of my time at the party and the next morning. Did I talk with Gwen? Did I see anyone else talk with Gwen, and did I see you talk to Gwen?"

"They asked about me?" Carrie questioned. "I hope they don't think I'm a suspect. I've been there and done that suspect thing."

"Jenco wanted to know if I saw Gwen come in from the garden and buy a book. I reminded him I never saw or spoke with her. But he doesn't seem satisfied," Joanne said. "Then he put Dan through the same drill. They even asked him if he knew Gwen before the event, implying they had a prior relationship."

"I understand your situation. Jenco assembles his case through intimidation," Carrie said. "If it makes you feel better, Charles and I started interviewing people who knew Gwen and researching their backgrounds."

"Do you have any results, like suspects, other than Dan and myself?" Joanne asked, sounding desperate.

While they hadn't made much progress, Carrie didn't want to tell Joanne that. "Don't worry. Charles and I will figure this out. We always do," Carrie said. "Put the investigation out of your mind and enjoy the rest of the day with Dan."

"I'm sorry to vent, but it's frustrating. Thanks for listening." Joanne rang off.

"I take it that was Joanne," Charles said.

"Jenco had more questions for her and Dan. I'm sure you figured out from the conversation that she's worried," Carrie said. "I sounded positive for her sake, but I'm frustrated that we haven't made more progress. I'm not sure what to do next. Any suggestions?"

"I have a suggestion," Charles said. "I'm hungry."

Carrie raised an eyebrow as she questioned her husband. "Help me understand how you're being hungry, helps us solve the case," Carrie said.

"If we go to the Train Stop, we'll have a chance to chat with Gloria."

"That's not a bad idea," Carrie said. "Now that the funeral is over, maybe she can offer other leads."

***

At the Train Stop, Carrie and Charles ordered black and blue salads consisting of thinly sliced steak and blue cheese crumbles on a bed of greens with assorted toppings. Had Charles been eating alone, he would have probably ordered dishes that were higher in calories, like fries and onion rings. Although tall and thin, Carrie encouraged him to order healthier options.

Gloria ran in and out of the kitchen, serving customers, and waved when she spotted Carrie. As they finished their lunch, Gloria stopped by their table.

"Sorry it took so long for me to visit, but Saturday mornings are always busy," she said. "Did you enjoy your food?"

"We had the Black and Blue Salad," Carrie said. "Delicious."

"That's our most popular salad."

"This is my husband, Charles," Carrie said.

"Nice to meet you," Gloria said. "Did you come for the food, or do you have an update on the case?"

"We've run into a wall trying to find your sister's research materials from her Brighton project," Charles said. "We believe that project may hold some clues as to what happened to your sister."

"We checked her office at the university and found someone searched it before we arrived," Carrie said. "The searcher emptied and threw papers everywhere."

"No one told me this." Gloria sat, shocked by the news. "Do you know what they wanted? More importantly, could you tell if they took anything?"

"We don't know for sure, but based on our conversation with Emily Hopkins, your sister always protected her research materials," Charles said. "We don't think they found what they wanted."

"Since we checked Gwen's university office, could we look at her home office? That's assuming the police finished with it," Carrie said.

"The police gave the all-clear for her condo, and I've started to remove things," Gloria said. "Can you go now? I have a break before the dinner crowd."

"We're free," Charles said.

"Give me a few minutes to change my clothes."

***

When they entered Gwen's condo, Carrie saw a large room with an open floor plan, windows overlooking the park, and contemporary Danish furniture. It wasn't to Carrie's taste, but she respected the design.

91

"I've looked through the contents of her desk and removed any documents to pay her bills and put her finances in order. Everything else is how Gwen left it," Gloria said. "Are you looking for something specific?"

"We hoped to find Gwen's final report for Mrs. Brighton-Stanford. Or if that's not available, find the original research on her computer," Carrie said.

"I'm afraid you're out of luck," Gloria said. "Her computer isn't here."

"Do you think someone took it?" Charles asked. "Any signs of a break-in?"

"Her condo wasn't disturbed the way you described her university office with papers tossed around," Gloria said. "But I had a feeling someone searched the place. Several drawers weren't completely closed in the bedroom and in her office. I didn't leave them that way."

"Any signs of her phone? Several people mentioned that Gwen used her phone to capture photos and documents," Carrie said

"The police asked me about that. Since I didn't have it, the detectives assumed Gwen's killer took it when he...," Gloria started to tear up. She took a deep breath and continued, "I'll be in her bedroom if you need me. I'm still gathering her clothes to donate."

Once Gloria left the room, Carrie searched the filing cabinet and the closet while Charles investigated Gwen's desk.

They worked quietly except for the sound of drawers opening and papers rustling. After several minutes, Charles said, "Here's something interesting."

Carrie joined him at the desk and placed her hand on his shoulder as she looked at where he pointed. "What did you find?"

"Gwen made notations here on her blotter. A sort of a to-do list with everything from picking up laundry, paying bills, checking birth, death, and divorce records at the historical society, and B.C.," Charles said.

"Checking for records sounds related to her research." I wonder who or what B.C. is?" Carrie asked.

"Don't know, but this list is the only thing I've found related to her work," Charles said. "Her digital recorder is in the drawer, but there's nothing on it."

"Does that seem unusual?" Carrie asked.

"Not necessarily. Many of our reporters use this same model. They transfer what they record onto their computer and then delete the files."

After several more minutes, Charles and Carrie decided there was nothing more to see in Gwen's condo. They called to Gloria to say that they were about to leave. As they passed by the bedroom, Carrie saw Gloria sitting on the edge of the bed with her hands covering her face.

"Charles, wait for me in the living room," Carrie whispered as she entered the bedroom.

Gloria wiped her tears with a wet tissue. Carrie handed her a fresh tissue and sat beside Gloria on the bed.

"I'm sorry. It isn't easy. Everyone feels sadness when there is the loss of someone close. Losing a twin sister is worse," Gloria said. "And I lost her at the hands of a killer."

"Believe me, I understand. Do you know why I returned to Tri-City?" Carrie asked.

Gloria shook her head.

"It was to find the killer of Charles's brother, Jamie. Solving the case closed a sad event but also brought Charles and me together to start a new family chapter," Carrie said. Even though years had passed, Carrie found it challenging to tell the story.

"I heard you had solved crimes. I didn't realize one of the cases involved a member of your family. I appreciate you sharing this," Gloria said. "I'm feeling lonely and isolated with the realization that no one cares about Gwen's death."

"Charles and I care," Carrie said. She put her arm around Gloria's shoulders and hugged her.

After a moment, Gloria regained her composure. "There's no rush to sell the condo. I find it easier to pack a few things each time I come."

"Do you want us to stay with you while you finish?" Carrie asked.

"No, I've done enough for today. I can only handle a little bit at a time. I'll take this pile to the local charity and return to the restaurant to help with dinner preparations."

As they left the condo, Carrie turned to Gwen, "Remember, you are not alone. Charles and I are committed to finding who murdered your sister."

14

Three weeks after the murder, Carrie lectured on "How to Get Started Writing" at the monthly Lady's Guild country club luncheon. After lunch, Carrie and Marilyn Armstrong sat in chairs on a raised platform as Marilyn interviewed her. In the end, the attendees had the chance to ask questions, and they asked so many questions the event ran over.

Carrie was surprised and grateful so many women attended. She saw Marge and Maddy give a thumbs up, indicating they sold out of her book. After the event, Carrie and Joanne stopped by the bar for a glass of wine.

"Whew. I'm glad that's over. I'm not fond of large events, especially when I'm the main attraction," Carrie said. "But I got through it, and it was almost as good as this wine we're enjoying."

"You gave a great talk. You even made me want to start writing," Joanne laughed.

"There's no reason you can't. Everyone has a story to tell," Carrie said.

Joanne shook her head, but Carrie could tell writing had crossed her mind.

"You impressed me with how you handled all the questions from the ladies," Joanne said. "They certainly had a lot of them."

"I wished more of the questions had to do with how to get started writing instead of the latest news about Gwen's murder." Carrie never understood why people always wanted the details of a murder.

"I noticed, and those questions made me uncomfortable. The ladies probably wanted me on stage with you, giving specifics about finding a dead body," Joanne said. Carrie saw Joanne close her eyes tight as if she remembered the event. "Speaking of the case, anything new?"

"We picked up a few tidbits from Jim Albright about how he helped Gwen find certain documents, and Jake added some information," said Carrie.

"Jake, our friendly bartender?" Joanne asked, tilting her head to where Jake stood.

"Gwen stopped by the bar after she met with Jim," Carrie said. "At their last meeting, she told Jake she had information that would impact several people's lives."

"That sounds like a real clue. Perhaps that answers why Gwen wanted to contact you," Joanne suggested. "Maybe she thought a fellow writer could provide some insight on how to present sensitive material. Anything else?"

Carrie could tell Joanne was anxious to get every tidbit concerning the case. Joanne felt she and Dan were still under the police microscope.

"We checked out Gwen's condo with Gloria."

"Any clues?"

"Not positive ones. Gwen's computer and phone are missing, meaning all her research has disappeared."

"Did Mrs. Brighton-Stanford shed any light?" Joanne asked. "After all, Gwen worked in her home sorting documents to create her report."

"That's the other piece of news. Henrietta had an intruder who searched Gwen's workspace at her home," Carrie said. "There are so many boxes of documents we can't tell if anything is missing. Our only hope is to find Gwen's report."

"It sounds like what she uncovered frightened someone enough to break into the various locations to find her materials," Joanne said.

"Charles, and I agree with you. And who knows how much they have destroyed," Carrie said. "That's why we started to retrace Gwen's research."

They finished their wine and were ready to leave when Joanne's phone rang.

"Mrs. Collins. How are you?" Joanne asked. "That's interesting." Joanne touched Carrie's arm and pointed to her phone. "I'm finishing lunch at the country club and should be home within 15 minutes."

Carrie detected excitement in Joanne's voice as she waited to get the details.

"Get this. That was Mrs. Collins, my neighbor whose home adjoins the back of our property. She has those big hedges separating our properties," Joanne said. "Her gardener was trimming the hedges and discovered a phone."

"A phone! Could it be Gwen's phone?" Carrie asked.

"There's only one way to find out," Joanne said.

***

When they arrived at Joanne's home, they walked a few hundred yards to the sprawling rancher of Mrs. Collins. Mr. and Mrs. Collins were two of the older residents in the neighborhood. They often talked about downsizing and moving to a smaller place but had remained in their home.

When Mrs. Collins answered the door, she said, "That didn't take long. You both look so lovely. I've been sorting out some closets and haven't had time to change. I hope you'll excuse my appearance," she said.

Mrs. Collins looked acceptable to Carrie in a loose-fitting baby blue top and jeans.

"We only look this way because we were at a club luncheon," Joanne said. "I hope you don't mind. I brought my friend. Carrie, this is my neighbor, Mrs. Collins."

"Please call me Emma. I was sorry to miss your book signing at Joanne's, but we had an out-of-state family wedding and then vacation. We only returned home last night." Emma said. "I bought a copy of your book from Marge and Maddy. Can't wait to read it." She pointed to Carrie's book sitting on the coffee table.

"That's very kind of you. Would you like me to sign it?" Carrie asked.

After Carrie signed the book, Emma said, "I knew you had the book party and thought it might belong to one of your guests."

"It could be," Joanne said. "One of our guests did lose a phone."

Carrie admired how Joanne explained the phone without indicating it belonged to a dead woman. Carrie also realized that since Emma only returned to town last night, she might not be aware of the murder. After one day, the story had dropped from media coverage.

Emma went to the sideboard, retrieved the phone, and handed it to Joanne. "Don't know much about these things. I didn't know how to find out whose phone it might be," Emma said.

"Emma, do you mind showing us where you found the phone?" Joanne asked.

"Not sure how it ended up in the hedges, but yes, I can show you where the gardener found it," Emma said.

Emma led them out the back patio door to the end of her property, where a gate opened onto a large field surrounded by trees.

"Where does this go?" Carrie asked. "I mean, who owns all this land?"

"It's a land conservation area, but the homeowners can reserve the property for events. Last month, one of the neighbors held their daughter's wedding out here," Joanne said. "Most of the surrounding homes have a gate that provides access to the field."

"My gardener said he found the phone in the hedge outside our back gate," Mrs. Collins said, pointing to the hedge near her back gate.

Gwen could have been meeting someone outside Mrs. Collin's property. Carrie decided the hedge was the perfect hiding place if she felt she was in danger and wanted to protect her phone.

"Thank you for having the foresight to think the phone might belong to one of our party guests," Joanne said.

"Glad to help," Emma said.

"Thank you, and let's get together for lunch," Joanne said.

"It was a pleasure to meet you, and I hope you enjoy the book," Carrie said. "Joanne, if you have a gate to the open area, we can leave this way."

Joanne looked surprised by Carrie's request but said, "We can do that."

They headed for Joanne's house, walking along the edge of the common area.

"Why did you want to come this way?"

"Remember, we thought the body was moved and positioned in your garden. If this is where the gardener found Gwen's phone, it means she could have met her assailant here," Carrie said.

Joanne's face brightened. "If someone murdered her here and not in my garden, maybe Dan and I can get off Jenco's suspect list."

They had only gone a short distance when Carrie stopped.

"Joanne, look. I'll bet these brown spots on the grass and fence are blood splatter," Carrie said. "It's a good thing it hasn't rained since the murder, or this evidence could have washed away."

Joanne followed where Carrie was pointing. "If you're correct, this is the actual crime scene. Why didn't the police find it."

"They concentrated on where you discovered the body," Carrie said. "You can ask Detective Jenco why he missed this, but I wouldn't say anything that might annoy him. He isn't very tolerant."

Carrie took several pictures with her phone to show Charles, then they both hurried back to Joanne's kitchen.

"Do you want to call the police, or should I?" Joanne asked.

"You can, but let me verify this is Gwen's phone. We don't want to irate Jenco by having him make an unnecessary trip," Carrie said.

Carrie held the phone with a napkin to avoid adding her fingerprints. She turned on the phone, and it restarted without a problem. For all of Gwen's concerns about project security, her phone had no passcode. It took Carrie only seconds to identify that it was Gwen's phone since the first contact listed was Gloria.

"We found our missing phone," Carrie said. She reached for her bag, found a cord, and transferred Gwen's files to her phone.

"I can't believe you carry phone cords with you," Joanne said.

"I'm a writer. I often need to transfer files when researching a story," Carrie said.

Carrie scrolled through the various files on the phone, especially the gallery of photos. In seconds, she had downloaded the information.

"All done," Carrie said, "Call Detective Jenco. Hopefully, giving him Gwen's phone will get you on his good side. A suspect wouldn't turn over a murdered woman's phone."

"Are you staying?" Joanne asked as she dialed the detective's number.

"I don't have a choice. If Jenco verifies your story with Emma, she'll tell him I was with you," Carrie said. "I don't want to trade places with you on Jenco's suspect list."

15

"Mrs. Faraday," Jenco said, emphasizing her name. "Why am I not surprised to find you here?"

Carrie didn't miss his sarcasm and wasn't looking forward to another encounter with him. While she was thinking about how to answer, Joanne jumped to her defense.

"We were finishing lunch at the club when my neighbor Mrs. Collins called to say her gardener found a phone outside her back gate," Joanne said. "Carrie thought it might be the victim's missing phone and suggested I call you. Does that explain her presence to your satisfaction?"

Joanne didn't like Jenco, and Carrie realized she needed to make sure Joanne didn't agitate the detective. Jenco ignored Joanne and addressed Carrie.

"It didn't occur to you that you might leave fingerprints?" Jenco snapped.

"I used a napkin," Carrie said. "I'm sure you realize, Detective, that the gardener, or one of his crew, discovered the phone, handed it to Mrs. Collins, and then she handed it to Joanne. And I'm sure you'll find Gwen's prints, but you won't find mine." Carrie had worried about Joanne annoying the Detective, and here she was doing the same thing. She noticed a slight smile on Sergeant McCall's face as he made notes on his tablet.

"Was it Gwen's phone?" Jenco asked.

Carrie said. "I restarted it, and her sister was the first name on her contact list. And several of the photos represented her Tri-City research."

Jenco interrupted. "You're sure the phone wasn't on?"

"I thought it unusual, but the phone was off," Carrie answered. Had Gwen expected trouble, turned the phone off, and hid it to keep her assailant from taking it?

"And you didn't think to call me immediately when you learned about the phone?" Jenco asked as he attempted to keep his tone even.

"The gardener discovered the phone in an area accessed by all the neighborhood homes. We didn't want to call you and have you make an unnecessary trip if it belonged to someone else," Joanne said.

Carrie handed Jenco a napkin, which he used to place the phone in an evidence bag.

"Why are you interfering with my case? What do you hope to accomplish playing amateur detective?" Jenco asked. "I went to the Brighton-Stanford home to find that you and your husband visited with her. I followed a lead at the country club and learned that your husband already talked to Jim Albright about Gwen's research," Jenco said. "A neighbor finds Gwen's phone, and here you are."

Carrie remained quiet for a moment. Then, she decided on a different approach that might placate Jenco. "Let's level with each other. You're interested in solving Gwen's murder. I'm a writer and interested in her research," Carrie said. "After meeting Mrs. Brighton-Stanford and hearing about her family's history, I decided it would make a fascinating article. Tri-City's Founders Day is just around the corner."

"That's a wonderful idea. You would write a great story about Tri-City, and Charles could publish it in the Tri-County magazine," Joanne said eagerly. "The entire community would be interested."

Carrie realized their comments probably made them sound ditzy, but that might have been a good thing. She saw a smile on McCall's face. Jenco stared at the two ladies and shook his head.

"You can write your story. But if you find anything related to the murder, stay away, and call me IMMEDIATELY," Jenco demanded. "Even if you had doubts about the phone, you should have called me. I would have picked the phone up from your neighbor and determined who owned it."

"You should be glad we retrieved the phone. We left the Collins property by the back gate, which you wouldn't have done," Joanne said politely.

"What's your point?" Jenco asked.

"We found the spot where Gwen's murder happened that your team missed. There are blood stains on the pathway between the two houses," Joanne said excitedly.

Carrie wasn't happy. Joanne threw this in Jenco's face. She waited to see how he reacted.

Jenco straightened. They had his undivided attention. "What do you mean you found the murder scene?"

"After getting the phone, we returned to Joanne's house using the back pathway. There's a section where the grass appeared flattened, and it looked like blood stains on the fence," Carrie said.

"We can show you the spot," Joanne offered.

Jenco and McCall had no choice but to follow them out the French doors and down the pathway toward Mrs. Collins's property. Carrie touched Joanne's arm as they got closer to stop her from charging ahead.

"We'll stay here so as not to contaminate the area. "You'll see the matted grass and the blood spatter on the fence next to it," Carrie said.

Jenco spent only a few minutes looking at the spot and then returned to the women. "I need to call for a forensic team. If you ladies will wait for me in your kitchen, I'll be with you shortly."

While waiting for Jenco to return, Joanne and Carrie drank multiple cups of coffee and devoured too many cookies. Finally, Jenco returned to the kitchen. He was non-committal about whether they had discovered the murder scene, but Carrie understood he was waiting for the forensic team to finish their work.

"Mrs. Faraday, you can leave. And remember what we decided. Your job is writing. My job is solving crimes."

As Carrie headed to her car, she ran into Dan.

"Don't tell me the police are back," Dan asked, wrinkling his forehead.

"They are, but it might be positive this time. Today's discovery may eliminate you and Joanne as the prime suspects," Carrie said. "Joanne will tell you all about it."

Dan's arrival meant it was dinnertime. Carrie focused on what she could pull together for a meal. When she got home, she found Charles on the patio preparing the grill.

"I stopped by the seafood market and picked up a flank of salmon. I hope you're in the mood for fish," Charles said.

"I'm in the mood for whatever you're preparing," she said, relieved Charles solved the dinner decision.

While fixing side dishes and setting the table, Carrie told Charles about the discovery of Gwen's phone and the probable murder site. She showed Charles the photos of the possible crime scene.

"At first, Jenco was his usual snarky self and asked why I interfered with his case. But once we gave him the phone and guided him to the murder scene, he became more receptive," Carrie said.

"Maybe he felt embarrassed that his team didn't examine a wider area," Charles said. "In their defense, you indicated this spot was outside a neighbor's property, hidden by a hedge near an open field."

"That's true. There's something else. Jenco and I reached an understanding." Carrie said. "We can continue our story research but not investigate the murder. And if we uncover anything that would help his investigation, we notify him immediately."

After dinner, they enjoyed coffee on the patio and watched the sunset.

"Forget your promise to Jenco for the moment. Let's talk about the murder scene." Charles said.

"Good idea. What have we learned?" Carrie asked.

"We assume that Gwen left Joanne's garden and met the person you observed having the animated conversation with her," Charles said.

"I agree," Carrie said.

"I also believe Gwen and her assailant did not leave the party together," Charles said.

Carrie thought about what Charles had said. "Right. If they left the party together, her assailant would have seen her hide the phone in the hedge. But why leave Joanne's garden?"

"The assailant and Gwen may have realized their argument was getting out of hand and didn't want to alert the other party attendees," Charles said.

"They saw the back gate, the pathway, and the open field beyond the property. They agreed to meet there at a certain time. That gave Gwen time to hide her phone," Carrie said. "They met, the argument continued, and the murder occurred."

"This suggests something else. Gwen mustn't have felt her life was in danger because she agreed to meet the person," Charles said. "However, she worried the person might snatch her phone with all her research, so she hid it."

"Something else. Gwen told Jake and others that she struggled with her final report to the client because it could change lives. Could her attacker have been someone affected by her discovery?" Carrie suggested. "It's time we look at the files on her phone."

Carrie grabbed her laptop, and Charles stood next to her. She started scrolling through the documents.

"I saw many of these photos on Henrietta's wall and in Jim's file," Charles said.

"I don't see anything that stands out. Tomorrow, I'll go through the documents more slowly and make a list," Carrie said, as disappointment showed in her voice.

"There is one thing I saw. Is it just me, or does the Founder's Day Picnic photo keep appearing everywhere?"

"Wait, there was something else in Gwen's notes. She has a document with the letters A, B, C, D, etc. Next to the letters are names," Carrie said. "Could these be the people in the photo?"

"You're right. Henrietta said these two people were her grandparents," Charles said, pointing to the two people on the far left. "But there were lots of names missing."

"Then that's where we start. We find out who these people are at the picnic," Carrie said. "And perhaps it will lead us to the murderer."

16

The following day, Carrie couldn't wait to start her research. She reviewed the online information about the founding of Tri-City and compared that information to Gwen's files.

After several hours, she found almost nothing beyond what she already knew. It was a familiar story about the three villages that formed the new city.

She switched her focus from the city's history to discovering more about the three founders. Allwin and Dorchester were local farmers. The communities tapped them because they held the most extensive landholdings, and the communities' names came from their ancestors. Brighton was a wealthy local banker, and the Village of St. Thomas selected him to represent their interests.

All three men were married with children when they formed the new city. Carrie found the Brighton ancestry the easiest to trace to Henrietta, Henry, and Hansen. They were the only remaining members of the Brighton family. As Jim had told

Charles, the Dorchester family had all died. Carrie traced the last member to a great-granddaughter who had never married and had no descendants. Allwin was the most difficult to follow. He had a son, Steven, with his first wife before she died. She found the marriage certificate for his second wife, Rebecca, but that's where the information stopped.

She felt frustrated not finding information that would explain the reason for Gwen's murder. Carrie debated what to do next. Perhaps a trip to the state archives. She put her decision on hold when Charles arrived home unexpectedly.

"What brings you home in the middle of the day?" Carrie asked, "Are you feeling alright?"

"I'm fine. I had an appointment in the area and thought I would stop in for lunch and share some information," Charles said. "What have you been doing?"

"Trying to discover more information about the founders," Carrie said.

"We were thinking along the same lines."

"I hope your information is more informative than what I found. I'm getting nowhere," Carrie said.

"First, tell me what you found?" Charles asked.

"I concentrated on the founders. Only the Brighton family have clear lines of their descendants. The other two gentlemen present more problems because I can't find descendants. And nothing that would have changed lives," Carrie said. "How about you?"

"Tri-County Monthly magazine published a story about the city reaching its one-hundredth anniversary."

"I don't remember that story," Carrie said.

"That's because we were on our honeymoon. Anyway, it seemed logical that the magazine would have covered the anniversary, and when I checked the archive," Charles dropped a copy of the magazine on Carrie's desk. "There's more good news. Gerald Benson, who wrote the article, is still one of our reporters."

"Did he have some inside info to share?" Carrie asked.

"He did. Before I share, let me get a sandwich," Charles said. "I need to get back to the office for a meeting."

"That's not fair to tease me by making me wait. I guess we can talk over lunch," Carrie said.

"I stopped at the deli and picked up our favorite braunschweiger and a loaf of rye bread," Charles said.

The couple headed to the kitchen and made sandwiches.

"What did Mr. Benson have to say?" Carrie asked.

"Benson was a young reporter. The editor gave him the Tri-City anniversary assignment because it was an easy story. Although then, like now, he was a thorough investigator and had a way of having his subject reveal details," Charles said.

"Did he interview any family members?" Carrie asked.

"He did. He interviewed the elderly great-granddaughter from the Dorchester clan. She was the last family member. She has since died, and Jim confirmed that the country club no longer had to pay rent for the land."

Carrie waited while Charles took another bite of his sandwich.

"He interviewed Henrietta, and she told him what we already knew. Benson said she was proud of her family's role in founding Tri-City," Charles said.

"I had the same impression when I talked with Henrietta while you were upstairs with Rachel," Carrie said. "Not to mention the wall of photos and documents on display."

"The Allwin family was the most difficult, according to Benson. Steven Allwin declined the interview. When he asked about the remaining family members, Steven said there was no one."

"That's what I found. Nothing but dead ends," Carrie voiced her disappointment.

"Ah, but I've saved the best for last," Charles said with a twinkle in his eye. "Benson interviewed a lady named Betty Canton. She was not a member of the three founding families, but her grandfather was the lawyer who handled the legal documents for the city's incorporation."

Carrie stared at Charles.

"What's the matter?" He asked.

"You said her name is Betty Canton. Didn't Gwen have a B.C listed on her desk blotter?"

"Oh, my heaven, you're right. I didn't make the connection," Charles said.

"That's why we're a team. Did Betty have any juicy bits to add to the story?" Carrie asked as she took a sip of iced tea.

"Did you know there was a scandal associated with the founders that the public never heard? It never made it to our story because we don't print gossip," Charles said.

"It may not have made it to your story, but I hope it will make it to your wife's ears," Carrie said, laughing.

"Allwin's first wife died, and he married again. His second wife was a local girl from a good family who was well-known in the community. They weren't married too long before she became pregnant," Charles said. "Her pregnancy was a scandal because Allwin was not the child's father."

"That was a scandal, especially for that period," Carrie said. "Did Betty know who the father was?"

"That's the juicy part. According to Betty, the rumor was that Henry Brighton was the father." Charles waited for Carrie's reaction.

Carrie was swallowing a mouthful of iced tea, and it was all she could do to swallow it. "Do you think Gwen discovered this scandal?"

"I do."

"Since Henrietta employed Gwen, perhaps Gwen had concerns about revealing this information in her final report," Carrie said. "It also explains why Gwen had 'check historical society' on her desk blotter."

"Maybe, but there has to be more. Today, people would accept what happened and move on," Charles said. "It might deflate Henrietta's admiration for her grandfather, but that's not a reason to murder someone."

"I wonder if Mr. Canton is in the picnic photo?" Charles asked.

"We keep coming back to that photo," Carrie said. "That photo is our only real clue. We should try to identify the people."

17

"We should see if Ms. Canton is still around," Charles said.

"You mean alive, don't you," Carrie responded.

"Not necessarily. Benson said she was elderly when he interviewed her. But he was in his 20s at the time," Charles said. "You know how that goes. Young people often think individuals like us are elderly."

"Very funny. Why don't you call Benson and see if he knows what happened to her?" Carrie suggested.

After the call, Charles said, "Good and bad news. When Benson interviewed her, she was about to move to a retirement community. We'll need to do some extra work to find her."

"Hopefully, she remained in the area," Carrie said as she opened her laptop. "We don't have that many retirement places in Tri-City."

Carrie printed a copy of the list, and they divided the task.

After a few calls, Carrie waved her hand to get Charles's attention. "I understand you don't give out residents' phone numbers, but could you ask Ms. Canton to call me?" Carrie gave the listener her number and said, "Tell her I'd like to talk with her about Tri-City's history."

"I take it you found Ms. Canton?" Charles asked.

"Betty Canton is at Ridgely Woods," Carrie said. "To protect the residents from unwanted solicitations, they will put my message in her mailbox. She can decide if she wants to get in touch."

Charles returned to work, but soon after his departure, Carrie received a call from Betty Canton.

"I'll be delighted to meet with you," she said. "Can you come here to Ridgely Woods?"

***

The next day, on their way to Ridgely Woods, Charles stopped at the BonBon Chocolatier. He returned to the car with two bags.

"Weren't you cutting down on your sugar intake," Carrie said.

"I am cutting down. I got us a one-pound box in case of a chocolate emergency."

"Really, a chocolate emergency," Carrie said, laughing. Charles had a sweet tooth, and Carrie kept an eye on how much he consumed. On the other hand, having a box of fine chocolates in the house would be a nice treat.

To quickly change the subject, Charles said, "I bought a two-pound box for Betty."

"I hope she's allowed chocolate," Carrie said.

"She is. While you were getting ready, I called Ridgely Woods," Charles said. "I was thinking about taking flowers, but the concierge told me Ms. Canton loves chocolate."

They arrived at Ridgely Woods and found the correct building. Ms. Canton arranged to meet Charles and Carrie in a community area with comfortable chairs surrounding a fireplace. It provided a warm and cozy atmosphere for talking.

Betty Canton was tall and stood straight as an arrow as she approached the couple. She looked in her early seventies and dressed in a stylish pale blue top and dark blue slacks covered with a small flower print.

"You must be the Faradays," she verified.

"Please, call us Charles and Carrie," Charles said.

"And I'm Betty. It's exciting to meet you. I'm the last of my family, so I rarely have visitors," Betty said. "I understand you want to talk about local history."

"My husband is the publisher of the Tri-County Monthly magazine..."

Betty interrupted. "The magazine interviewed me for the Hundredth Anniversary article. Is that why you're here? Are you doing another story on Tri-City?"

Charles took the lead. He told Betty about Carrie's book signing, briefly mentioning Gwen Smith's murder. "We're continuing her research on Tri-City and the original families."

"We felt a story focusing on the founders would make an interesting story for the readers," Carrie said.

"Did you know she called me?" Betty asked.

"Gwen Smith contacted you?" Charles asked. He wondered how Gwen found her. Maybe Gwen read the article in the

Tri-County Monthly. They were following in Gwen's footsteps. Was the murderer doing the same thing?

"Gwen said she was writing a report for a client about the founding of Tri-City. She probably meant Henrietta Brighton-Stanford," Betty said.

"That's correct. Did you share specific information about the Brighton family with her?" Carrie asked.

"Never met the woman because she didn't keep her appointment. I tried calling her," Betty said. "Now I realize her appointment with me was after her murder."

To lighten the mood after mentioning the murder, Charles said, "Then I'm glad we found you."

"You've come to the right person if you want Tri-City historical information," Betty said. "My grandfather, Anthony, was the lawyer who handled the incorporation documentation, and I have all his papers from that period."

"We learned your grandfather was the legal counsel but didn't realize paperwork still existed. We've had difficulty finding additional documentation," Charles said, pleased about this revelation. Charles remembered the boxes of papers at Henrietta's home that yielded little, and here was Betty with more documents.

"Let me correct that," she said. "We residents don't have much storage space. Before I moved here, I scanned all the important documents and put them on DVDs."

"I'm so pleased you had the foresight to do that," Carrie said. "Did you donate the DVDs to our historical society?"

"Not yet. I still have the DVDs in my apartment, but I've directed in my will that they go to the historical society," Betty said. "While I'm alive, I wanted to keep the files in case someone contacted me and wanted copies. And here you are."

Charles looked at Carrie. It was hard to hide his excitement that Betty could provide them with documents. "However, since we're here with you today, we would love to hear some of the details you found," Charles said.

"Where do I start?" Betty asked. She thought momentarily and then said, "My grandfather was the personal attorney for the three founders, in addition to acting as the lawyer for the new city."

"That seems a little unusual that your grandfather did corporate and personal legal work for the founders," Charles said.

"You must remember that Allwin, Dorchester, and Saint Thomas were small villages back then. Lawyers, like doctors, were few and far between, so my grandfather had most of the legal business," Betty said. "Then his son, my father, took over the practice and continued serving the city's and the founders' needs."

"Did you follow in their footsteps? Are you a lawyer?" Carrie asked.

She shook her head. "No, my field was history. I sometimes helped my father if he had a case that needed research. I enjoyed those opportunities that involved history."

Betty stopped speaking as she waved her hand to get the attention of a staff member pushing a drink cart.

"Hello, Betty. Do you want your usual tea?" The staff member asked.

"I do indeed, and my visitors, I'm sure, would like something to drink."

Charles and Carrie ordered coffee. Charles started to pay for the drinks.

"You can't pay. The staff doesn't accept payments. It gets added to my monthly food account," Betty said.

"In that case, we'll pay for our drinks with a trade. Our coffee for chocolate," Charles said as he handed her the candy box.

"How lovely. Bonbon Chocolates are my favorite. They've been around almost as long as Tri-City. Should I open it now?" She asked.

"No, this box is for you. My husband bought a second box for us in case of a chocolate emergency," Carrie said.

Betty gave a hearty laugh. "I'll have to remember that the next time I want a box of chocolates. I'll tell the staff it's an emergency," Betty said. "Now, where were we?"

"You were about to share some stories," Carrie said.

"Ah, yes, the beginnings were straightforward. Farmers from the three areas would come to a central location to sell their goods. In addition to farm products like eggs, meat, and produce, the women sold quilts and clothing items," Betty said. "That central location is where they built our city hall."

"Why did they decide to incorporate?" Charles asked.

"One word, Money. By incorporating the new community, the founders could petition the state for unclaimed land and money for buildings," Betty said. "The state-owned thousands of acres sitting idle, meaning the government wasn't collecting taxes."

"That's interesting. I never realized the founders built Tri-City on state lands," Carrie said.

"My grandfather represented the communities with the state to get thousands of acres transferred," Betty said as she sipped her tea. "There was one stipulation that the three villages agreed to the incorporation. I found the correspondence between my grandfather and the state."

"And that's how Allwin, Dorchester, and Brighton became village representatives," Carrie said. "What do you know about the three men?"

"Dorchester was a farmer and widower with two daughters. Allwin was a farmer who had a son with his first wife. After she died, he remarried a local girl named Rebecca. The names of these villages came from their ancestors," Betty said. "Brighton was a banker and married with two children. St. Thomas held an election and picked Brighton as the representative."

"Since the state offered so many acres, why buy the country club land?" Charles asked.

"Oh, you heard about that. The Dorchester land was in the center of the new city, and the farmhouse was the first building," Betty said. "The new city had no money to purchase the land outright. Instead, they created a lease agreement. Dorchester used the lease payments to buy shares in the newly formed Tri-City Building Corporation."

"And those payments ended when the last Dorchester relative died," Carrie added.

"The country club thinks so," Betty said without explanation as she sipped her tea.

Charles didn't miss the inference but decided to start with the scandal Betty mentioned previously. "During your magazine interview, you hinted at a scandal. It involved a rumor that Henry Brighton had fathered a child," Charles said.

"Since you published that story, I discovered something different," Betty said.

"And that was," Charles prodded

"When your reporter interviewed me, I foolishly repeated the rumor that Henry Brighton was the father of Rebecca Allwin's child," Betty said. "When Gwen called for an appointment, I reviewed the legal documents I scanned. I discovered my grandfather handled Allwin's divorce. I also discovered that Samuel Dorchester was the father of a child named Richard, who he had with Rebecca."

"Samuel Dorchester," Carrie said, surprised at the revelation.

"You have proof?" Charles asked.

"I discovered the marriage certificate. My grandfather became a judge and performed a quiet civil ceremony between Samuel and Rebecca. They kept it quiet because Allwin was still alive," Betty said. She sat back and finished her tea as Charles and Carrie digested this new information.

"If they didn't want anyone to know, including Allwin, why get married?" Charles asked.

"Dorchester was a decent man. He admitted he was the father so that the child had a legitimate birth. That was important in those days," Betty said. "My grandfather changed the birth certificate to acknowledge Dorchester's paternity."

"Could you email the certificate and any other paperwork you think may add to our research.?" Carrie asked.

Betty nodded, and Carrie wrote out her email address.

"That means there's a possible unknown Dorchester heir the country club should be paying," Charles said thoughtfully.

"Perhaps. After Dorchester's great-granddaughter died, the club assumed there were no additional heirs and didn't look any further," Betty said.

"Do you know what happened to Rebecca and the child?"

"I don't. I'm sure you could answer that question by doing more genealogy research. Maybe Gwen discovered this information and wanted to verify it with me," Betty said.

Betty looked at Charles and Carrie for a moment. "You have a reputation for solving crimes. I assume you're doing more than following the dead girl's research. Perhaps you're searching for why someone murdered her."

"We're doing research for a story. We promised the police that if we come across anything that would help solve the murder, we would pass it along," Carrie said.

"Betty, I don't want to frighten you, but I want you to alert me if anyone else contacts you wanting information," Charles suggested.

"I understand. You think the murderer may want my materials," Betty said. "Don't worry. We have great security at Ridgely Woods, and if anyone contacts me, I'll let you know."

Charles said, "Good. And I'm glad you're sending us the material, so hopefully, we can stay one step ahead of the murderer."

18

The day after they met with Betty, Carrie stared at the photo of the Founder's Day Picnic. She realized it would take time to find the names of everyone pictured. Where to start the search? Then Carrie had an idea. She would call Henrietta.

"Hello, Carrie. I was just about to call you," Henrietta said.

"What can I do for you?" Carrie asked.

"I belong to a book club. After reading your book, I suggested to the club ladies we discuss your book at our next meeting," Henrietta said. "Then I got another idea. Could you attend our meeting? It would enrich our discussion to have the author present. What do you think?"

Henrietta's request for a book club appearance surprised Carrie. She thought the call might be something about Gwen's research.

"Thank you for recommending the book, and I would be happy to chat with your club members," Carrie said.

"I'm afraid it's short notice. We meet the day after tomorrow at 3:00. We discuss the book while enjoying light refreshments," she said. "I'll warn you that the ladies won't be afraid to tell you what they didn't like."

"I want to know what my readers think. It's beneficial if I write another book."

"Then I'll see you..." Henrietta stopped. "Wait, you said you were calling me. Did you have something you wanted to discuss with me?"

"Charles and I are following up on leads surrounding Gwen's research. We had a question about one of the photos we found," Carrie said. "If you have time, I can discuss the photo with you after the book club meeting."

"I'll be happy to talk with you. See you Wednesday," Henrietta said.

***

The ladies at Henrietta's book club provided Carrie with a new experience. Unlike a book signing where the attendees hadn't read the book, these ladies were ready to discuss her book in detail. Carrie joined them in a lively discussion about the characters and how she developed the plot.

The ladies liked that the detective solved the crime by discovering a hidden clue behind a picture. One of the ladies stated that the most significant part of the story was when Carrie's detective had to tell the client the truth about what he had discovered. This comment struck a nerve with Carrie. Was that why Gwen wanted to talk with her? She needed to tell Henrietta a truth she might not like to hear.

After the ladies left, Rachel cleared the refreshments and started to straighten the room.

"You said you wanted to talk to me about a photo," Mrs. Brighton said.

"We keep hitting dead ends with Gwen's research. As you know, someone searched the research materials upstairs," Carrie said. "Someone also searched Gwen's office at her condo. There's no sign of her computer."

"I wonder what they're after," Henrietta said, shaking her head. "Any idea what it is?"

"No, but I have news. The neighbor next to the Quinn property found Gwen's phone."

"Did you find information on the phone, or did the police get it first?" Henrietta asked.

"I downloaded all the files before I gave the phone to Detective Jenco," Carrie said. "Many of the documents on her phone were the same ones we saw here or at the country club. One thing we noticed was that one photo kept appearing in multiple places. You have the same photo."

"I do? Which one?" Henrietta asked.

"It's the photo of the founders you have hanging on your wall," Carrie said, pointing to the picture. "Gwen started to identify the people pictured."

Carrie noticed that Rachel's clean-up seemed to be taking a long time. Was she deliberately lingering to hear the conversation?

Henrietta walked across the room to her wall of photos. "You mean this elongated shot of over a dozen people at the picnic," she said, pointing to the picture.

"Yes, that's the one," Carrie said.

Henrietta took the photo from the wall and returned to where Carrie was seated. "I can help with a few of the names. Here's my grandfather, Henry Brighton, and his wife, Clarissa, my grandmother," she said, pointing to the first two people. "The two youngsters are my father, Henry, and his sister, Henrietta. My parents named me for her."

Henrietta stared at the photo for several seconds. "Based on other photos, I'm sure the second man in line is Mr. Dorchester and his daughters. He was a widower, so there was no wife," Henrietta said. "One of the other two men must be Mr. Allwin and his wife. I'm unsure about the others, but they must be family members."

Carrie stared at the photo. "Do you think Allwin is with his first or second wife?" Carrie asked.

"I knew he married a second time, but I don't know which wife is pictured," Henrietta said as she examined the picture. "This frame is quite old. I should have it restored." As she turned the frame over to look at the back, it slipped off her lap and onto the floor, breaking the glass.

At the sound of the glass breaking, Rachel ran to Henrietta. "Are you all right?" Rachel asked. She started to pick up the pieces of glass and frame.

"Rachel, be careful. Don't cut yourself," Henrietta said,

"These glass pieces are fairly large, but I'll get a broom for the fragments," Rachel said. She picked up the photo and headed to the door.

"Wait, don't take the photo," Henrietta said. "Mrs. Faraday and I want to look at that."

Carrie sensed that Rachel was reluctant to relinquish the picture.

"I wanted to be sure there are no glass pieces on it," Rachel defended.

"It's fine," Henrietta said as she took the photo and shook it. "It's such a long photo we can lay it flat if we sit at the table."

Carrie thought she saw something attached to the picture as they moved to the table. "There's something on the back," Carrie said.

Henrietta flipped it over. "There's a handwritten note," Henrietta said.

"It looks like a list of names identifying the people in the photo," Carrie said. "This may be our first break in the case."

The list verified that Henry Brighton, his wife, and their children were the first two people pictured. Samuel Dorchester and his two daughters were next. Then, Anthony Canton, his wife, Maribel, and their girls. Edwin Allwin and his wife, Rebecca, were last in line.

"Even though it doesn't identify the children's names, it's good to have the adults identified," Carrie said.

"I know Dorchester, Allwin, and my great grandfather, but who was Anthony Canton?" Henrietta asked.

"Mr. Canton was the lawyer who did the incorporation paperwork for the three villages and other legal work for the founders," Carrie said. "A reporter for the Tri-County Monthly interviewed his granddaughter, Betty Canton, for a hundred-anniversary article."

"Amazing. That picture hung on my wall all these years, and I had no idea who they were," Henrietta said. "Have you found Betty Canton and talked with her?"

"We did. Betty provided a different perspective based on information from her father's legal files." Carrie hesitated to consider revealing Betty's gossip, especially the update about Dorchester fathering the child. She wanted to see what Henrietta had to say.

"Did she reveal some piece of information that you're hesitant to share with me?" Henrietta asked. "I read that article but don't remember anything other than the known history."

Carrie was always impressed by people of Henrietta's age who maintained their ability to assess a situation. She hated it when others assumed older people couldn't think critically. Henrietta Brighton-Stanford was sharp as a tack.

"You're right. This information didn't appear in the article because Charles doesn't print unsubstantiated facts and gossip," Carrie said. "Ms. Canton initially told the reporter the paperwork to form the new city almost didn't go through," Carrie said. "It had to do with a rumor concerning your grandfather."

"You mean it almost stopped because of a scandal, don't you?" Henrietta laughed heartily. "Don't worry. Carrie, you're not telling me anything that I didn't know. The rumor was that my grandfather fathered a child with Mrs. Allwin."

"Yes, but I'm surprised you know. Betty thought she told the reporter a deep secret hidden for years." Carrie said.

"Indeed, they kept the rumor quiet, or maybe I should say they buried it," Henrietta said, leaning back in her chair and folding her hands. "When I was a grown woman, and my grandmother was nearing the end of her life, she told me about the scandal. My granny worried that I might have to deal with rumors I couldn't answer after her death," Henrietta said. "She assured me that it was false. My grandfather loved her and had never strayed. There were only two children, my father and his sister, my Aunt Henrietta."

"What happened to your father's sister?" Carrie asked.

"She died in the 1919 flu epidemic," Henrietta said. "It was a sad story. She was engaged to be married to a captain in the army. He came home from the war with the flu. He survived, but she didn't."

Carrie looked at the photo. "The woman with Mr. Allwin is named Rebecca," Carrie said.

"My grandmother told me his first wife's name was Doris, so Rebecca must be his second wife who became pregnant with another man's child," Henrietta said. "They look happy in this photo."

There was something about Rebecca that looked familiar. The discoloration on the picture made it hard to distinguish facial features. She would see if a computer program she had could clean up the photo.

"As the rumor goes, Mr. Allwin had an accident with a piece of farm equipment, which kept him from having additional children. When his wife became pregnant, Allwin knew it wasn't his."

"Did they discover the father?" Carrie asked, not wanting to reveal she knew the answer.

"There were all kinds of rumors. Most thought it was a young farmhand. Allwin fired the farmhand and divorced his wife," Henrietta said. "His wife moved away to live with relatives, and the truth became hidden in history."

Had Gwen discovered more information about Rebecca and her descendants? There was movement on the far side of the room. Rachel was slowly sweeping up the remaining debris from the broken frame. How much had she heard? Rachel saw Carrie looking at her, quickly tied up the trash bag, and left the room. Was it curiosity, or was there another reason? Carrie decided not to tell Henrietta about Dorchester being the father until she checked the documentation.

"There was a bigger scandal than who fathered the child that almost derailed the founding," Henrietta said. "According to my grandmother, the men fell out over money."

"Money?" Carrie said, noting that Betty used the same word. "Weren't the founders all wealthy men, and that's why the communities selected them to represent them?"

Henrietta went to a sideboard and brought a decanter of sherry and two glasses to the table. She poured the liquor and settled back into her chair.

"My grandfather was a banker, inherited money, and had personal investments. Our family was probably the wealthiest of the three founding members," Henrietta said. "Dorchester and Allwin were both farmers. While they had extensive land holdings, they didn't have liquid assets."

"What happened?" Carrie asked. "How did money affect the relationship between the men?"

"My grandfather and Mr. Dorchester formed the Tri-City Building Corporation to help finance buildings for the new city. It all started with the stone farmhouse at the country club. Did you know that story?" Henrietta asked.

"Charles learned from the country club's historian that Dorchester leased a large piece of land," Carrie said.

"The initial lease payment he received for the property gave him the money to join the corporation," Henrietta said.

"Betty said they received additional land from the state for municipal buildings," Carrie said.

"The old courthouse, city hall, and the original Tri-City hospital were some of the facilities they built on state lands," Henrietta said. "And they offered low-cost construction loans to residents for offices and retail spaces."

"Then how did the men fall out?" Carrie asked.

"Allwin decided not to join the corporation. He said he was a farmer and not a businessman. He didn't want to use his time or money to help the city beyond what he had already provided," Henrietta said.

"Was it only Dorchester and your grandfather in the corporation?" Carrie asked.

"No. Any family living within the new city's boundaries could buy shares. As the structures were built, sold, or rented, the investors received dividends," Henrietta said. "Once they started paying dividends, Allwin felt he should have been given shares as a founding member."

"How did it end?" Carrie asked.

"Allwin was so mad about not getting payments that he never spoke to Dorchester and my grandfather again. They parted ways. His son, Steven, wanted to participate, but his father blocked him."

Carrie sat in her chair, thinking about Henrietta's words as she sipped her sherry. "Thanks for sharing this information. Did Gwen come across some of this history during her research?"

"She never mentioned it or asked for more information about the corporation. My grandmother told me this story in the last days of her life. I've never shared this story with anyone until today. My mother and father never mentioned it, and I never saw any paperwork," Henrietta said. "Did Betty Canton mention any records from the building corporation she can share?"

"She's sent me some files. We'll have to see what they contain," Carrie said.

Then, as an afterthought, Henrietta added, "Do you think this research had anything to do with Gwen's murder?"

"In all honesty, I have no idea. We keep gathering information, but nothing points to why anyone would want to murder Gwen over a research document," Carrie said. "As they say in police investigations, it's early days."

19

When Emily Hopkins asked Carrie to present a lecture to her journalism students, she felt honored. Her former mentor now considered Carrie a professional who could share her knowledge with a new group of writers. While it wasn't an opportunity to sell books, she thought interacting with the kids and seeing what interested them would be fun and educational.

Because the lecture wasn't on the regular class schedule, Professor Hopkins held the talk at the end of the day in a large lecture hall. She opened it to all students, regardless of their major. Charles tagged along in support of his wife.

When the couple entered the lecture hall, they bumped into Penny Stevens, Gwen's admin.

"Hello, Penny. Are you coming to my lecture?" Carrie questioned her attendance since she knew her interest was history.

"Yes, I'm working at sharpening my writing skills. I must publish to maintain my position when I secure a full-time teaching position."

"I'm glad you came. This is my husband, Charles," Carrie said, touching Charles's arm.

Penny nodded. "I better grab a seat. It looks like a full house."

"Penny Stevens was Gwen's administrative assistant," Carrie said as they watched her take an aisle seat. "I'm glad you decided to join me for this event. Having at least one friendly face in the audience is always nice."

"I'm glad to be your friendly face, but I had an ulterior motive."

"What might that be?" Carrie asked.

"I'm hoping to take the speaker to dinner."

"That will be a nice treat to boost my morale," Carrie said.

"You'll do fine. You're a former student who's a successful writer," Charles said, kissing her on the cheek.

After greeting Emily Hopkins, Charles sat at the back of the auditorium. Carrie and Emily stepped onto the platform as the hall filled. Carrie noticed Brian Amberson and Hansen Stanford took seats several rows behind Penny. How did Brian and Hansen know each other, or was she reading too much into this? She put these thoughts aside as Emily introduced her.

Since this was a journalism lecture, Carrie presented information on article structure, the types of articles magazines wanted, copy preparation, and many more tips. She noticed that most of the students took notes as she spoke.

At the end of the session, Carrie answered questions. The students seemed most concerned about who had the right to review their work and the ethics of revealing their information sources. The same questions Gwen found challenging.

"If you do a good job with your research, document your sources, and follow the directions the editor gave you, there are rarely issues," Carrie said. "Remember, the editor's job is to ensure the article fits the publication. Study the magazine, write what the editor requested, accept the changes or make a strong case for challenging them, and rack up publishing credits."

When she finished, she received a standing ovation but noticed that Charles, Penny, Brian, and Hansen were all missing. Carrie thanked Emily for the opportunity and went to find Charles. She reached the back of the hall just as Charles reentered the room.

"What happened to you? Was my lecture that boring that you had to go out for fresh air?" Carrie asked in good fun.

"Your lecture was great. I saw Penny Stevens leave when the questions started," Charles said. "Don't ask me why, but I followed her."

"Where did she go?" Carrie asked.

"She's in the student union."

"Good, because that's where we are going. The bookstore is in the student union, and I want to see if they'll stock my book," Carrie said.

Charles stayed in the lounge area while Carrie checked the bookstore. She discovered they already had her book for sale.

"Mrs. Faraday, I'm glad I got to meet you. I'm a journalism major, and that was a very informative talk," the bookstore clerk said. "Can I help you find something?"

"I wanted to ask if you could order a few copies of my book to sell, but you already have them."

"Professor Hopkins asked us to order them." She looked at Carrie and smiled. "We've sold several, and I'm sure we'll sell more to those who attended the lecture."

***

After Carrie entered the bookstore, Charles spotted a coffee bar. While waiting for his drinks, he scanned the seating area. He saw Penny Stevens sitting with two young men he had spotted at the lecture. They seemed thoroughly engrossed in conversation.

Charles paid for the drinks and turned to find Carrie beside him.

"Guess what? They're already carrying my book. Professor Hopkins asked them to order them."

"That's a nice surprise," Charles said. "I knew I liked Emily." He handed her a cup of coffee.

"You have a surprise for me, too. I could use a cup of coffee."

"We could drink our coffee here before I take you to dinner. Penny is sitting over there," Charles said. "We could see if she liked your lecture."

Carrie followed Charles's gaze to the far side of the room. "Do you know who's sitting with Penny?" Carrie asked.

"I haven't a clue," Charles answered.

"That's Hansen, Mrs. Brighton-Stanford's grandson, and Brian Amberson, Gwen's student intern," Carrie said. "Penny and Brian worked together, but I wonder how they know Hansen?"

"Remember, Rachel told me Hansen hosted college friends at his grandmother's house. Maybe they attended a party," Charles suggested.

"Let's find out," Carrie said.

Penny noticed the couple only when they stood beside the table.

She looked up and seemed startled. "Oh, Mr. and Mrs. Faraday, err..., nice to see you again."

"Do you mind if my husband and I join you?" Carrie asked, pulling out an empty chair.

"Not at all," Penny said, quickly recovering.

She waved her hand towards her companions. "Carrie, you met Brian at Gwen's memorial service, but have you met Hansen Stanford?"

"We haven't met, but I saw you at Gwen's memorial service with your grandmother and again at the Tri-County bookstore last week," Carrie said. "And this is my husband, Charles."

Charles saw Hansen stiffen when Carrie mentioned the bookstore. Did he leave the note on their car? But why.

"Mrs. Faraday, I enjoyed your lecture," Hansen said.

"I found it informative, especially about the ethics of sharing information," Penny said. "It's a topic that always comes up when writing research reports." She ran her hand through her short-cropped blond hair.

Charles didn't miss Penny's comment about ethics. Was she referring to the same ethics issue that Gwen discussed with Emily?

"I'm glad you enjoyed it. Journalism can be tricky. Some writers want to reveal everything, whether it's top secret or hurts people," Carrie said.

Brian and Hansen nodded.

"It was interesting to hear how you started writing," Hansen asked.

"You might say I came to writing through the backdoor," Carrie said. "I originally made my living as a photographer. Photo captions were all I wrote. Then, I created longer pieces to accompany the pictures. But writing a book was a new challenge."

"It seems a natural progression. I hope your book is a success," Brian said.

"Thank you. Brian. You and Penny worked for Gwen, but how did you meet Hansen?" Carrie asked.

"Hansen took several of Gwen's classes, and since I'm her intern for the year… I mean, I was her intern," Brian said. "Anyway, we ran into each other in class, discovered we drank at the same bar and had mutual friends. We've been friends ever since."

"Brian helped me with the papers I had to do for Gwen's class," Hansen said, then he quickly added. "Not writing them for me but helping me understand what Gwen wanted in her assignments."

"Your grandmother is interested in documenting your family's past," Charles said. "Are you interested in pursuing a career in history, or do you prefer journalism?"

"I enjoy history, but I would rather be a journalist," Hansen said.

"No reason you can't do both," Charles said. "Many of the articles we publish in our magazines have a historical flavor."

"My husband," she turned towards Charles, "owns Faraday Press, which publishes several magazines. I have an inside contact when I have an article to publish." Carrie winked at the group.

"Don't believe her for a minute. Her articles get published because she's a good writer," Charles said. Charles put his arm around her shoulder and hugged her.

"I never made the connection that your husband was the magazine's publisher," Hansen said as he knocked over his coffee. "Sorry, sorry," he said as he panicked and grabbed napkins to wipe the spill.

Charles decided the time was right to ask the next question. "Did your grandmother tell you she received poison pen letters asking her to stop Gwen's work?"

Hansen shook his head.

"Here's another interesting fact. The font used to create the words in the letter was the same font we created specifically for the magazine," Charles said.

Charles watched the faces of the people. Penny sipped her coffee. Brian didn't seem interested, but Hansen started to fidget.

Hansen quickly changed the subject from the letters. "Mrs. Faraday, Grandmother said when you visited with her that you planned to continue Gwen's research."

"I didn't know you were taking over the project," Penny said, sounding concerned.

"Penny, were you interested in continuing Gwen's work?" Carrie asked.

"I helped her source documents for her outside clients. I learned her process," Penny said. "I worked on the Brighton-Tri-City materials with Gwen, and I could easily handle the project if Hansen's grandmother wanted to continue."

"I'm not using Gwen's research since no one can find it," Carrie said. "Instead, I'm writing a story about Tri-City's founders for the magazine. The anniversary for the city is fast approaching."

Charles noticed Penny relaxed when Carrie indicated she was only writing a story and not continuing Gwen's project. It might also explain why she wanted to know Hansen so that she could get closer to his grandmother.

"Dredging up all that old stuff about the founders doesn't attract today's audiences. Stirring up the past serves no purpose and is boring," Hansen said.

Charles had seen or heard that line before. Charles looked at Carrie, but she didn't have the same reaction. He sat there trying to remember while the conversation continued around him.

"Because of Gwen's murder, it's good to hear you're not following her steps," Brian said. "It could be dangerous."

"I agree. Carrie is a writer, not a detective," Charles said with emphasis.

20

Carrie and Charles finished their coffee and left the young people. When Charles looked back, he saw them huddled in conversation.

"Thanks for telling them I'm a writer, not a detective. That stopped any additional questions about Gwen's research and murder," Carrie said.

"Glad to help," Charles said.

They opened the door to leave the student union and bumped into Emily Hopkins.

"Oh, hello again," Emily said. "I was delayed by several students wanting to continue your discussion. Always good when the speaker leaves the students thinking."

"I enjoyed it. It was an educational experience to hear the questions and what topics are important to today's students," Carrie said.

"Are you finished for the day?" Charles asked.

"I'm grabbing a cup of coffee and a sandwich and then back to work. I must finish grading papers and get the grades recorded by the end of the day," Emily said. "I'm looking forward to tomorrow evening when I can enjoy a nice hot meal."

"If you're looking for a delicious meal, let me suggest the Train Stop," Charles said.

"I knew Gloria owned the restaurant, but I've never had the opportunity to eat there. Gwen often brought food for us to share when we got together, and it was delicious," Emily said. "It's time I visit in person, but I'm afraid it'll have to wait until another day."

Charles knew Emily wanted to eat her sandwich and finish work, but he needed more answers.

"I don't want to keep you, but I have another question," Charles said. "We talked with Brian Amberson, Penny Stevens, and Hansen Stanford after the lecture. Do you know why they came to Carrie's lecture?"

"This is an assumption, but Gwen might have mentioned she wanted to meet Carrie. This comment piqued the interest of her two associates. And they might also have been curious to see if Carrie discussed the murder," Emily said.

"What about Hansen?" Charles asked.

"Hansen is rather an interesting young man. He's one of the many students searching for what they want to do. The Stanfords are a wealthy family, but Hansen's trying to find his way without relying on his family's name," Emily said. "He took history classes with Gwen but is also interested in journalism. The papers he's written for my classes are good. Journalism could be a future career if he pursued his studies."

"Emily, I promise this is the last question," Carrie said. "How are student interns selected? Specifically, how did Brian Amberson get his position?"

"It's a straightforward process. The students apply to a professor with an intern opening," Emily said.

"I assume, as part of the process, Brian would have indicated he was interested in pursuing a career in history," Carrie said.

"That's correct. Usually, the student candidate attended courses with the professor, so the professor is familiar with the applicant," Emily said.

"The intern is a volunteer with no financial compensation," Charles said.

"True, but these are highly sought-after positions. The students receive credit for their work, and if they're applying to graduate school or seeking a job, it looks great on their resume. We always have more applications than positions."

"What about Penny's position?" Charles asked.

"The college advertised the position. Penny applied and interviewed just like anyone else seeking a paid job," Emily said as she fidgeted with her watch band, trying to be discreet about checking the time. "The instructor also needs to feel comfortable working with the person."

"Would an admin position also need a background in the subject?" Carrie asked.

"Not always, but Penny has a master's degree in history and is working on her doctorate here at the university. Why are you two asking questions about Gwen's associates?" Emily asked.

"We're gathering information about Gwen's research and the people she knew as we look for a solution to her murder," Charles said.

"Gwen told me Penny did an excellent job. She was very efficient in managing her schedule and the extra workload when Gwen started taking consultant jobs like her Brighton-Stanford project," Emily said. "Gwen also said Penny was a good researcher, but she needed help when writing reports. I've seen her at several journalism lectures. Perhaps she's trying to improve those skills."

"Thanks for the information and the opportunity to speak to your students. Don't work too hard on those student grades. If you give them all an "A," it will go much faster," Carrie said, laughing.

In the car, Charles turned to Carrie. "What did you think of those three?"

"I don't know. If Penny wanted to continue Gwen's research, I could understand why she came to my lecture to see if I mentioned the Brighton-Stanford project," Carrie said. "But I can't see her hanging out with Brian and Hansen."

"Hansen's explanation seemed logical. He likes history but thinks he might want to be a journalist," Charles said.

"Brian said they had several classes in common. We should have asked Emily if Brian took journalism classes," Carrie said.

"One other thing. Did you notice the phrase Hansen used when discussing his family history?" Charles asked. "I remembered where I heard it before."

"What did he say?" Carrie responded.

"He used the exact phrase in one of the poison pen letters, 'stirring up the past serves no purpose.'"

"That was astute of you to catch that phrase." Carrie reached out and patted Charles on the shoulder. "Wait. That doesn't make sense. Why would Hansen write poison pen letters to his grandmother?"

"Haven't a clue. But that's not a common phrase," Charles said.

"Like Gwen, Hansen had access to the family records. Perhaps he discovered a family secret he wanted to keep hidden," Carrie said.

"Maybe. But Hansen doesn't strike me as an original thinker for sending poison pen letters. Could Penny or Brian have influenced him?" Charles asked. "Maybe that explains why the three were meeting after the lecture."

"It also brings up another interesting point. Rachel had mentioned that Hansen held parties at his grandmother's house. If Brian attended the parties, he could slip away and search the room where Gwen worked," Carrie said.

"That's the thing about this case," Charles said. "Each time we learn something new, it raises more questions. We need to learn more about these three."

21

Charles and Carrie were in their study enjoying an evening together. Charles relaxed on his recliner as he watched a ball game while Carrie stretched out on the sofa with a book and Baxter on her lap. Suddenly, the computer buzzed, indicating that the security cameras in the driveway had picked up motion. Charles jumped up to check the footage.

"Do we have a deer crossing the path again?" Carrie asked.

"No. We have a car in the driveway," Charles said.

"It's probably someone who's lost and using our driveway to turn around," Carrie suggested.

"I don't know about that," Charles said. "Remember, I had the cameras moved back forty feet two weeks ago. There's plenty of room for someone to turn around without triggering the system."

To Baxter's annoyance, Carrie got up and joined Charles to view the screen. "How long is the car going to sit there?" Carrie asked.

"If they're lost, maybe they're checking the directions," Charles said.

The couple continued watching. Finally, the car slowly proceeded up the driveway.

"Can you see who it is?" Carrie asked.

"Not yet. The willow tree is blocking my view," Charles said.

The young man exited the car in front of their door. He leaned on the car and looked at their house. Charles manipulated the screen and zoomed in on the image.

"That's Hansen Stanford," Carrie said.

"Let's see what he wants," Charles said as he left the study for the front door.

"Charles, be careful. We don't know what Hansen's involvement is in all these events," Carrie called after him. She heard the front door open.

"Hello, Hansen. What brings you here tonight?" Charles asked in a friendly tone.

"Mr. Faraday, I'm, I mean, since you're home, I wondered if I could speak with you?" Hansen said.

Charles and Hansen entered the study.

"Hello, Mrs. Faraday. I hope you don't mind me dropping in unannounced," he said in a raspy voice that erupted in a dry cough.

Carrie thought the cough might be nerves, "Not at all. Can we get you something to drink?" Carrie asked.

"Would you have a soda?" Hansen asked.

Charles went behind the bar and opened the refrigerator. "Cola, root beer, or ginger ale," Charles offered as he placed the cans on the bar.

Hansen selected a root beer and climbed on one of the bar stools. He took several gulps of soda with a shaky hand. After a few moments, Hansen said, "I have a problem, and perhaps you could offer some advice."

Charles felt he needed some encouragement. "Could your dilemma have something to do with the poison pen letters you sent your grandmother?"

"You knew," Hansen said, astonished by the revelation.

"We strongly suspected. When we met you and your friends in the student union, you said, 'stirring up the past serves no purpose,' when I asked about your interest in history," Charles said. "It was the exact phrase in one of the letters. I also noticed your discomfort when we talked about the letters."

"What possessed you to do this?" Carrie asked.

Hansen began to twist his hands together. "I don't know. Brian and I were at a party and were drinking beer. Lots of beer," Hansen said. "I started talking about Professor Smith's research and how much my grandmother paid her."

"How did you discover Gwen's compensation? Did your grandmother tell you?" Carrie asked.

"No, grandmother and I never discussed the project. Brian saw a copy of the contract in Gwen's office and saw the amount," Hansen said. He squirmed on the bar stool to find a comfortable position.

"I take it the amount of money bothered you?" Charles prodded.

Carrie went behind the bar. She opened a snack package from the refrigerator containing sliced meat, cheeses, and crackers. She placed the plate before Hansen, hoping the snacks would help him relax.

"It seemed like a massive amount to me. My grandmother and father don't want me to work while I'm in school. They give me an allowance, but some weeks I'm scrapping by," Hansen said. "They could have paid me to do the research. I live in the house and have access to all those records."

Hansen's comment made Carrie wonder if he searched the boxes from the attic. But why would he dump the contents around the room? No, the person who searched the boxes didn't have time to be neat.

"Hansen, your grandmother paid Gwen for her knowledge of gathering the research and putting together a professional report," Carrie said.

"Was it only the money?" Charles asked, sensing there was more.

"I guess I had a little resentment about my family's heritage. I've heard about my great-grandfather's founding of this city all my life. Who cares? Does he make me unique?" Hansen said. "I need to find my way and not rely on what my ancestors did. That's why I used that phrase about stirring up the past."

Having blurted out this information, Carrie sensed he seemed relieved. His shoulders relaxed. He sat back, took another gulp of soda, and started consuming the snacks. Although Carrie didn't condone the letter writing, she appreciated Hansen's attitude about finding his way without his family's help.

"Tell me more about the letters. Did you come up with the idea?" Charles asked.

"As I said, we had been drinking beer. I don't know who thought up the idea. We stupidly rationalized that if we sent letters to my grandmother, she would show them to Gwen and stop the research," Hansen said.

"Your grandmother never showed them to Gwen? She felt guilty that by not telling her about the letters it may have caused her murder," Carrie said.

"I didn't realize she didn't tell Gwen. Wait a minute! Do you think..., wait, I had nothing to do with her murder," Hansen screeched as he banged his hand on the bar. His cough returned.

"I don't, but you can see why your grandmother and others might assume the letter writer could be the killer," Charles said.

"We only sent a few. Then I realized it was stupid. When my grandmother sets her mind to something, there is no stopping her," Hansen said. He paused and added, "Aside from fearing discovery, I realized the letters would only draw more attention to the family."

"Carrie saw you in the bookstore the night your grandmother came to buy her book. Did you place the threatening note on our windshield when you left?" Charles asked.

"Not me." Hansen shook his head. "I was with friends at a restaurant down the street. I walked to the bookstore to catch a ride home with my grandmother."

If it wasn't Hansen, who else knew the wording from the letters? Carrie thought of two other people—Penny and Brian.

"Did Penny know what the two of you were up to? I'm only asking because you were talking with her in the student union," Carrie said.

"Brian told her. She encouraged us to stop. Penny felt tracing family origins was an essential part of history. Since I'm currently a history major, she said I should have more respect for the past," Hansen said. "Penny wants to take over the project and get the research fee."

"You said you're a history major. Is there something else you want to do?" Carrie asked the question, hoping to relieve the tension in the room.

"I was thinking about switching my major to journalism. That's why I attended your lecture," Hansen said.

Hansen finished the entire plate of snacks.

"Would you like me to make you a sandwich?" Carrie offered.

Hansen looked embarrassed as he saw the empty plate. "No, thank you. I didn't mean to eat everything."

"Don't be silly. That's why I put the snacks out for you," Carrie said.

"Are you going to tell my grandmother?" Hansen asked nervously.

"It's not up to us to run to your grandmother and report this conversation," Charles said. "We're going to leave that up to you."

"I'm sure you'll feel much better after you tell your grandmother. I haven't known Henrietta that long, but she seems understanding," Carrie said. "And she thinks the world of you."

"Tell her it started as a prank. You stopped when you realized it was wrong. But she needs to hear it from you," Charles said.

Hansen finished his soda and thanked them for their hospitality. Charles escorted Hansen to the door and watched him leave their property.

"What do you think?" Carrie asked as she stood next to Charles.

"He's a young man who made a mistake. He regrets his actions and will make it right."

"I agree that he will tell his grandmother," Carrie said.

"There's only one problem with that," Charles said.

"What's that?" Carrie asked.

"Hansen Stanford is not the killer. Gwen's murderer is still at large."

22

Charles turned off the road by the city's main library branch into a narrow lane. As Charles guided the car up a steep hill, a family of deer grazed on the lawn, unfazed by the couple's car. At the end of the driveway sat a large stone building housing the Tri-County Historical Society.

"Have you been here before?" Carrie asked.

"I was often here when I worked as an editor for my father before I took over as managing director of the business," Charles said. "Articles in our magazines have always had a historical flair, and I used the society's documents to fact-check the research of our reporters."

"Now, everyone uses the internet," Carrie suggested.

"True, but not everything online is accurate. Some records are only available in places like historical societies."

The car bumped along a road that needed repairs.

"I knew we had a historical society, but I've never visited," Carrie said. "How long has it been here?"

"Not that long. The county purchased the old almshouse twenty years ago," Charles said. "It's a win-win. The building is listed on the historical registry and can't be demolished, giving the society a permanent place to operate."

"Isn't almshouse another word for the poor house?" Carrie asked as she grabbed onto the car's ceiling handle. Charles swerved to miss a pothole.

"This road is awful. I'll call one of my contacts at Public Works and request a repair. Anyway, it's a massive farmhouse with multiple rooms. They housed families on one floor, women on another, and single men in a dormitory in an outbuilding on the property," Charles said. "Our city was one of the first municipalities to create a place for those struggling to make ends meet."

"Did the residents work the farm?" Carrie asked.

Charles nodded. "In addition to lodgings and daily meals, the residents received a payment for their labor. That was a radical idea at the time," Charles said. "The men worked the farm, and the women made clothing, jams, and canned fruits and vegetables. They sold whatever they didn't require to maintain the community. The shared income from what they sold helped many residents get a fresh start."

"A bright spot in our history," Carrie said. "Was the almshouse built by the Tri-City Building Corporation?"

"That I don't know, but we can ask one of the volunteers," Charles said as he parked the car.

Before they entered the building, Carrie removed her camera from her bag and took several photos of the building from different angles, along with the society's hand-painted sign. They climbed a series of steps that led to a wrap-around porch. Carrie imagined the residents sitting on the porch after a hard day's work, watching the sunset over the fields.

"The history of this place would make an interesting article," Carrie said as they entered the building.

Inside, a woman stood at the greeter counter. She had snow-white curly hair, wire-rimmed glasses, and was so small in stature that she barely reached above the counter. Her face lit up as she recognized Charles.

"Mr. Faraday, it's been such a long time since you've visited with us," the woman said. "Are you researching a story?"

"Mrs. Franklin, how wonderful to see you again. I don't think you've met my wife, Carrie," Charles said. "Mrs. Franklin is the assistant director of the Tri-County Historical Society and a woman who knows everything about our city's history."

Mrs. Franklin looked at Carrie from head to toe. Carrie had the impression she was evaluating her suitability to be Charles's wife. She must have passed because Mrs. Franklin gave her a warm smile.

"Thank you. There's a lot I don't know, but we have many historical records that fill those gaps," Mrs. Franklin said, amused by the compliment.

Carrie was always amazed at the number of people who knew Charles. He liked people, and people liked him. And he was a good-looking man and a favorite with the ladies. Mrs. Franklin was no exception.

"Can I direct you towards specific records, or are you just browsing?" Mrs. Franklin asked.

"We're preparing an article on Tri-City's formation. We would like to see any documents concerning that period," Charles responded.

"You've come to the right place," Mrs. Franklin said. "Most of what we house concerns Tri-City's history, but we'll need to narrow your search."

"We're particularly interested in the founders and their descendants," Charles said. "We would also like information about the Tri-City Building Corporation. We wondered if the building corporation was responsible for building the almshouse?"

"Once the city was incorporated, they could apply for state funding to erect community buildings like hospitals and schools for the good of everyone. But the funds didn't cover something as progressive as an almshouse for a small segment of the community," Mrs. Franklin said. "Brighton and Dorchester used their corporation's funds to purchase the farm. Once the project produced revenue, the almshouse sent rent payments to the corporation."

"That's informative. I bet few people know this about our founders," Carrie said.

"Are you writing a story for our upcoming anniversary? There's always renewed interest when the city's anniversary rolls around." Mrs. Franklin said.

"Have you had others ask recently for information?" Carrie asked.

"One of the history professors from the university did research here," Mrs. Franklin said. "I can't remember her name, but I have it written down in the visitor log."

"Was it Gwen Smith?" Charles asked.

"That's it, Smith. You would think I could remember an easy name like that," Mrs. Franklin laughed. "She came several times alone, and then her assistant came. Her name was Polly something."

"Maybe Penny Stevens," Carrie suggested.

"That sounds right. Amazing, I can remember all the details of our city's history, but I'm terrible with names," she said. "Do you know these women?"

"Mrs. Brighton-Stanford hired Gwen Smith to prepare a family history." Carrie didn't want to tell Mrs. Franklin that they were searching for someone with a reason to murder Gwen. Carrie was glad Mrs. Franklin changed the subject,

"I've been after Mrs. Brighton-Stanford for years to prepare a family history and give us any documents she might have. I'm glad she finally hired someone to help her," Mrs. Franklin said. "But how can I help you two?"

Charles said, "I want to begin with the founders' birth, death, and divorce records."

"I'll show you how to access those records. Carrie, what documents would you like to find?" Mrs. Franklin asked.

"I'm interested in any newspaper clippings from the period. I want to get a feel for the writings of the time and local activities," Carrie said.

"Follow me, and I'll set you up in one of our research rooms," Mrs. Franklin said.

Charles and Carrie followed Mrs. Franklin down a long hallway that had initially housed dorm rooms for the tenants. Today, the rooms provide visitors with individual spaces for research.

Each room had one table with a computer on each side. Mrs. Franklin helped Carrie and Charles log into society's system.

"This is very modern. The last time I was here, I remember microfiche machines on the tables," Charles said.

"We had the microfiche transferred to computer files," Mrs. Franklin said. "Unfortunately, there is no way to sort the records. It's just like microfiche, where you select a year and then scroll through the names line by line until you find the record you want."

After they spent several hours searching, Mrs. Franklin popped her head into the room.

"How are you two doing? You're so quiet I assumed you're engrossed in our history," Mrs. Franklin said.

"Slow going, but we're getting there," Charles said.

"I have a question. We know the three villages formed the city, but do any of the original buildings remain where the villages once stood?" Carrie asked.

"The original main street from St. Thomas is now Brighton Boulevard, and you'll still find a few old buildings along that thoroughfare. The village of Dorchester had a general store, a feed store, and a gas station, but they are all gone," Mrs. Franklin said as she made a tick, tick sound and shook her head.

"And Allwin," Charles prodded.

"Allwin had a train station for transporting people, milk, and other farm products into the city center. The trains no longer run, but the original station is now a café and gift shop that services tourists, locals, and bikers who ride on a path next to the train tracks," Mrs. Franklin said. "The main street in Allwin still has the original Phillips General Store and other original buildings that house stores and offices. They've maintained their quaint village atmosphere."

"It's time we visit Allwin and take some photos of the village," Carrie said.

"Call the Allwin library when you go and see if Harold Keegan is working. He knows as much about Allwin's history as anyone. He has a wonderful collection of early photos," Mrs. Franklin said as she left the room.

A few minutes later, Carrie said, "Here's an article about our earlier question. The headline reads, 'Tri-City Building Corporation Creates a Place for Citizens in Need.' Mrs. Franklin said they paid rent, but I imagine it took decades before the corporation got any return on their money."

"You raise an interesting point. We should research the corporation's current status and see if they are still collecting rents and paying dividends," Charles said. "Are you finding other information about their buildings?"

"A lot. There were newspaper stories each time the corporation purchased property or broke ground for a new building. There's also one article that announced the corporation made their first dividend to the stockholders," Carrie said. "How about you? What have you uncovered?"

"Mrs. Franklin was correct that the files are tedious without search capabilities," Charles said. "I'm using computer searches to find family names and then checking historical files for the birth and death records for those names."

"How many have you done?" Carrie asked.

"I finished the Brightons. They were the easiest because they had fewer descendants, and I knew the names. I completed

Dorchester once I found his daughter's names," Charles said. "I'm tracing Rebecca and her son with Dorchester now."

They continued their work until Charles said, "Well, I'll be."

"Found something?" Carrie asked, noting the excitement in his voice.

"Rebecca took her maiden name after Allwin kicked her out. The name was Pembrook," Charles said.

"The same last name as Rachel, Henrietta's companion," Carrie said, unable to hide her astonishment. "Does that mean that Rachel is a Dorchester descendant?"

"Give me a few more minutes to double-check my research," Charles said.

Before Charles finished, Mrs. Franklin entered the room, "I hate to disturb your research, but it's closing time."

"I need a few more minutes to finish this founder," Charles said, looking up and smiling at Mrs. Franklin.

"I knew that's what you would say. Whenever you worked here you always needed a few more minutes. " Mrs. Franklin laughed. "You can have the time it takes me to close down the other areas."

"While I'm finishing up with Rebecca Pembroke, can you download these additional Allwin files on your laptop?" Charles asked Carrie.

Carrie quickly loaded the names of the files Charles gave her and anything mentioning the Allwin and Pembroke names from the newspaper records.

Charles shut the computer down, and the couple said their goodbyes to Mrs. Franklin.

As they walked down the steps, Carrie said, "Well."

"There is no doubt that Rachel Pembroke is a Dorchester descendant," Charles said. "I made a copy of her birth certificate. It lists Richard, the son of Rebecca and Dorchester, as her father."

23

"Should we assume that Gwen found the same information?" Charles asked as they left the historical society parking lot, and he maneuvered the car along the bumpy road.

"With Gwen's background in research, I'm sure she did," Carrie said.

"Now that we know Rachel Pembroke is a descendant of Samuel Dorchester, do you think she's the killer?" Charles asked.

"I met her at the book signing and then again at Henrietta's house. Somehow, she doesn't strike me as a murderer."

"You know what they say. Anyone is capable of murder under the right circumstances," Charles said.

"That may be true, but what's her motive? If Gwen proved Rachel was a Dorchester descendant, she could submit a claim to the country club for lease payments," Carrie said. "Why reject the money and kill Gwen?"

"Does she have another motive, like endearing herself to Henrietta? Maybe she's after a larger payout," Charles said.

Carrie thought about Charles's comments. Could Rachel's motivation be related to her feelings for Henry Stanford? "What should we do next? Do we go to Jenco and tell him what we found? Let him confront Rachel? Or should we alert Henrietta that Rachel might pose a threat?"

"I don't have an answer, but let's get something to eat and discuss it. All that research made me hungry," Charles said.

"Since we're on this side of town, how about the Train Stop?" Carrie asked.

"Sounds good to me," Charles said as he turned onto Railroad Avenue.

The couple arrived at the restaurant to find a crowd. They were lucky to get a table at the back of the dining room. At least it offered privacy from the larger booths loaded with families.

Charles said. "Looks like everyone in the area chose the Train Stop for food."

"The town appreciates a nice place to eat with good food, and I'm sure staying busy distracts Gloria from thinking about Gwen," Carrie said.

When the waitress arrived, Carrie recognized Cindy Russell, Gloria's cousin.

"Hello, Cindy," Carrie said. "Do you remember me?"

Cindy stared and said, "Oh yes, you're Mrs. Faraday. I met you at the memorial service."

"The place is bustling," Charles said.

Cindy looked around as if seeing the crowds for the first time. "This is normal. We fill up at this time every day," Cindy said with little emotion. "With food costs rising, it's cheaper to eat out. And everyone gets to pick what they want to eat."

"Plus, someone else fixes the meals and washes the dishes," Carrie said.

Cindy laughed. "I understand what you mean. I always take food home from here for the same reason." She took their orders and hurried off to the kitchen.

"Rather than contact Henrietta, perhaps we should talk to Rachel first. Confront her with what we found," Charles suggested.

"That's a good idea. And we may have our opportunity sooner rather than later," Carrie said.

"What do you mean?" Charles asked.

"Rachel Pembroke just walked in the door."

"No time like the present," Charles said as he bounced up from the table to invite Rachel to share their table.

"It's very kind of you to let me join you. I hate eating at the counter, and I don't know how long before a table for one would be available," Rachel said as she sat beside Carrie.

"Glad to have you," Carrie said. "Do you eat here often?"

"Gwen recommended it," Rachel said. "When Henrietta has an outing that doesn't require my assistance, I enjoy coming here for my meals."

"I take it you have the night off," Charles said.

"Henrietta and a group of her friends had theatre tickets and are out for the evening. I could have eaten at the house, but it's nice to get out and try something different," Rachel said. "Enough about me. How did you find this place?"

"We discovered the restaurant because of ..." Carrie hesitated, "Gwen's death."

Charles raised his hand to get Cindy's attention. Carrie watched when Cindy arrived at the table to see if Rachel recognized her.

"Cindy, we have another order for you," Charles said.

"No problem. Do you know what you want?" She asked Rachel.

"I believe you waited on me the last time I ate here," Rachel said. Cindy only smiled but didn't seem to recognize her. "I'll take an iced tea and the blackened salmon salad with blue cheese dressing."

"Cindy is Gloria and was Gwen's cousin," Charles said after Cindy headed to the kitchen.

"I didn't know that, but she looked familiar. That's why I thought she may have waited on me previously," Rachel said.

"She was at the memorial service and is a student at the university," Carrie offered.

"I don't remember seeing her at the memorial service," Rachel said. She thought for a moment. "If she attends the university, I might have seen her at one of Hansen's weekend parties."

Here was another connection between the Brighton-Stanford family and Gwen. Carrie focused back on Rachel. "I haven't tried the blackened salmon salad. Is it good?"

"Delicious. The chef grills it on a wood plank for added flavor," Rachel said. "Mrs. Lancaster, our housekeeper, isn't big on salmon. I love it and often order it when I'm out."

The Train Stop kept the food and the customers moving, and it wasn't long before Cindy brought their order. Carrie and Charles decided to enjoy their food before confronting Rachel with their discovery. The conversation was pleasant, and Rachel seemed relaxed and friendly.

"How did you come to work for Mrs. Brighton-Stanford?" Charles asked.

"I have no family of my own. All my relatives have passed," Rachel said. "I wanted to find a job with either a small company or a family. I couldn't believe my luck when I saw an ad in the community paper that Mrs. Brighton-Stanford wanted a secretary/companion. I applied and got the job."

"How long ago was this?" Carrie asked.

"I've been working for Henrietta for almost ten years. And I've enjoyed every minute," Rachel said. "The work is interesting, and I have plenty of free time to pursue my interests."

"Why do you say interesting? What sort of things do you do for Henrietta?" Charles asked.

"For a woman that's up in years, she's quite active. She heads up several charities and sits on multiple boards. Not to mention all her personal activities like the book club," Rachel said. "I manage her schedule and handle all her correspondence and paperwork."

"Speaking of the book club, I was surprised you didn't join us for the discussion," Carrie said.

"Henrietta wouldn't object if I sat in, but the club members are her long-time friends," Rachel said. "Speaking of books, I'm glad to have the opportunity to chat with you about writing."

Carrie immediately assumed she wanted to discuss Gwen's report, but Rachel's answer surprised her.

"I'll share a secret. I want to be a writer. Let me change that. I am a writer," Rachel said.

"What sort of things do you write?" Carrie asked, taking a new interest in the conversation.

"I've had two short stories published, which was an absolute thrill. And I'm working on a novel."

"That's a great start. What's your novel's genre?" Carrie asked.

Rachel looked embarrassed and quietly said, "I've been writing a cowboy romance."

"Cowboy romance," Charles said, surprised. "That's one I haven't heard before."

"It's currently a popular category of romances," Carrie said.

"I didn't write it because it's popular. I've always been a romance reader, but the idea of having a rough and ready cowboy in the story fascinated me," Rachel said with pleasure. "But I've reached the point where I don't know if I'm on track with the rules for the genre. It's one thing to get a short story published. It's another to finish a complete book and hold the reader's attention."

"You should attend the Tri-City Writers' meetings. They have critique groups that could provide feedback," Carrie said, adding, "If you feel comfortable, I'd be happy to read your writing and offer suggestions."

"My wife is a good writer and an excellent editor. She's one of the few writers the magazine employs whose work is ready for publication when it arrives," Charles said. "She would give you an honest appraisal."

"Ignore my husband's compliment. The next meeting is Thursday, and you're welcome to go with me," Carrie said.

"I would love your feedback along with a ride to the meeting," Rachel said.

The conversation grew quiet. Carrie had mixed feelings about Rachel. How could someone who wrote romances be a murderer? Or was she being swayed because Rachel was a fellow writer? Carrie knew her conclusion made no sense, but that's what she thought.

Charles interrupted Carrie's thoughts. "Research is a big part of writing. I'm sure you learned that assuming you don't have a background as a cowboy."

"I grew up on a farm with horses, but we didn't have cowhands. Since I've always lived on the East Coast, I needed to study the Old West," Rachel said.

"I'm glad you agree. Carrie and I were at the historical society this afternoon going through some of the archives and found some interesting facts about the Tri-City founders."

The color in Rachel's face drained. She gently pushed her plate away and gulped her iced tea.

"Really, what did you find? I have a feeling it concerns me," Rachel said.

"I'm going to be frank. We discovered that you are a descendant of Samuel Dorchester. Your grandmother was the woman who had a child with Dorchester. And that son was your father," Charles said bluntly. "Isn't that correct?"

Rachel checked that none of the nearby tables showed interest in their conversation. She lowered her voice. "It's all true. I am a descendant of the Dorchester family. That was another reason why I wanted to work with Henrietta. I felt I could learn more about my grandfather," Rachel said.

"Why haven't you made this known?" Carrie asked.

"I had several reasons for not wanting to reveal this. I didn't know my father. He died in the Iraq war, and my mother passed away soon after I graduated from college."

"You said there were several reasons," Carrie said.

"I wasn't sure how Henrietta would react to having a member of the Dorchester family working for her in light of the rumor of a relationship between her grandfather and my grandmother," Rachel said. "My past wasn't as important as my job."

"Dorchester's lease with the country club stipulated that the club pay a fee to any descendant. You would be entitled to that money," Charles said.

"I'm not concerned about the money. I get paid an excellent salary, and I'm quite happy. I don't want to lose my job," Rachel emphasized.

"You must realize that your background and work with Henrietta make you a suspect in Gwen's murder," Charles said gently.

"Murder! I had nothing to do with Gwen's murder," Rachel said defiantly. "When Henrietta hired Gwen, I hoped she might uncover something new about my family, but that isn't a reason for murder. As you discovered, the records are readily available in the historical archives."

"You need to have a conversation with Henrietta before she learns this information from someone else," Charles suggested. "There's a murderer out there, and I wouldn't want you or Henrietta to be in their sights as the next victims."

Rachel nodded her head. "I hadn't thought of the potential danger. I'll talk to Henrietta as soon as she gets home tonight."

Rachel paused and then asked hesitantly. "Can I still go with you to the writers' meeting?"

Carrie made a quick decision and answered, "Yes."

"Is your investigation providing any other leads to the murder?" Rachel asked.

"We're leaving the murder investigation to the police, but we researched the city's founders for a story. That's how we traced you," Carrie said. "One piece we came across was the formation of the Tri-City Building Corporation started by Brighton and Dorchester. Do you know if that corporation still exists?" Carrie noticed a slight arch in Rachel's eyebrow.

"Oh, yes, it still exists. Henrietta sits on the board, and her son Henry is the CEO," Rachel said. "Henry is an excellent businessman and has expanded the holdings beyond Tri-City."

Carrie sensed Rachel's admiration of Henry. Was there more between them? Maybe Charles was right that there was a bigger prize than the club's lease payment.

"Then the corporation has been active for a long time," Carrie said.

"It's operated continuously since Brighton and Dorchester formed the company," Rachel said with pride.

"We need to reach out to Henrietta and learn more about the Brighton-Dorchester corporation's history," Charles said.

24

Carrie wanted to spend the morning looking at the files they downloaded from the historical society. Her plans changed when Maddy from Tri-County Books called.

"They continue to sell. Like hotcakes," Maddy said. "All the publicity about that poor girl's murder. No doubt, it's helping sales."

Because of her short, choppy sentences, Carrie had to listen carefully to understand what Maddy said.

"Sorry to hear that," Carrie said. "I don't mean the book sales. That's great news. I meant that someone else's tragedy caused the increased sales."

"Your book has nothing to do with Gwen's murder," Maddy said.

"You and I know that, but I'm not sure the general public knows this," Carrie answered.

"Doesn't matter why they're buying. I need you to sign more copies. Can you come over to the store?" Maddy asked.

"I'd be happy to," Carrie said. "I'm leaving now."

***

When Carrie arrived at the store, it wasn't busy. Students were in school, and parents were at work. Carrie found Maddy training a staff member at the register. Carrie noticed the next person in line had a copy of her book, which warmed Carrie's heart.

"Mrs. Tompkin, you're just in time to meet the author of your book, Carrie Faraday," Maddy said. "Would you like her to sign your book?"

Mrs. Thomkin accepted her change and gushed at Carrie, "Oh, yes, that would be wonderful. I have a collection of signed books."

Carrie signed Mrs. Tompkin's book. "I hope you enjoy the book, and don't forget to tell all your friends," Carrie said.

"I'm afraid I'm late to the party. Most of my friends already bought the book and recommended it," Mrs. Tomkins said as she gathered her purchase and left.

"Word of Mouth," Maddy said.

Carrie wasn't sure what she meant, "Word of mouth," she repeated.

"One friend telling another friend they liked the book. That's the key to sales," Maddy said.

"Not to mention the huge display you gave me at the front of the store," Carrie added.

"Glad to help." Maddy looked embarrassed and changed the subject. "You came at a good time. Bit slower," Maddy said. "Makes it easier for me to leave the floor."

"Where's Marge?" Carrie asked, not seeing Maddy's sister on the floor.

Maddy lowered her voice even though no one else was around. "New boyfriend. Do you know John Perkins?"

"Sounds familiar, but I can't quite place him," Carrie said.

"Perkins Antiques," Maddy added.

"I remember. A few years back, I wrote a story about antique shops in the area," Carrie said. "I interviewed John."

"John came in looking for books on antiques. Marge and John are dating. I believe it's serious." Maddy said with no emotion as they walked to the office at the back of the store.

Carrie realized Maddy didn't seem upset with what the future might hold for the bookstore if Marge went off to sell antiques with John. Maddy appeared flighty compared to Marge, who had a solid business sense. But that wasn't fair of Carrie. If Marge found someone special, then that was a good thing.

"Here we are," Maddy said. "You don't mind signing them in the office? I haven't put the books out."

"I'll sign as many copies as you want in any location," Carrie said.

Carrie sat at one of the two office desks, one for each sister. A stack of two dozen copies waited for her signature.

"I hope you won't get stuck with all these signed copies," Carrie said.

"We would only get stuck if we wanted to return them. Not happening," Maddy said. "They'll sell."

While Carrie continued signing books, Maddy asked, "Have you and Charles made progress with solving Gwen Smith's murder?"

"What makes you think we're investigating her death?" Carrie asked.

Maddy raised an eyebrow. "It happened at your book signing. At your best friend's house. Of course, you're investigating."

Carrie questioned how much she should tell Maddy. Maddy had a way of divulging sensitive information to everyone without even realizing she was doing it. There were a few things Carrie could share. After all, Maddy had another two dozen books for her to sign.

"We started following Gwen's research path. We decided to focus on the three founders," Carrie said. "The Brighton history is an open book because you have Henrietta, her son, and her grandson still active with boxes of family documents available. Then we found a Dorchester heir from a historical society document, and now we're concentrating on the Allwin family."

"I heard Rachel Pembroke got money. The Dorchester country club payments," Maddy said.

Carrie told Maddy about what they discovered from Betty Canton concerning Rachel since it was now public knowledge.

"What about the Allwins?"

"Still working on that," Carrie said.

"Aren't they all gone? I remember seeing the death notices when Edwin and Steven died."

Carrie was amazed at how much Maddy knew, but then the bookstore tended to be a center of community life and gossip.

"The grandfather and father are gone, but Steven had two children, and we're currently trying to track where they are," Carrie said.

"Do you think they did the murder?" Maddy asked. "Maybe they're looking for money, too."

Carrie's eyes blinked. It amazed her how quickly Maddy returned to the murder. But was she any different from the rest of the population? No one liked having an unsolved murder in the community.

"We haven't discovered any clues to the murder, but we're still working on the theory that Gwen's research led to her death," Carrie said.

Maddy said nothing, but her facial expression changed as she remembered something. "I forgot to tell you something. Gwen worked in one of our private rooms several times."

Carrie looked up from her work. "You're kidding. Why didn't you mention this before?"

"It was several weeks before I saw her picture in one of the newspapers. That's when I realized it was her," Maddy said. "Then I forgot."

"You never told the police?" Carrie asked, still astonished at this new information.

"Nothing to tell. Many people come to the bookstore and use our rooms," Maddy said. "Besides, I don't like that, Detective Jenco. The way he treated you in the Barrington case."

Carrie thought more about Gwen using one of the rooms. "Maddy, you're a bookstore, not a library. Why did Gwen come here to work?"

"Gwen wanted a place to work away from the students, and she wanted to order history books from us," Maddy said. "Marge is good at knowing available historical books, especially about Tri-City."

"Charles mentioned that there was only one book when he looked in the Tri-City section. It talked about families living in the area and how they coped in the early days," Carrie said.

"That's the other interesting thing. A book disappeared. Had two copies. Gwen bought one, one disappeared," Maddy said. "We're trying to replace that book and order others. People will be interested with the upcoming anniversary."

"What book disappeared?" Carrie asked, trying to keep up with Maddy's chaotic speaking style.

"Book of interviews. It included Brighton, Dorchester, Allwin, and other early families," Maddy said. "Written by a local historian. Hope we can find another copy."

Carrie closed the cover of the last book she had signed. "All done."

"I remembered one more thing. Gwen had a confrontation one of the days she was here," Maddy said. "Looked like a student."

"What do you mean by a confrontation? How do you know? Aren't those rooms soundproof?" Carrie questioned.

"They are. I was putting out new arrivals on a shelf nearby. Became aware of motion," Maddy said. "A kid with his back to me. Couldn't see his face. He waved his arms, and I saw him raise a fist at one point. Hadn't thought about it until I started talking with you."

"You said a student. What made you think that?" Carrie asked.

"Wearing one of those hoodies with the university name on the back."

"Could it have been a woman?" Carrie asked.

"Could have been. The kids all dress alike," Maddy answered.

"What happened next?"

"Nothing. I went to the storage room for more books. I came back. The hoodie kid had left."

Maddy started putting the books Carrie signed back in the cartons.

"Did Gwen stay or leave after the encounter?"

"She finished her work. Bought two books before she left," Maddy said.

"Was that the last time she worked here?"

Maddy screwed up her face as she taxed her memory. "Maybe, one more time, but not sure. Do you think I should call the cops?"

"While there isn't much to tell since you can't identify the kid, you should still let the police know that Gwen had this encounter. It may offer another motive for her murder," Carrie said. "I need to get going. The Tri-City Writers meet tonight."

Carrie left the store anxious to tell Charles what she had learned about this additional confrontation. Was it the same person who confronted Gwen in Joanne's garden?

Maybe there was another angle to the murder. Could it be a disgruntled student, where the situation escalated into murder?

25

Thursday night, Carrie picked Rachel up for the Tri-City Writers meeting.

"I appreciate you inviting me and taking me to the meeting," Rachel said. "I'll confess I'm a bit of a loner. Going to social events by myself has always been a challenge. Maybe all writers feel this way."

"As writers, we spend so much time alone that it's difficult to come out of our shells and be little social butterflies." Carrie agreed. "This outing won't be too taxing since we're in a comfort zone with fellow writers."

"How do they run these meetings?" Rachel asked. "Will I have to introduce myself?"

"The word meeting is a bit of a misnomer. No formal group business or reports," Carrie said. "There's time to network. Then the president calls the meeting to order and introduces the speaker."

"No reports and the focus on writing is my kind of meeting," Rachel said, looking pleased.

"I believe you'll enjoy tonight's speaker. He's a professional editor and gives step-by-step tips for self-editing," Carrie said.

"Something I need to learn," Rachel said.

They drove quietly for some time, and then Rachel broke the silence.

"You're too polite to ask," Rachel said. "I talked to Henrietta. She couldn't have been more gracious, and I felt a weight lifted from me."

"Was she surprised that you were a Dorchester descendant?" Carrie said.

"Yes and No. After you told Henrietta about Betty Canton over at Ridgely, she arranged a luncheon with her," Rachel said. "Betty verified Dorchester, not her grandfather, fathered a male child."

"And when you told her you were the descendant..." Carrie left the sentence hanging.

"She never suspected I was a Dorchester," Rachel said. "Then she said the nicest thing. She always felt we had a special bond. And was glad I was the descendant."

Carrie couldn't see Rachel's eyes. But when she heard the catch in her voice, she knew she had welled up emotionally.

"Henrietta strikes me as a woman who doesn't let things upset her," Carrie said. "She faces issues head-on and deals with them."

"You're right about that," Rachel said. "Henrietta already called the country club and notified them there's another Dorchester descendant. She's arranging for me to receive the lease payments."

"There's no reason why you shouldn't have the money. It isn't a fortune but designed to provide for future descendants," Carrie said.

"Everything's worked out fine, thanks to you and Charles," Rachel said. "My job is secure. I feel closer to Henrietta, and she's happy she can officially put a family rumor to rest."

Within a few minutes, they arrived at a local pub.

"The meeting is at a pub," Rachel said, showing surprise.

"We can't drink at a community center or other county buildings without applying for a costly permit each time. This pub has a private room and is happy to provide a cash bar," Carrie said.

Carrie and Rachel paid for glasses of wine. Then, Carrie introduced Rachel to several romance writers.

After leaving Rachel in a discussion about romance writing, Carrie networked until she spotted Hansen at the bar.

"Hello, Hansen. Good to see you again. Are you pursuing your interest in writing," Carrie said.

Hansen spun around. "Mrs. Faraday, hello, um, it's good to see you," Hansen said. "Professor Hopkins recommended this group. She said the presenters have strong writing credentials, and I would find these presentations helpful."

"Professor Hopkins is right. This group attracts good speakers."

"I'm surprised you came to a lecture on editing since you already published your book," Hansen said.

"I haven't stopped writing, so the learning doesn't stop," Carrie said. "I'm here tonight because I want more editing tips."

"I guess we're all learning." Hansen took a sip from the beer he purchased and looked at Carrie. "Don't worry. I'm having only one beer. I won't be inspired to write any letters when I leave."

"I'm not worried about you. Did you tell your grandmother?" Carrie asked.

"I did. She was disappointed in my behavior but recognized it as a foolish prank," Hansen said. "We had a long talk. She told me things I never knew about my family's history."

Carrie wondered if Henrietta had told Hansen the revelation about his grandfather and Rachel's ancestry. She decided not to press Hansen.

"Grandmother said being a founding family member was only important if we implemented the lessons learned from the past. She told me she felt the same way when she was growing up but learned how much we could accomplish when people worked together for the good of everyone," Hansen said. "For the first time, I saw our history in a different light."

"I'm glad you had the courage to talk to her," Carrie said.

"Having first told you and your husband made it much easier," Hansen said, fidgeting. "Thank you."

The awkward moment was interrupted when the president announced that the program would start shortly.

"I guess I better find Rachel and get seated."

"Is Rachel here?" Hansen asked, scanning the room. "Is my grandmother here, too?"

"Only Rachel," Carrie said. "Did you know she's a writer? She published several short stories and is working on a romance novel."

"I didn't know that," Hansen said as he walked away.

Carrie found a table on the far side of the room, and soon Rachel joined her.

"This is remarkable. Several of the romance writers invited me to join their critique group," Rachel said.

"Critique groups provide great feedback," Carrie said.

"I saw you talking with Hansen." She lowered her voice. "Did you know he was responsible for the poison pen letters?" Rachel asked. When Carrie didn't respond immediately, Rachel added, "I can tell by your response that you already knew this."

"Hansen contacted my husband and me after my lecture at the college. He knew he made a mistake and needed to talk with someone," Carrie said. "We advised him to tell his grandmother."

"I respected Hansen for owning up to what he did," Rachel said. "For once, he realized his actions could have consequences."

Carrie realized Henrietta trusted Rachel since she told her about Hansen's poisoned pen prank. It meant Rachel had a special place in Henrietta's life.

"Did you know Hansen also wants to be a writer?" Carrie asked. "You should talk to him."

Astounding, Carrie thought. Two people who lived in the same house had no idea they had similar interests. Rachel became distracted as she looked across the room.

"Isn't that the waitress, Cindy, from the Trolley Stop with Hansen?" Rachel asked.

Carrie followed her gaze. "You're right."

"Now, I'm sure I met her at one of Hansen's parties. I guess the university crowd is smaller than we think," Rachel said.

Was this a chance meeting between Hansen and Cindy, or were they more involved? Carrie reflected on other recent events. Henrietta Brighton-Stanford had a busy week. She heard the confession from Hansen and put the poison pen issue to rest. She met Betty Canton and got the proof that eliminated the stigma that her grandfather had fathered a child. She learned that Rachel

Pembroke was a descendant of the Dorchester family, and she called the country club to get Rachel's lease payments started.

The president made opening remarks and introduced the speaker. As late arrivals found seats, Carrie saw Penny Stevens slip in and sit at a table in the back. Hansen, Rachel, Cindy, and Penny at the same meeting. The only one missing was Brian Amberson. Carrie scanned the room but saw no signs of Brian.

When the meeting ended, Rachel wanted to get contact information from the group of writers she had met. Carrie returned to the bar and again met Hansen, ordering two beers.

"What did you think of the talk?" Carrie asked.

"It was good. Not everything applied to my writing, but I picked up hints I can use."

"That's how it's supposed to work," Carrie said. "You're here with Cindy. How did you two meet?" Carrie asked.

"We both took a class with Professor Hopkins. That's when I found out she was Gwen's cousin."

Cindy walked up to the bar and joined them. "Hello, Mrs. Faraday. Good to see you."

"Are you interested in writing?" Carrie asked.

"I'm not sure what my focus is. I'm only a sophomore. I still have time to decide on my major," Cindy said. "I attended several legal classes and liked them. I took a journalism class with Professor Hopkins and liked it."

"That's a great approach," Carrie said as she paid for her glass of wine and picked up the tab for Hansen and Cindy.

"Thanks, Mrs. Faraday, that was nice of you," Cindy said. Hansen nodded while taking a sip of his beer.

"I saw Penny at the start of the lecture, but I didn't see Brian. He also expressed an interest in writing." Carrie said.

Carrie saw the look that passed between Hansen and Cindy.

"He's unsure about joining a writer's group," Hansen said hesitantly.

"Hansen, we should be honest with Mrs. Faraday. Brian and I were casually dating, and then I met Hansen. It's like choosing a major. I'm exploring different opportunities," Cindy said, laughing while giving Hansen a gentle punch in the arm.

"There's another reason I invited Cindy to join me," Hansen said. "If you're not aware, this pub makes a mean burger, and I promised Cindy one if she tagged along."

"Then go order that burger and enjoy the rest of your evening," Carrie said.

After Carrie dropped Rachel off and drove home, she realized the same small circle of people who knew Gwen kept showing up. Was one of them a murderer?

26

The evening after the writers' meeting, Carrie finished an article on a deadline while Charles reviewed the quarterly financials for the business. The work distracted them from thinking about the case, which had hit another dead end.

"It's a warm evening, and we need a break. How about we go for some ice cream?" Charles suggested.

Carrie emphasized dramatically with her fingers as she typed the last words. "I finished my story, so your timing is perfect." She closed her laptop and put it in the carry case.

In the car, Charles asked, "Why did you bring the laptop?"

"I thought I might have the opportunity to review our information on Gwen while we ate ice cream. I feel we're missing something."

The local ice cream parlor was at the end of Brighton Boulevard, near the Tri-County bookstore and the local park and athletic fields. Visitors to the bookstore, teams after their games, and neighbors cooled all off with a homemade flavor at the ice cream parlor. The place overflowed with customers, and Carrie left her laptop in the car, knowing they would have to wait until later to discuss the case.

Carrie settled for a small dish of pistachio ice cream, and Charles had a double-dip black raspberry cone. Every picnic table scattered around the large yard outside the shop overflowed with young families. The couple debated whether to take their treats home when they heard a voice calling them.

"Charles, Carrie, over here."

Charles saw the Quinns at one of the tables.

"Come join us," Dan said. "We're getting lots of dirty looks since only two of us are at this big table."

"We're willing to share with a deserving couple," Joanne said with a laugh.

They joined the Quinns. After a few pleasantries, Dan asked, "What's the latest with the case?"

"We haven't heard a thing from the police," Joanne said. "Although I'm not complaining. Since they're not talking to us, I assume it means we're not at the top of the suspect list."

"We saw Jenco dining recently at the club," Carrie said. "Not that he shared any details with us."

"Forget the police. What have you two discovered?" Dan asked as he took a spoonful of his chocolate fudge nut sundae.

Charles looked enviously at the sundae and made a mental note to try one next time. "Carrie and I continue trying to find leads in the historical documents," he said.

"You mean Gwen's research?" Joanne asked.

"No. Gwen's work is still missing. No paperwork, no electronic files." Carrie said. "But we're interviewing her sources and trying to figure out what she discovered."

"Do you think her killer has her work?" Dan asked.

"Don't know for sure, but we don't think so. There are still no signs of Gwen's final report," Carrie said. "Like us, they are still looking for information."

"How about her phone files you downloaded?" Joanne asked. "Anything there?" Joanne finished her milkshake and threw her cup in the nearby trash can.

"Gwen had a picture of the founder's picnic and seemed to focus on their backgrounds. One of the men pictured was the man who served as the lawyer for the group," Charles said.

"From a previous Tri-County magazine article, we found the granddaughter, Betty Canton," Carrie said. "She sent me files of the firm's legal documents. I'm still sorting them, but nothing has surfaced to explain a reason for Gwen's murder."

"Betty discovered Henry Brighton didn't father the child with Allwin's wife. It was Dorchester," Charles said.

"That verifies the club's grapevine. Rumor has it that Mrs. Brighton-Stanford filed a claim to resume the lease payments to a descendant of the Dorchester family," Dan said.

Charles looked at Carrie, debating whether to tell the Quinns what they knew about the claim.

"I can tell you know. Out with it," Joanne said.

"I guess with the rumor swirling, it won't be long before everyone knows," Carrie said. "Mrs. Brighton-Stanford's companion is a Dorchester descendant."

"You don't mean Rachel Pembroke?" Joanna questioned.

"Correct. Rachel's grandmother, Rebecca, was Allwin's wife and then had a son with Dorchester."

"Does she have a claim if Dorchester never acknowledged the birth?" Dan asked.

"You're asking that question because you sit on the finance committee at the club," Charles said. "But I'm afraid the club may be out of luck. Dorchester married Rachel's grandmother and had the birth certificate changed, showing he was the child's father."

They stopped their discussion as a gang of young children chased each other around their table until the parents gathered them and headed for their car.

"I have to ask," Joanne said. "Did Rachel take the job for the opportunity to get closer to the Brighton family records and Gwen?"

"She's been working for Henrietta for ten years, long before Gwen came on the scene. And she would have no reason to kill Gwen because it benefits her to have her ancestry revealed," Charles said. "If anything, she wanted to learn more about her past. Her mother and father are dead, and she has no other relatives."

"She genuinely enjoys her job, and if it hadn't been for Betty Canton's discovery, Rachel would never have sought the lease payment. That's Henrietta's doing," Carrie said.

"You two have made a major discovery. Anything else?" Dan said.

Before either Charles or Carrie could answer, Charles's phone buzzed. He showed concern as he immediately started tapping the keys.

"What's wrong?" Carrie asked.

"It's an alert from the security company that we've had a break-in," Charles said while playing with his phone. "I'm having trouble pulling up our security camera images. We better go."

"Let us know what happened," Joanne called after them.

***

When the couple arrived home, they had to show identification to the police officer guarding their driveway.

At their front door, Perkins, a security officer from the alarm company, said, "The police officers are checking the perimeter and inside. Once they give the "all clear," you can enter and see if anything is missing."

Shortly, two police officers appeared, each coming from opposite sides of the house. "The intruder disabled the camera in the back and entered through the French doors. But it's all clear now if you want to go inside."

Charles immediately went upstairs to their bedroom, where they had a safe. It took only a few seconds to see that it wasn't disturbed. He heard a soft mewing sound and found Baxter peeking out from under the bed. He picked him up and stroked him as he returned downstairs to find Carrie in the study.

Carrie felt violated as she saw open drawers and papers thrown on the floor from both desks.

"What a mess," Carrie said.

"Any idea what they were looking for?" the officer asked.

"Haven't a clue. We don't keep money or valuables in the study. The papers represent stories I'm writing or papers from my husband's business," Carrie answered.

"How about you, sir? Anything disturbed upstairs,"

"No, the safe wasn't touched," Charles said. "The TV and other electronics are all here."

They all reacted to a sound behind them. Carrie and Charles were surprised when Detective Jenco popped into the study.

"Detective, I didn't know you responded to security alarm issues," Charles said.

"I don't," Jenco said, annoyed at the inference. "However, when I heard the address, I wanted to stop by."

Perkins entered the room. "Mr. Faraday, you can set the alarm code tonight as usual to protect the rest of the house," he said. "We added a lock bar to the French doors and will be back tomorrow to install a new camera and fix any damaged wiring."

"We'll write up a report, but there's nothing more we can do tonight." The officer nodded at Jenco.

After Perkins and the officers left, Jenco said, "Let me see if I understand what I heard. Someone broke in, rifled the study, but took nothing."

"Our intruder tried to breach my computer, but the security codes stopped them," Charles said.

Jenco looked at Carrie.

"My laptop was with me. Our burglar had no opportunity to take it," Carrie said. "Let's cut to the chase."

Charles admired how Carrie could get to the heart of the matter.

"By all means," Jenco encouraged.

"Whoever broke into our home wasn't looking to steal anything. They were looking for information."

"I agree with my wife," Charles said. "Considering the response time between the security company and your officers, they had very little time to complete their search."

"What did they expect to find?" Jenco asked.

"We all know," Carrie said. The look on Jenco's face indicated he agreed with her. "I believe they were looking for any information we had concerning Gwen's research."

Carrie and Charles sat on the sofa, and Charles pointed to an adjacent chair for Jenco.

"Have you two discovered something I should know about?" Jenco asked.

"Nothing that would provide a clue to Gwen's murderer, but we discovered some historical facts not previously known," Carrie said.

"As my wife told you when we met at the club, we've been concentrating on the founders," Charles said. Charles explained their findings about the Henry Brighton rumor.

"Did you discover who was the father?" Jenco asked.

"It was Samuel Dorchester, and we know that Rachel Pembroke, who works for Mrs. Brighton-Stanford, is a descendant," Carrie said.

Charles watched as Jenco processed the information. "There would be no reason for Rachel to kill Gwen. This discovery means the country club must start paying her lease money for the property," Charles added.

"Interesting. I'll have a conversation with Rachel Pembroke, but I agree it doesn't appear she has a motive,' Jenco said. "Anything else?"

"We interviewed Betty Canton. Her grandfather was the lawyer for the incorporation of Tri-City and the personal attorney for the founders," Charles said. "Besides verifying a Dorchester heir, she said Gwen made an appointment to meet with her. Regrettably, Gwen never got to keep it."

"How did you discover this Canton woman?"

"I remembered my magazine interviewed her for an article for the city's hundredth anniversary," Charles said.

"That's good work," Jenco said.

Charles couldn't believe Jenco had complimented them. He decided it might be a good time to get some information from Jenco. "Have you made any progress on the case?" Charles asked.

"As you know, there was nothing other than a few historical records, photos, and a list of names on Gwen's phone," Jenco said.

This statement made Charles realize that Jenco knew Carrie had downloaded files from Gwen's phone. Maybe Jenco was more intelligent than they gave him credit.

"Are you still assuming the motive for Gwen's murder was her research for Mrs. Brighton-Stanford?" Carrie asked.

"I can't say for sure, but her research is the only lead we have. She lived a quiet life as a college professor, and her students admired her. She wasn't dating anyone, so no other motive has surfaced," Jenco said.

"Mrs. Brighton-Stanford said Gwen nearly finished writing her final report, but the report hasn't surfaced. Maybe that's what our burglar wants," Charles said.

"That's assuming there was a final report," Jenco said.

"I believe there was, and if we find that report, we'll have more answers," Carrie said.

Jenco nodded. "I guess there's nothing more we can do tonight. I'll inform the patrol cars to run extra checks in the area." Jenco stood to leave and added, "The case has gone cold. Without some new information, we may never find who murdered Gwen Smith."

27

It was unusual for the couple not to be up early. But after the break-in, they enjoyed a few extra minutes of sleep until Charles's phone rang.

"Good, I'm glad you're there. Hope it's not too early to be calling."

"No, it's not too early," Charles answered through a yawn, as his mind raced through possibilities of who was on the other end. The voice was energized and sultry. Then, he recognized the caller. "Betty, is that you?"

"Yes, it's me. Oh, that wasn't polite. I should have identified myself," Betty laughed. "I'm calling to invite you to a meeting."

Charles played along. "I love meetings."

"I doubt that. No matter. Penny Stevens, Gwen Smith's assistant, wants to meet," Betty said. "Do you know her?"

"I've met Penny," Charles said. Betty sounded like Maddy, talking in short, almost incoherent sentences. It must be the excitement surrounding the upcoming meeting.

"Penny contacted both me and Henrietta. She wants to continue Gwen's project."

Carrie was now awake and sitting up next to him. Charles placed his phone on speaker.

"Are you still there? I heard a click," Betty said.

"Carrie's joined us, so I've placed you on speaker."

"Hello, Carrie."

"I could understand if Penny contacted Henrietta, but how did she get your name?" Carrie asked.

"She said she kept Gwen's calendar. Knew of the appointment with me to discuss my father's papers. Asked me if I could make a copy of any of my father's papers and send them to her," Betty said.

Charles could hear the doubt in her voice. "I assume you didn't do that."

"Absolutely not. I told Penny we should meet and discuss the project. That's when she told me she also contacted Henrietta," Betty said. "And since you told me to let you know if anyone showed interest in my father's paper, I'm calling you."

"How does Henrietta feel about continuing the project?" Carrie asked. "Does she want to start over since she doesn't have any of Gwen's completed work?"

"I asked Henrietta that same question. I cataloged my father's records, so the city's history isn't lost, and Henrietta felt the same," Betty said. "You get that way as you get older. You want to leave a record for the next generation."

"I understand," Charles said. Perhaps it was time he and Carrie talked about how to maintain the future of Faraday Press. He wasn't sure that Christopher was interested in continuing the family business, which would require a different plan for the future. "Where and when is this meeting?"

"Since I don't drive, we'll meet at Ridgely Woods tomorrow at three. Rachel will bring Henrietta. I've reserved a private room where we can discuss the project without disturbing other residents or them disturbing us, "Betty said. "Will you and Carrie come?"

Carrie nodded her head. "We'll be there," Charles said.

Charles remembered Emily's comment about Penny's limited writing skills.

"When you call Penny to verify the meeting, ask her to bring some writing samples."

"That's a good idea. Help us decide if Penny is qualified to take on this project," Betty said.

***

The next day, a few minutes before three, Penny arrived at Ridgley Woods. Henrietta, Rachel, and the Faradays were already seated. There was no hiding the surprise on Penny's face when she saw the couple.

"Mr. and, err, Mrs. Faraday," she stumbled, regained her composure, and said, "How nice to see you."

"You too, Penny," Carrie said.

Charles sensed Penny wanted to know why they were there. He responded before she could ask. "You're probably wondering why we're here. Since Carrie is working on the story for the Tri-County Monthly, we wanted to ensure that we weren't interfering with what you had in mind."

"Thanks for the clarification. I knew you indicated you weren't interested in continuing Gwen's project when we talked after your lecture," Penny said as she relaxed her shoulders.

The Ridgely Woods staff rolled in a cart with tea, coffee, and snacks for the group.

"Help yourself to refreshments. Then we'll get started," Betty said.

Everyone grabbed something from the cart and then took their seats.

"Let's begin," Betty said. "Penny contacted Henrietta about continuing Gwen's work and me about getting copies of my father's paper concerning Tri-City."

"Not only the city but the founders, too," Penny added.

"I meant to say the city and the founders. We all have access to different pieces of research. By getting together, we could help Henrietta decide whether to continue."

"I appreciate everyone coming. Since I never received any of Gwen's work, it means starting over," Henrietta said.

"Not from the beginning," Penny said. "I helped Gwen and knew her methodology. I gathered most of the records from the historical society for her and edited some of her early drafts."

Charles looked at Carrie and knew what she was thinking. He seriously doubted Penny did the editing based on her limited writing skills. How much of this draft had Penny seen?

"Did Gwen email you these drafts?" Carrie asked.

"I wish. She only gave me paper copies that I had to return. She was protective of her work until she completed the final report," Penny said. "But I'll have a head start over someone new."

After a moment, Rachel asked, "Mr. and Mrs. Faraday, you've done research at the historical society and other sources. Are you able to write a report based on your findings?"

Charles saw Penny look away as she tried to hide the annoyance that showed on her face.

"Our research focuses on a story, not a report, and is limited to the founders," Carrie said.

"That's my point. I'm more than qualified to handle the assignment, and it would make sense for one person to handle both the city's beginnings and the founders," Penny stressed. "If everyone could send me what they have discovered so far, I can get started immediately."

"Before we make any decision, did you bring some samples of your writing?" Betty asked.

"Yes, of course. Not knowing the others would be joining us, I only made two copies," Penny said, handing a copy to Betty and Henrietta.

Henrietta handed her copy to Charles. "Charles, you can make a better decision than me because of your work at the magazine."

Charles accepted the pages. "I'll review your work later today and touch base with Betty and Henrietta. Can we get back to you tomorrow?"

"Yes, of course. Thank you for meeting with me. "Remember, the sooner you make your decision, the sooner I can get started," said a confident Penny as she left the room.

"What do you think?" Charles asked the group as he started reading Penny's writing sample.

"As Gwen's administrative assistant, Penny would be the logical choice to continue the work. She would have an edge over someone new," Henrietta said. "She certainly thinks she's qualified."

"That's assuming she had access to as much of the research as she indicated," Betty said.

"What do you think of her writing?" Rachel asked.

"Based on the few paragraphs I read, Gwen's assessment was correct. Her writing needs work," Charles said. "But that's not a showstopper. A good editor could fix that."

"Could I get a copy?" Rachel asked.

"I'll make you one before you leave," Betty offered.

"Would all of you be available to join me for dinner on Saturday? We can review the facts, and you can help me decide what to do." Henrietta stood to leave. "Penny will have to wait a little longer before I decide whether to continue this project."

28

Saturday at six, Carrie and Charles arrived at Henrietta Brighton-Stanford's home. When they rang the bell, they expected Rachel to open the door, but instead, they were surprised to see Hansen.

"Hi, Hansen," Charles said.

"You too, Mr. Faraday. My grandmother is waiting for you in her sitting room."

As they walked down the hall, Carrie said, "We thought Rachel would answer the door. Isn't she joining us for dinner?"

"Rachel picked up Betty Canton at Ridgely Woods and is putting the car away," Hansen replied.

In the sitting room, Henrietta and Betty Canton chatted amiably. Charles heard snippets of reminiscences about people they knew and stores where they shopped in the past.

"Hello, Carrie and Charles. "I was just about to offer Betty a cocktail," Henrietta said. "Charles, since my son Henry is running late, would you mind serving as a bartender?"

"I'd be delighted," Charles said. "What would you ladies like?"

"A glass of sherry for me," Henrietta said.

"That would suit me as well," Betty said.

Charles fixed and delivered the sherry for the ladies. Charles held up a gin bottle and waved it to get Carrie's attention. Carrie licked her lips and nodded her head.

When Rachel arrived, she saw the exchange between the couple. "I'll take one," she said.

"Hansen, can I get you something?" Charles asked.

"Got a soda," Hansen said, holding up a can of root beer.

Charles wondered if Hansen chose a soft drink rather than a beer when he was with his grandmother.

Once everyone had their drinks and seats, Henrietta said, "I want us to share what we know about Gwen's research. I need to decide whether to hire Penny to continue the project."

"Between my father and grandfather's files, the records you have, Henrietta, and what Charles and Carrie have uncovered, I believe we have sufficient information to create a comprehensive historical document," Betty said. "What we need is someone to pull it all together."

"I don't know what you thought," Rachel said, looking at the Faradays. "I wasn't impressed with Penny's writing skills."

"We agree," Carrie said.

"And if you don't think Penny is the right person to continue the project, I accept your advice, but I'm concerned about something else," Henrietta said. "I still believe somewhere in the work Gwen completed is a reason for her murder."

"Grandmother, maybe you're mistaken that Gwen's research of our family history caused her murder," Hansen suggested.

"You might be right. Each of us, indeed, has a piece of the puzzle. That's why, having this discussion, we might find another reason for the murder," Henrietta said. She turned to Charles. "Are the police looking at other possibilities?"

"Detective Jenco told us they have no other leads, and without something new, the case may go cold," Charles said.

Charles debated whether to mention the break-in at their house. The thief didn't take anything, so he couldn't prove that the incident had anything to do with the murder. On the other hand, it was better to alert everyone to the possible danger.

"I don't want to frighten everyone, but Carrie and I had an intruder at our home this week," Charles said. That's when the detective mentioned the case status.

"Do you think it's related to Gwen?" Rachel asked.

"We don't know," Charles said. "The security company and the police were there within minutes. The burglar searched our study but stole nothing."

"Let me add that I had my computer with me during the break-in, so it wasn't available to steal. It had all of my Tri-City and Gwen research on it," Carrie said.

"If they took nothing of value, then it sounds like they were looking for something else like research documents," Henrietta said.

The group sat quietly for a moment, digesting this new information.

"Rachel mentioned that the Tri-City Building Corporation founded by your father and Samuel Dorchester is still active," Charles said. "I understand Henry is the current CEO."

"Henry does a wonderful job. He's taken the corporation beyond the boundaries of Tri-City with real estate holdings all over the state," Henrietta said. "About 15 years ago, when we were expanding the company, we had a public offering. Did you know your mother owns shares?" Henrietta asked Charles.

"I had no idea," Charles said, surprised.

"With the public offering, you attracted new stockholders, but are there still original stockholders or their descendants?" Carrie asked.

"Oh yes. I don't remember the exact number, but several descendants still receive dividends," Henrietta said. "If it's important, we can ask Henry for the number when he arrives."

"I still receive dividends," said Betty. "My grandfather was an original stockholder, and his shares have passed to me."

"How foolish of Mr. Allwin not to purchase shares," Carrie said. "I understand his reasoning. Being a farmer, he probably found the business aspects of starting a corporation and buying shares beyond his comfort level."

Charles noticed a change in Henrietta's demeanor. She looked out the window when Carrie mentioned Allwin's foolish behavior. Was there something she knew but hadn't shared?

"Henrietta, is there information about Edwin Allwin and the corporation you haven't told us?" Charles asked.

The others waited as Henrietta finished her sherry and placed her glass on the table.

"When I told Carrie the launch of the building corporation caused a rift between the partners, that part was true, but I failed to mention something else," Henrietta said. "My grandfather and Mr. Dorchester always felt bad that Allwin didn't have the foresight to join the corporation, and they set shares aside for his heirs."

Hansen exclaimed, "You're kidding."

The information surprised Rachel, Carrie, and Charles, but they said nothing.

Betty said, "That sounds like something they would do."

"Was there any legal documentation supporting what they did?" Betty asked.

"My father told me his father and other board members signed a handwritten document indicating their intentions," Henrietta said. "My father also said they never told Allwin what they had done. They thought if a descendant of Edwin came forward, they would tell them about the shares. I know it sounds vague, but that's how they designed it to avoid any contact with Allwin."

"Grandmother, why would the men give him free shares since Allwin opted out?" Hansen asked.

"Several reasons," Henrietta replied. "Their consciences got the better of them. They appreciated Edwin's hard work helping them start the city and didn't want his family to suffer because of his shortsighted arrogance."

"You said there were several reasons," Charles said.

"They wanted to avoid any future lawsuits if an heir came forward and claimed they had a right to shares in the corporation," Henrietta said.

"Do you think Gwen found this document?" Hansen asked.

"Gwen never mentioned it or asked any questions about the corporation," Henrietta said.

"That's the problem. Gwen never mentioned anything specific about her work," Rachel said. "She always indicated everything she discovered would be in her final report."

"If Gwen found the documentation, what did she do with it?" Henrietta said. "I'll have to ask Henry if there is anything in his files at the office."

"I remember my father saying the partners protected Allwin even though he was a bit of a scoundrel, Betty said. "But he never explained what he meant."

What an incredible revelation. Charles gave Carrie a questioning look. Could this information mean an Allwin descendant tried to find information about this document? But how would they have known it existed?

The discussion stopped as Mrs. Lancaster entered the room and announced that dinner was ready.

"Rachel, could you help me bring the food into the dining room?" Mrs. Lancaster asked.

"Should we wait for Henry?" Rachel asked.

"Hopefully, he will arrive in the next few minutes. If not, Mrs. Lancaster will keep a plate for him," Henrietta said. "We senior ladies are hungry and need to eat," she said, laughing as she patted Betty's arm.

Charles extended arms to Betty and Henrietta and escorted them to the dining room.

Henry Stanford arrived as Rachel and Mrs. Lancaster finished placing dishes on the table.

After introductions, Henry said, "Mrs. Lancaster, as always, you've outdone yourself. You cooked all my favorites."

Mrs. Lancaster's face reddened. "Thank you, Henry, but I always make this for the family."

Charles looked at Henry, a man in his early 50s with gray-framed glasses that matched his hair. He had his mother's eyes and a chiseled jaw and nose that must be from the male side of the family. Charles looked at Hansen and saw the same characteristics.

Dinner was pleasant as Charles asked Henry about his real estate business and shared details about running a magazine. Henrietta talked about the comedy she saw recently at the theatre. Charles noticed the one topic that they all avoided was Gwen's murder.

When they finished the main meal, Henrietta suggested they return to the drawing room for dessert. Over their cake and coffee, the conversation returned to Gwen.

"Henry, before you arrived, we discussed the document my grandfather and Dorchester wrote putting stock shares aside for the Allwin family. Have you ever seen the document?" Henrietta asked.

"I never saw it, Mom, but Dad told me there was such a document," Henry said. "The corporation is holding shares in a trust fund, and they've earned dividends all these years. Should a descendant come forward, they would receive a tidy sum."

"Assuming the document still exists, where do you think it might be?" Hansen asked.

"When we moved to larger offices, early papers were boxed and put in a storage room. I'll start a search of those boxes," Henry said. "When we ran out of room, I stored boxes in Mom's attic."

"Then there's a chance that Gwen found it, or perhaps there are files that Gwen hadn't searched," Carrie suggested.

"I know there are more boxes in the attic that Gwen never searched," Rachel said. "We should start with them."

"Betty, do you remember seeing a handwritten document in the files from your family's law practice?" Carrie asked.

"I don't. But as it got closer to my moving date, I scanned documents in bulk without reviewing each one," Betty said.

"I'll search the files you sent me. It should be quick now that I have something specific to find," Carrie said.

"It sounds like we all have our work cut out for us, Henrietta said. "Hansen and Rachel, can you two work together and go through the remaining boxes upstairs?"

They nodded, and Hansen said, "I would enjoy doing that. I want to be part of this project."

Charles realized that Hansen and Rachel working together was a positive development. And maybe their work would produce another clue.

29

The morning after Henrietta's dinner party, Carrie searched the files she received from Betty Canton. She didn't find the handwritten note granting building corporation shares to the Allwin heirs.

"Even though you didn't find the document, we should do more Allwin Village research," Charles suggested.

"Good idea. Let's head to Allwin," Carrie said.

***

The beautiful day reminded Carrie of when she had driven a convertible with the top down and the wind blowing through her hair. Today, she settled for the open moon roof on their SUV.

The Village of Allwin was at the southernmost tip of the Tri-County metro area and farthest from Center City. Using GPS, Charles found the village with a main street resembling the early photos from the last century. They pulled into the library parking lot at the end of Main Street. The library was old, with solid, dark furniture and bookcases. They asked to speak to Harold Keegan, the librarian Mrs. Franklin mentioned.

Harold Keegan was an elderly gentleman, thin as a rail, with unruly wisps of snow-white hair protruding at angles from his scalp. He wore a flannel shirt and jeans. Carrie wondered if Harold's shoulder stoop resulted from all the years spent leaning over the books he read. He had a look of contentment on his face.

When he saw Carrie and Charles, he said, "You must be the Faradays. Mrs. Franklin said you would be stopping by. I understand you're writing an article about Tri-City for its anniversary."

"We are, but instead of emphasizing the city and its progress, we wanted to take a closer look at the founders," Carrie said.

"We discovered many materials about Henry Brighton and Samuel Dorchester, but there's less information on Edwin Allwin," Charles added.

Harold stared at the couple, and Carrie felt he was determining their genuine interest in the village or looking for gossip about Edwin Allwin. "What publication assigned you this article?" Harold asked.

"Tri-County Monthly magazine," Carrie said.

Hearing the name of the magazine changed Harold's attitude toward the couple. "That's a fine publication," Harold said. "And you're correct. There's less information about Edwin Allwin and our village. While his ancestors may have founded the village, Edwin kept to himself and avoided publicity."

"Perhaps it's because he didn't join the other two founders in forming the building corporation," Charles said.

Harold nodded. "It's a sore point for the local villagers," Harold said.

"Why do you say that?" Charles asked.

"Early villagers faced a double-edged sword. A few residents bought stocks in the building corporation and did well with their investment," Harold said. "However, most villagers thought the new corporation ignored the village because Edwin didn't join."

"Research indicates Allwin preferred farming to construction," Carrie said.

"That's what outsiders thought, but villages knew Allwin was a skinflint and a curmudgeon," Harold said. "He didn't want to spend money to join."

"That's interesting," Carrie said. She didn't reveal she already knew this about Edwin.

"It was also a point of contention with his son. Steven wanted to join because he didn't want to be a farmer and wasn't good at it," Harold said. "When Edwin ignored what the other founders were doing, most people think that sealed the village's fate for future development."

"Can you give us an example?" Charles asked.

Harold thought for a moment. "Lots of building occurred over the years in the areas originally represented by Dorchester and Brighton, but I guess the biggest loss for our village came when they built the beltway to connect Tri-City with the other areas," Harold said.

"I'm confused," Carrie said. "We used the beltway to come to Allwin."

"But you got off at an exit that isn't marked for Allwin, and then, assuming you knew where you were going or used GPS, you retraced your steps south to find our village," Harold said sarcastically.

Carrie tried not to look guilty, knowing they had used GPS to find their way to the village. "On the positive side, you have a lovely quaint village with more charm than many of the modern buildings in Tri-City," Carrie said.

"That's our current plan to reinvent our village and attract tourists. We've developed hiking and bike trails that follow the old rail tracks. The town converted the train station into a café, and the original general stores offer various items that remind people of the past," Harold said. "We're also trying to attract individual boutiques, stores, and restaurants that our potential tourists would find attractive."

The conversation paused as a woman approached the desk and asked for help.

"Excuse me. I'll help this lady and then grab one of my photo books you might find interesting," Harold said as he led the woman to shelves on the other side of the room.

"What are your thoughts?" Carrie asked Charles.

"Harold may be one of the old-timers looking for an excuse for their lack of progress. And Edwin Allwin is the scapegoat," Charles said.

"It does seem unfair they didn't get an exit ramp from the highway," Carrie said.

"If I remember correctly, the village didn't get an exit due to the cost of building a bridge over a river. But there's no reason the town council couldn't authorize signs," Charles said.

"I wonder if the whole town feels this way," Carrie said.

Harold returned carrying a thick photo album. He placed the book on a nearby table.

"Thanks for waiting. Even though we're not busy, when some-one needs help, duty calls," Harold said. "The photos will give you a flavor of our history. Why don't I give you a few minutes to review the album."

The couple passed over the photos they had previously seen to concentrate on the new ones. They found a picture of Brighton and Dorchester seated at the desk, signing a document with Allwin standing behind them.

"This is when Dorchester signed over the golf course land to Tri-City. The caption reads *Tri-City's First Building*," Charles said. "I bet Jim Albright would like a copy of this picture for the club archives."

Many of the remaining photos showed Allwin's main street during various community events. Carrie recognized Edwin Allwin on a tractor, and next to him was a young man with two small children leading the 4th of July parade. After a few minutes, Harold joined them at the table.

"Did you have questions about the photos?" Harold asked.

"We haven't seen many of these pictures. I assume the peo-ple next to Edwin were his son and grandchildren," Charles said, pointing to the July 4th picture.

"Yes, that's Steven and his two children," Harold said, shaking his head. "Those kids had it tough."

"Why do you say that?" Carrie asked.

"You probably discovered that Steven's stepmother left the area in disgrace. Allwin was left to raise his son with no help," Harold said.

Carrie nodded but said nothing. She wanted to hear Harold's version of the facts.

Harold continued, "Steven married and had a boy and a girl. Then, his wife died from cancer. Many villagers blamed Edwin for not getting her the medical help she needed."

"That must have been difficult. Based on this photo, the children look young," Charles said.

"The little girl was ten and her brother two or three when their mother died. Edwin and Steven were left raising these youngsters," Harold said. "The other kids ostracized them because they wore second-hand clothes bought at a thrift shop. And their grandfather wouldn't let them participate in school activities. He had chores waiting for them on the farm."

"That's sad," Carrie said.

"I forget her name, but when the girl graduated high school, she left to live with her mother's sister. Several years later, the boy joined them," Harold said. "I heard the girl received a college scholarship, but that was the last I heard of her. I have no idea what became of the boy."

"Are there any pictures of the children when they were older?" Carrie asked.

"I only have the one from the 4th of July parade," Harold said.

"It's a shame we don't know more about the children," Carrie sighed. She was thinking about the shares of stock they were entitled to receive.

"If you head down to Phillips General Store, they've got photos on the wall, including many graduation class pictures. You might find a later picture of the kids," Harold said.

"One last question, Harold, and then we'll let you get back to work. Does the Allwin farm still exist?" Charles asked.

A change came over Harold's face, and he made a tick, tick sound,

"I take it it's no longer there," Carrie prompted.

"Oh, it's still there, but there's a change coming that may not be good for the village. It was foreclosed and sold." Harold said. "We haven't heard what will happen to that piece of prime real estate."

"Where's it located?" Charles asked.

"It's about six miles outside town on the main road. You can't miss it," Harold said, adding, "You'll see the real estate sign at the entrance."

The couple thanked Harold and headed to the general store. In addition to selling an unbelievable assortment of products, the store offered a deli. While they waited for the sandwiches they ordered, Carrie looked at the photos that covered the walls. Like Harold's album, most were photos of village events but didn't identify the people pictured.

Then, Carrie found a section with graduation class pictures. At the bottom of each photo was the year. Carrie tried calculating the year the Allwin children graduated when a staff member stood beside her.

"Were you looking for a specific person in the photo?" she asked.

"Oh, hello," Carrie said, startled, "My husband and I were chatting with Harold at the library about the village's history and the Allwin farm. He mentioned Steven Allwin's children, and I was curious if they were in one of these pictures."

"I'm afraid not. The school didn't start taking these group shots until the year after the daughter, Lorna, graduated," she said.

"Steven, Jr. went to live with an aunt in seventh grade, so he didn't graduate from Allwin High School."

Carrie decided to take advantage of the moment. "What do you think about the sale of the Allwin farm?"

"It has to be better than abandoned land," she said. "If it's developed commercially, it will bring jobs, and if it's housing, that will bring families and new life to the community."

"That certainly is a positive approach. Thanks for the information," Carrie said.

When they left the general store, the couple followed Harold's instructions. They saw a leaning mailbox with a faded Allwin name about six miles from town. Next to the box was a 20 by 12 foot for sale sign with the word "SOLD" posted across the center.

Charles turned in the driveway and started down the lane.

"Do you think we can get down to the house?" Carrie asked.

"Let's see," Charles said.

They discovered a faded white clapboard farmhouse at the end of a bumpy ride. The barn had a missing roof section and wallboards falling off. A chain-link fence surrounded the farmhouse with the windows and door boarded. Carrie agreed with the general store worker that any development would be better than this abandoned property.

"No one has lived here in quite a while," Charles said as he turned the car around. "We need to find Steven Allwin's children."

"I wonder why the Allwin children didn't claim the property. They could have sold it rather than having it foreclosed," Carrie said.

"Since it was a foreclosure, it probably means there was a tax issue," Charles said. "Even if the children had a claim, they may not have been able to pay the back taxes."

Once they were heading home, Carrie asked, "How can we find out who bought the property? Don't you know some folks in the real estate business?"

"I do. But if I ask a real estate agent about a particular property, I will stir up unwanted interest. But I have an idea," Charles said.

"What's that?" Carrie asked.

"Henry Stanford buys and sells properties." Charles dialed Henry Stanford.

"Charles, what can I do for you?"

"Carrie and I were taking a little ride. We found the original Allwin family farm, with a sold sign posted. We wondered if you knew anything about who bought it?" Charles asked.

"Can you stop by the office rather than talk over the phone?" Henry said. "I'll tell you about the Allwin property and something else that occurred."

30

Within twenty minutes, Carrie and Charles reached Henry's Tri-City Building Corporation offices housed in one of the oldest buildings in the city. However, when the elevator reached Henry's floor, Carrie looked at Charles in disbelief. The décor was modern, with a large reception area and glass offices on each side of the hallways.

"This isn't what I expected," Carrie said.

"I agree," Charles said. "Since this is one of the oldest companies in Tri-City and housed in a historical building, I expected the office would reflect the past."

The staff bustled between offices as the couple introduced themselves to the receptionist. She spoke briefly on the phone, and within a few minutes, Henry Stanford greeted them.

"Carrie, Charles, thank you for coming here. I wanted you to see the office set-up," Henry said. "Would you like something to drink?"

"I could use a cup of coffee if you have some available," Charles responded.

Carrie nodded, and Henry led them to an alcove with single-pod coffee machines and an espresso maker. After fixing their coffee, they followed Henry to his office. While all the glass made office activities and everyone visible, Carrie noticed the silence and sense of privacy once Henry shut his office door. They sat in an area on the far side of the office with several overstuffed chairs and a round table in the center.

"We can enjoy our coffee while I answer your questions about the Allwin property."

"I take it you know something about the property?" Charles asked.

"That I do. You see, I bought it, or I should say the Tri-City Building Corporation bought it," Henry said.

Carrie was glad she didn't have a mouthful of coffee because she would have choked upon hearing Henry's news. She responded with, "You bought the property?" Then she realized how stupid that sounded since Henry just said that. "I mean, we didn't expect, we had no idea…"

"It's all right, Dear," Charles said as he patted his wife's arm. "Henry took us both by surprise. Why did you buy the Allwin property?"

"We didn't purchase the land because it was the Allwin property. It's more about the property's location, the number of acres, and the price," Henry said.

"I assume you got a good price because it's a foreclosure," Charles suggested.

"I did, but that doesn't always happen. If it's a property in a 'hot' location, there can be a bidding war with a foreclosure," Henry said. "Because the Village of Allwin has had limited development, there weren't many bids. I got the property for an excellent price."

"Was it foreclosed because of taxes?" Charles asked.

"Correct. No one had paid property taxes in years," Henry said.

"In Allwin, we learned that Edwin's son Steven had two children. The two children moved away to live with their aunt, and no one has heard from them," Carrie said. "I assume the kids would have inherited the farm."

"When it went up for sale, the state owned the property, not the family. If the kids were around, it wouldn't have affected the sale. Unless they had money, the kids probably couldn't have afforded to pay the back taxes," Henry said. "However, if heirs exist, they could claim the Allwin shares from the building corporation. After visiting Allwin, do you have any additional information about any family members?"

"Not yet. We just discovered this information earlier today, and I haven't had a chance to do any research," Carrie said. "Our next project is to try to find them."

"Are you going to divide the property and sell or lease parcels? The For Sale sign listed the farm as 400 acres," Charles said as he drained his coffee.

"In the past, the corporation purchased buildings, renovated them, and either sold or leased them. That's not our plan with this purchase," Henry said. "We're developing a resort destination with event and conference facilities, a golf course, and hotel rooms. At the end of the project, we'll build a few single-family homes around the edge of the golf course."

Henry went to a cabinet, returned with a plan of the future site, and placed it on the table for the couple to see. He pointed to locations on the document and explained what each building represented. As Henry discussed his project, Carrie noticed how excited he became.

"This development will create many jobs, and we will run shuttle buses to the village to increase their sales. It's a win-win for everybody," Henry said eagerly.

Carrie knew the villager she spoke with in the general store would be happy. She got both her wishes—business development to bring jobs and housing to lure new families to the area. "Your project is in line with the village's plans to reinvent itself as a tourist attraction," Carrie said.

He paused and then rolled up the project document. "I probably shouldn't have shared this since we haven't announced our plans," Henry said. "I'm so excited about the development; I got carried away."

"Don't worry, we won't say a word," Charles said. "When you're ready to announce your plans, we can do a feature in the Tri-County magazine for you."

That's my husband, Carrie thought. Always on the lookout for a good story

"Thanks, I appreciate that. And don't think I won't remind you," Henry said.

"While this all sounds good, I hope you're planning on adding an exit sign on the beltway," Charles laughed. "It can be a challenge to find the village."

"We're presenting our proposal for an additional exit at the next council meeting. It would be below the existing exits, but it would eliminate the need for a bridge over the widest part of the river," Henry said. "In the meantime, we'll add signage at the current exit to help visitors find their way."

"When we saw a fence around the house, we thought construction had begun," Charles said.

"I had the fence installed and the doors and windows boarded after my site manager saw signs that someone had been in the house."

"Do you mean someone was living there?" Carrie asked.

"Not exactly. The state turned off the water and electricity, but there were paper plates and cups, soda cans, and snack items in the kitchen," Henry said. "We added the fence and posted signs because we didn't want to deal with squatters once construction started."

Carrie heard what Henry said about squatters, but was there another answer? Could it be an Allwin kid visiting their family home?

"When are you planning on starting?" Charles asked.

"In two weeks, we have a zoning hearing to change the property designation from farmland to allowing development. As soon as that's approved, we'll apply for the permits," Henry said. "Then we'll begin construction."

"I'm sure the zoning hearing will go well," Charles said. "The village of Allwin has waited many years for development, and I can't imagine there will be opposition."

"Henry, you asked us to come to your office," Carrie said. "Was there something you wanted to show us?"

Henry said, "We had a break-in."

31

"Unbelievable! Who's doing this?" Carrie exclaimed. "Did they take anything of value? Do you think it has to do with Gwen?"

Henry raised an eyebrow at Carrie's barrage of questions. "The burglar touched nothing except the boxes of historical documents. I don't know if it's directly related to Gwen, but someone is interested in old city documents."

Henry might not want to admit it, but Charles suspected these crimes were related to Gwen's research and murder. What had Gwen discovered? What document did the intruder want? Was this information a reason for murder?

"Do you remember my assignment from Mom's dinner party? I was to search the boxes we stored here from the original corporation papers and look for the document concerning the Allwin building shares," Henry said. "Let me show you what we found this morning."

"Did you find it?" Charles asked.

"Not the document, but something else. It's a slow process," Henry said. "We don't need to keep storing these boxes. I had two of our associates go through the boxes, scan each item, and sort them by importance. We'll send documents of value to the historical society and recycle the rest."

"That's a good idea," Carrie said. "I had no luck finding the missing document either, but the scanned files Betty sent me made it an easy search."

"Exactly. Scanned documents make more sense. The boxes for disposal were stacked in a conference room until we finished and notified the shredding company," Henry said, stopping outside a conference room. "We came in this morning to find the contents of every box turned out on the floor."

"Are there more boxes?" Carrie asked.

"A few, but they're locked in the safe, and our thief didn't attempt to open it."

"Aside from the safe, is there any other security?" Charles asked.

"Each employee has an individual key code they punch in when they enter the office. We don't have anything else, although the building has closed circuit cameras in the lobby," Henry said. "We've never needed extensive security. Besides our office electronics, there's no money, and we keep property documents in the safe."

"How do you think the intruder got in?" Carrie asked.

"We had a late meeting yesterday to discuss the new property and had sandwiches delivered. One possibility is that the intruder entered when the food person left because we can't see the main door from the conference room."

"Anything else?" Charles asked.

"If the intruder had arrived earlier in the day, he could have hidden and waited for us to leave," Henry said.

"With all this glass, wouldn't it be hard for someone to hide?" Carrie asked.

"Not necessarily. While the offices are mostly glass, we have storage closets, utility areas, and restrooms that provide cover," Henry said. "I was the last person to leave, but I didn't check the premises. I assumed I was the only one here."

"You mentioned each employee has an individual keycode," Charles said. "Are those codes tracked?"

Henry nodded. They returned to Henry's office, and he dialed a number and asked for the key code list. "How about another cup of coffee while we wait?" Henry suggested.

"Coffee always makes waiting better," Carrie said, laughing. "I'll fix it. Do you both want a cup?"

The men nodded, and Carrie returned to the coffee station. Out of curiosity, Carrie opened a door next to the station. She saw what Henry meant by places to hide. It was a large walk-in closet with several storage shelves but plenty of space for someone to wait until the office was empty. When she returned to Henry's office, his receptionist opened the door for Carrie and then handed Henry a paper.

As Henry scanned the list of names, the expression on his face changed. It was apparent to Carrie he had recognized a name.

"Did you spot something?" Charles asked.

"The person who entered the office at ten yesterday evening was my son Hansen."

Henry didn't wait. He placed his phone on speaker and dialed a number.

"Hey, Dad. What's happening?" Hansen asked.

"I'm here with Mr. and Mrs. Faraday. We were looking at the keycard log for yesterday. I was curious about what brought you to the office at ten last night." Henry asked his son.

"The log must be wrong. I wasn't there," Hansen answered definitively.

"Could others have accessed your code?" Henry asked.

"No way," Hansen said.

Carrie surmised that his father's suggestion offended Hansen based on what he said next.

"You can check with Rachel. We were going through document boxes from the attic last night. I never left the house."

"You don't need an alibi, son. I was curious when I saw your name, that's all," Henry said. "Thanks for the info. I'll check for a glitch in the program."

Carrie and Charles had remained quiet during Henry's conversation with his son. Carrie realized Henry had a good relationship with his son since he could ask Hansen sensitive questions.

Henry sat back in his chair with a frown on his face. "Contrary to what Hansen said, I have to believe someone stole his code. There's no other explanation."

"Could it be a program glitch?" Carrie asked. She liked Hansen and found him to be a decent young man. Carrie couldn't believe he would come to his father's office and dump boxes of documents.

"I guess it wouldn't hurt to check with the security company," Henry said.

"Speaking of checking security," Charles said, "You mentioned the building has cameras at the entrance. Any chance we could see the footage from those cameras?"

Henry dialed another number, and after a brief conversation, he informed the couple that building security would send him the camera footage from the previous night.

As they waited, Charles said, "There is something obvious. We have someone who showed no fear going to the third floor and searching Gwen's room in your mother's home. And now someone came to this office to search more boxes of historical paperwork."

"Are you saying the intruder in both cases is probably someone we know," Carrie said.

"It also sounds like you're implying this person is a member of my family," Henry said, sounding defensive.

"Not true. I understand Hansen often hosts parties with his college friends," Charles responded quickly.

"One of the guests could easily slip up to the third floor without anyone noticing they were gone," Carrie added.

Henry's computer pinged. "Here's the footage."

Carrie and Charles stood behind Henry and watched the footage that covered the lobby from nine to eleven. The camera only showed people leaving until a few minutes before ten when someone wearing a dark hoodie entered the building. They couldn't see the face, and it was only a couple of seconds before the individual was out of sight.

They watched the entire footage. Then Henry rewound it several more times.

"There's not much to see," Henry said. "But I feel confident that's not Hansen. Hansen is taller than this person."

"The clothes are so baggy it could be a male or female," Charles said.

"I can't put my finger on it, but there's something that seems familiar about the person," Carrie said. "Could you send me the file? I have some software that might enhance the image."

"You'll have it by the time you get home," Henry said as he punched a few computer buttons. "Let me know if you identify our intruder."

32

"What a day! We learned a little more from our visits to Allwin and Henry's office, but I'm glad to be back at our farmhouse," Carrie sighed.

They found comfort in the home that they had renovated together. They settled in their study with wine and cheese to discuss the case.

"I find it hard to believe that the Allwin heirs didn't come forward. They might have been able to work with the state to avoid foreclosure," Carrie said.

Carrie could see that Charles was pondering something. "What else are you thinking?"

"We need to find out what happened to Allwin's grandkids. If the kids are around and feel cheated out of their property, which someone else is developing for profit, this could be a strong motive for murder," Charles said.

"I agree. I'll start researching the children in the morning," Carrie said as she took a long sip of her wine and a bite of cheese. "Maybe tomorrow we'll have some new ideas on how to find them."

"I had an idea after we left Henry's office. Our thief broke into Gwen's college office and her condo, took out a security camera at our house, and entered through our French doors. Now they entered Henry's office and either stole Hansen's key code or breached the key code system," Charles said. "Our thief is someone with a security background."

"I hadn't thought of that. Our culprit does seem to be familiar with security systems," Carrie agreed.

"If we ever find a viable suspect, I will bet they have a security background," Charles said.

"Speaking of suspects. I like Hansen. Even though he pulled the prank with the letters, I don't want to think he's involved," Carrie said. "The problem is he keeps popping up."

"Everything that's happened centers around his family and Tri-City's founders, which would explain his popping up. And he's been honest when confronted about his activities. I don't think he's a suspect," Charles said as he finished his wine. "Aside from these delicious snacks, do you have something in mind for dinner?"

"I don't feel like going out for dinner. Why don't you fire up the grill, and we'll have hamburgers with all the fixings."

"Good suggestion," Charles said.

As they headed to the kitchen, Charles's phone rang. "Speaking of Hansen," Charles said as he saw the caller ID. "Hello, Hansen. I've got you on speaker so Carrie can hear."

"And Rachel and Cindy are here with me," Hansen responded.

In the background, they heard greetings from Rachel and Cindy.

"You were at my father's office when he called about the security code situation," Hansen said. "I know he was being vague, but it sounds like someone used my code while I was at grandmother's searching through boxes of documents with Rachel and Cindy. That concerns me."

Was Hansen protesting too much? Carrie avoided the discussion about the security code breach. Instead, she asked, "Did the three of you discover anything new?"

"We did. I didn't ask you this when Dad called because I knew his focus was on the key codes," Hansen said. "Could you two come over to grandmother's house? We'll show you what we found."

Charles looked at Carrie, and she mouthed, have them come here.

"Carrie and I have been out all day and were just about to fix dinner," Charles said. "We're grilling burgers. How about you three joining us? After dinner, we can discuss your findings."

There was only a moment of hesitation as Carrie heard the ladies agree to the invitation.

"That sounds good to us," Hansen said.

"Can we bring anything?" Rachel offered.

"Just yourselves. We have everything we need," Carrie said.

After Charles ended the call, Carrie said, "I agree with you. Hansen wouldn't share information with us if he were involved."

"In my opinion, he's an innocent bystander," Charles said.

Carrie raised an eyebrow, "Meaning."

"Hansen inadvertently said something or invited a guest to one of his parties who gained access to information about the family," Charles said as he went to the patio.

While Charles prepared the grill, Carrie sliced cheese, lettuce, tomato, and onions. She then assembled an assortment of condiments so each person could customize their burger.

"Should I do French fries or onion rings?" Carrie asked.

"Both," Charles responded.

"I should have known better than to ask you. But you're right, both go with burgers."

Carrie heated the oil, cooked the fries and onion rings, and placed them in the oven to keep them warm. She had no sooner finished her preparations when she heard a car coming up the driveway. Charles answered the door and returned with Hansen, Cindy, and Rachel. Hansen carried a brown envelope.

"Is everyone okay with eating on the patio rather than the dining room," Carrie said.

"Great idea," Cindy said. "It's a beautiful evening."

"What can I do to help?" Rachel offered.

"If everyone carries an item from the counter out to the table, we should be good," Carrie said.

As soon as Rachel took a seat on the patio, Baxter jumped onto her lap. She stroked the cat, and he purred in appreciation.

"Looks like Baxter found a new friend. That's unusual for him to cozy up to a stranger," Charles said.

"He probably senses that I'm a cat lover. I always had cats growing up," Rachel said. "I miss not having one. They're great companions."

"You should ask grandmother if you can have one. She had several cats when I was growing up," Hansen said.

"Maybe I'll do that," Rachel answered as she continued stroking Baxter.

Nice of Hansen to suggest Rachel ask Henrietta for a cat, thought Carrie. They had a new respect for each other.

When the burgers were ready and placed on the table, Charles took Baxter to the kitchen so Rachel could enjoy her meal without a cat on her lap.

"Please dig in," Carrie said as she followed Charles into the kitchen.

"Did you see Hansen brought an envelope with him?" Carrie whispered to Charles.

Charles nodded. "He placed it against the leg of his chair."

"I'm dying to know what's in it. I want to grab it and tear it open," Carrie said.

"Steady, Dear," Charles said. "We'll know soon enough what secrets it holds."

When they returned to the table, their guests were devouring the meal.

"You know, the night of the writer's meeting, I told you that the pub where they held the meeting was known for its burgers," Hansen said. "This Faraday burger gives them some real competition."

"I agree with Hansen," Cindy said. "This is delicious."

After a second burger for Charles and Hansen and brownies for dessert, they were ready to discuss the trio's research.

"What did you discover when you searched the remaining boxes of documents?" Charles asked.

"We finished checking every box from the attic and sorted them by category," Rachel said.

"It was a lot of documents, but it was also interesting to see all the work involved in starting a new city," Cindy said.

"Dad probably told you he scanned the historical documents in his office. We're going to do the same thing to get rid of storing all that paper in the attic," Hansen said. "It's a fire hazard."

"That's a good idea, but don't keep us in suspense. What did you three discover?" Carrie said. "Did you find the stock document for the Allwin heirs?"

"We didn't find the actual document but discovered the minutes from a meeting where the building corporation board discussed and approved the awarding of shares," Hansen said as he opened his envelope and handed a sheet of paper to Charles.

"There was also a notation that Allwin's son Steven wanted to join the corporation, but it caused a rift with his father," Cindy said. "That's why they decided to hold shares for the future heirs and not offer them to Edwin or Steven Allwin."

Charles passed the paper to Carrie.

"We also found this photo. We think it's Steven with his two children."

The children were older than in the photo Carrie saw at the library and Phillips General Store when they rode in a parade. It was a sharper picture, and Carrie stared at their faces. She didn't recognize the little girl's face, but something about the little boy reminded her of someone.

"Do either of the children look familiar to you, especially the little boy?" Carrie asked.

Charles, Hansen, Cindy, and Rachel passed the photo between them.

Then Charles said, "Wait a minute. The little boy looks a bit like Brian."

"You're right," Hansen said.

"What," Cindy exclaimed as she grabbed the photo. "Yes, I can see it—especially the eyes and the jaw."

"Age-wise, is it possible Brian Amberson could be this boy?" Charles asked.

"My great-grandfather was the oldest founder, and Allwin was the youngest," Hansen said. "Yes, Brian could be a grandson."

"If it is Brian, why wouldn't he have come forward and acknowledged his family ties?" Carrie looked at Hansen. "Has he ever asked you specific questions about the founders?"

"Occasionally, he asked questions about my family heritage, but I wasn't much help." Hansen squirmed in his seat as he added, "As you know, I avoided talking about my family's history."

"Remember Brian was Cousin Gwen's intern. If he didn't get information from Hansen, he probably had access to her research," Cindy said.

"Can I assume Brian also attended the weekend gatherings at your grandmother's house?" Charles asked.

"Brian and I both came, along with others, to Hansen's parties," Cindy said. "Is that important?"

"If an individual had access to your grandmother's home, the person might have searched the boxes in the room where Gwen worked," Charles said. "If Brian was at those parties, he could have easily slipped upstairs."

"It's certainly possible. We were in multiple rooms on the first floor, and no one was tracking anyone's specific movements," Hansen said.

Cindy and Hansen shared a guilty look. Cindy spoke first. "That's when Hansen and I were getting to know each other. There were many times when we were glad Brian wasn't in the room with us."

"Hansen, how did you meet Brian?" Rachel asked.

"Brian told you when you joined us in the student union that we met in one of Gwen's history classes. That wasn't quite true. He came to one of my weekend parties and suggested I take one of Gwen's classes," Hansen said. "After I signed up for the class, Brian applied for the open intern position with Gwen."

Brian's suggestion that Hansen take a history class with Gwen sounded innocent, or did Brian hope to get access to the Brighton documents? Carrie wanted to hear more about Brian.

"Before the job with Gwen, did Brian have another job?" Charles asked,

"He had a part-time job with a security company," Hansen said.

Carrie controlled her reaction to this news. Instead, she casually asked, "What did he do for them?"

"Initially, he answered phones at the customer service call center. Later, he helped the technicians with installations," Hansen said.

Cindy laughed, "He said he was learning how to break into all the best homes in Tri-City."

Carrie kept a poker face as she looked at Charles, and he discreetly nodded.

"Why did he leave?" Charles asked.

"I can answer that," Cindy said. "Response to security calls could occur any time of the day or night. He couldn't be on constant call once he got the internship with Gwen."

"Why are you asking about his work background?" Rachel asked.

"We've had several break-ins, and now an intruder searched your father's office. Security system knowledge would be helpful in these instances," Charles said.

"Someone broke into Dad's office. I didn't know that. When did it happen?" Hansen asked.

"Last night, a little after ten," Charles said.

"That's why Dad asked if I lost my key code and where I was last night," Hansen said.

"Any idea of who might have stolen your code?" Carrie asked.

"Brian was with me the last time I visited Dad's office," Hansen said. "It would have been easy for Brian to look over my shoulder and see the five-digit number I entered."

"It's hard to believe Brian is behind all this mayhem," Cindy said.

The group fell quiet as they thought about Cindy's comment.

Then Rachel said in a low voice, "Does that mean Brian murdered Gwen?"

33

Charles trained Baxter to walk on a leash, which was challenging for a cat. The leash protected Baxter. Charles could quickly rope him in if a dog from a neighboring house, a squirrel, or some other animal approached them while they walked.

One of their adventures was walking down to the mailbox. Charles gave Baxter time to roll in the grass and smell the different scents along the path. He gathered the mail and then leisurely returned to the house while Baxter batted an acorn along the driveway.

Once inside, Charles removed the leash, and Baxter immediately found his water bowl. Then he ignored Carrie and pranced out to the sunroom off the study. The couple opened windows in warmer weather, and Baxter could enjoy fresh air. Regardless of the season, Baxter would find a spot in full sun and curl up for a nap.

"Did you have a nice walk? Baxter seemed quite happy," Carrie said, looking up from the magazine she was reading.

"It's amazing how much pleasure he gets from rolling in the grass and batting an acorn," Charles said as he placed the mail on the coffee table in front of Carrie.

"You have a couple of interesting articles in this month's Tri-County magazine," Carrie said, "I realized what you meant when you told Hansen that many of the articles have a historical element."

"Then, the writer is doing a good job of blending history into the story. Most articles that feature a person, location, or a particular event have a historical element attached to it," Charles said. "But it's a balance between celebrating the past while informing readers about the present."

Carrie put her magazine aside and sorted the mail. She had almost finished when a letter caught her eye.

"Charles, look at this," Carrie said excitedly. "It's a letter from Gwen Smith. Or at least that's what the return address indicates."

"How on earth did Gwen Smith send you a letter almost four weeks after her murder?" Charles asked.

"She used the wrong zip code," Carrie said. "No doubt the letter floated around several post office departments until it got redirected to our zip code."

Charles handed her the letter opener, and Carrie read the single sheet of paper from the envelope. It was the second time she received a letter from a dead person. The first time was when Jamie, Charles's brother, sent her a letter imploring her to solve his death if it wasn't by natural causes. It wasn't natural. Now she was reading a letter from another murder victim.

"What does it say?" Charles asked. "You have me in suspense."

Charles's voice returned her to the present. "She wanted to meet with me and gave me her email and phone number. I'll read it," Carrie said.

Dear Mrs. Faraday,

We haven't met. I'm a history professor at Tri-City University and accept outside consulting work doing genealogy and family histories.

After reading your book, I compared what I discovered in my research and how your main character solved the crime.

I was especially fascinated when your detective discovered the answer to the puzzle by finding a clue hidden behind a photo. What a clever technique. Wouldn't it be wonderful if we could solve all our problems with a hidden clue?

I want to discuss a project I've finished for a client with you. I thought you might have some suggestions on how to present what I've discovered.

I look forward to meeting you and discussing your new book and my research report, which I might turn into a book.

Gwen Smith

"Maybe that's why she came to the book signing since I never contacted her," Carrie said.

"Seems a reasonable assumption," Charles said.

"What do you think of the letter?" Carrie asked.

"Seems rather cryptic. Why would someone who has never met you send a message and include a particular reference to your book?" Charles asked. "Is there something unusual about that passage?"

"Not that I'm aware of, but one of the ladies in Henrietta's book club also mentioned that same passage," Carrie said. "My hero discovered a clue taped on the back of a photo that reveals the culprit and solves the murder."

"I remember that scene," Charles said. "It's a shame the letter didn't reach you sooner. Now all we can do is turn it over to Jenco," Charles said.

Charles leafed through the piles of mail Carrie created. He tossed most of the advertising pieces in the trash and placed the other items aside to be dealt with later. Charles saw Carrie was still holding the letter. "What are you thinking?" he asked.

"Maybe the message wasn't that cryptic," Carrie said. "Maybe Gwen hid something on the back of a photo."

"It certainly sounds that way, but it seems odd that she would send a clue to someone she didn't know."

"Charles, stranger things have happened. If she felt she was in danger, and my book struck a note with her, she might take a chance and contact me," Carrie said. "Emily told her about me, and she asked Terry about the cases we solved."

"I remember seeing lots of photos on the wall in Gwen's college office," Charles said. "Sounds like we need to make another visit to the university."

"I'll call Emily to see if we can get another look at Gwen's office."

"And I'll scan a copy of the letter and send it to Jenco," Charles said.

34

Emily had a meeting and couldn't meet with them, but she promised to leave Gwen's office key with her administrative assistant. They picked up the key and headed to Gwen's office.

"It's eerie walking down these halls with no people," Carrie said as she held onto Charles's arm.

"The students are glad to have a spring break after exams, but it makes this a lonely place and makes us stand out," Charles said. "We need to be quick. Let's get in and out before anyone notices us, like the campus police."

Charles unlocked Gwen's door and carefully locked it after they entered. They looked around the room, and Carrie immediately went to the Founder's Day picnic photo. She removed it from the wall and turned it over but found nothing.

"That's one of my brilliant ideas eliminated. I was sure Gwen hid a message in this photo," she said.

"Let's not be so quick to assume failure. Maybe the Founders Day photo was a hint to get us looking," Charles said. "Lots more pictures to check."

Carrie nodded, and they started checking the backs of more photos. Near the end of their search, Carrie removed the image of the Tri-City ribbon-cutting ceremony.

"Charles, look! There's a thumb drive taped to the back," Carrie exclaimed.

Charles stood beside Carrie as she placed the photo on the desk and carefully untaped the drive.

"I can't wait to see what's on it," Carrie said, taking out her phone and transferring the cord.

"Let's do the file transfer when we get home," Charles said, putting the photo back on the wall. "It's time to go."

Carrie put her phone and the thumb drive in her pocket. The couple was so engrossed in finishing that they didn't hear a key in the door and were startled by a voice.

"What did you find?"

The couple spun around and faced Brian Amberson, pointing a gun at them.

"Brian, are you following us?" Carrie asked.

"No. Pure luck. I decided to search Gwen's office again, and here you are, interfering," Brian said. "You didn't answer my question. What did you find?"

"What makes you think we found something?" Carrie asked, trying to sound nonchalant.

"I heard Mr. Faraday say you should wait until you get home to check something. What is it you're going to check?" Brian asked, poking the gun towards her like a stick.

Carrie ignored Brian's question and asked, "Are you Edwin Allwin's grandson?"

"You two have been busy," Brian said. "Yes, I'm Edwin's grandson. Not that I ever mattered to him."

"What are you after?" Charles asked.

"It's simple. I want the inheritance that Dorchester and Brighton stole from my family," Brian said.

Carrie thought Brian tried to sound tough, but his face revealed someone who looked scared. Regardless of his demeanor, Brian still brandished a gun.

Brian continued, "Henrietta's companion, Rachel, got the Dorchester inheritance. Now, I want my share."

How did Brian know this information? It wasn't public knowledge. Only a limited number of people knew about Rachel's newfound wealth. Carrie assumed Hansen told him.

"Brian, you don't need to do this. We discovered shares from the Tri-City Building Corporation are in trust for your grandfather's heirs," Charles said. "That means you and your sister are entitled to money."

"I don't believe you," Brian said. "Why haven't we heard about this before?"

Brian's use of the word 'we' reminded Carrie about his sister. Where was his sister? Who was she?

"It sounds crazy, but the board of directors knew not investing in the Tri-City Building Corporation caused a rift between your father and grandfather. They also didn't like your grandfather's attitude." Carrie added. "They decided to bypass them and never told them shares were waiting for any heirs that came forward."

"Enough! Give me what you found behind that picture," Brian said carelessly, waving the gun.

Carrie saw a change in Brian's eyes, which looked determined. She reached into her pocket to give Brian the thumb drive. Then she saw Hansen and Cindy enter the office. Hansen had an umbrella.

In a deep guttural voice, Hansen said, "Drop the weapon. Put your hands up." Hansen poked Brian in the back with the point of the umbrella.

As Brian turned, Cindy snapped off the lights. A shot rang out, and Charles pulled Carrie to the floor. Carrie heard the gun drop and then the sound of running feet. Cindy turned on the lights as Hansen continued tightly gripping his umbrella. It would have been comic if it wasn't such a deadly situation.

"Glad to see you two," Charles said as he raced into the hallway and looked in both directions. There was no sign of Brian.

"What brought you to Gwen's office in the middle of the afternoon?" Carrie asked.

"We were sitting on the green enjoying the weather when we saw you two enter the building. A few minutes later, we saw Brian arrive," Cindy said.

"Based on what we learned at your home about Brian, we wanted to see why he was on campus," Hansen said. "We thought he might be meeting you."

"I can't believe Brian had a gun," Cindy said, bending to pick up the gun.

"Don't! Leave the gun where it is," Carrie declared. "The police will take care of it when they arrive."

Cindy jumped back and then nodded her head. The group listened while Charles placed a call to Detective Jenco.

After a brief conversation, Charles said, "The police are on their way. Jenco wants us to wait until he arrives."

Carrie noticed Cindy turned pale and worried she might faint. Carrie suggested, "We can wait in the hall."

Charles escorted Hansen and Cindy out of the office.

"I'll be right there," Carrie said as she pulled a cord from her handbag to transfer the thumb drive information to her phone. She also took the precaution of sending a copy to Charles's email. As she was putting her phone away, she took a quick look around the room but didn't see any signs of what the bullet had struck.

"Is that Cousin Gwen's missing research?" Cindy asked when she saw Carrie holding the thumb drive.

"I don't know, but just in case it is, I want a copy before I turn this over to the police."

Jenco and McCall must have been in the area because it was only a few more minutes before they arrived.

"Brief me. What happened here?" Jenco asked.

Cindy blurted out, "Brian Amberson held the Faradays at gunpoint."

Jenco raised an eyebrow at Cindy's statement and then turned to the couple. "Is this true?"

Carrie nodded.

"Let's start at the beginning," Jenco said.

Each of them recounted what happened as McCall took notes.

"What happened to the bullet?" Jenco asked.

"I didn't see it, but it should be in the wall near Gwen's desk," Carrie said.

"We'll get your statements prepared. I need you to stop by the precinct in the next few days to sign them," Jenco said. "You're all free to go."

Carrie handed Jenco the thumb drive. For a moment, she thought he might ask her if she had made a copy. Instead, he dropped it in an evidence bag and sealed it.

As Charles reached the door, he turned to Jenco, "We also sent you a copy of the letter we received from Gwen. Her comment about hiding something behind a photo brought us here this afternoon."

"I got it. That's why we were on our way here, but as usual, you got here first," Jenco said and turned away.

Carrie generally didn't give Jenco credit for his policing skills, but he figured out the clue from the letter.

Charles and Carrie walked back down the long hallway. They didn't see Hansen and Cindy leave, but they may have gone through a back entrance. When Charles opened the main door, they faced a crowd of people, mostly students, held back by a police barricade.

"What's going on?" Emily yelled to the couple as they left the building.

Charles and Carrie walked towards Emily, and a police officer lifted the tape to allow them through. Charles took Emily's arm and directed her away from the crowd.

"The police have asked us not to discuss what happened, but you have a right to know. Charles said. "Brian Amberson ambushed us in Gwen's office."

"We found a thumb drive hidden behind one of the photos on Gwen's office wall," Carrie said. "Then Brian entered the office with a gun and demanded we give him what we found."

"Brian," she said in disbelief. "Why would he do that?"

"He's the grandson of Edwin Allwin. He wants the money he believes he's entitled to from the founding families," Carrie said.

"Where is Brian now?" Emily asked.

"Escaped. The police are on Brian's trail. It won't be long before everyone knows he's wanted," Charles said. "You must take care until the police have him in custody."

"I was on my way home when I saw the crowd," Emily said. "I will lock myself in and pour a large glass of wine."

"We're planning on doing the same thing," Carrie said as they walked to the parking lot and saw Emily safely in her car.

"I'm finding it hard to believe that Brian killed Gwen," Carrie said as they drove away.

"Why do you say that? He held a gun on us, and he fired it."

"I don't think he intended to use it. I'm sure the gun went off accidentally when Hansen poked him with the umbrella," Carrie said.

"That was pretty daring of Hansen," Charles said. "Hansen is coming into his own."

"That was daring of you to protect me from Brian's bullets," Carrie said.

"I'm always here for you," Charles said, pulling her close and kissing her. Then added, "If you're right and Brian is not the killer, the murderer is still out there."

35

The couple was glad when they reached their home's comfort and safety. Charles took Carrie in his arms, holding her for a long time. They realized they had once again escaped danger in one of their investigations.

"Do you agree the gun went off accidentally?" Carrie asked.

"That doesn't excuse the fact Brian had a weapon. Things can happen when you point a gun at someone," Charles said.

"True. This incident was too close for comfort," Carrie said. "I'm sure it's the adrenaline letdown, but I feel lightheaded. I need something to eat before we start looking at the information on the thumb drive."

Carrie needed comfort food. She prepared cream of tomato soup and grilled cheese sandwiches and placed sweet pickles on the plate. That was the nice thing about cooking for Charles. He was as content with a cheese sandwich as a fine steak dinner.

After their meal, Carrie downloaded the thumb drive files from her phone to her laptop, and Charles opened the email

Carrie sent him on his desktop computer. They started reading Gwen's final report. Carrie scanned the pages until she found the attachments with all the supporting documentation at the back. Charles used a systematic approach of reading every page to grasp the complete picture. Both were looking for a clue that might explain Gwen's murder.

After several minutes, Charles said, "Gwen was a good writer. She knew how to weave the story to read more like a novel than a formal report. Henrietta would have been pleased with the result," Charles said.

"She might have written her report in this style since she wanted to publish a book. It also makes dry historical facts easier for her clients to read."

Carrie continued reviewing all the attachments. "Charles, I found it," Carrie exclaimed. "Gwen has a photo of the handwritten document indicating the board's intention to leave shares of the Tri-City Building Corporation to the Allwin heirs."

"I wonder if they formalized their intentions in a legal document. What page are you on?" Charles asked.

"I'm on page 31 of the attachments. I haven't found a legal document, but the attachments aren't in order. Looks like she photographed them as she found them," Carrie said. "It's sad. Had Brian waited just a little longer, he would have discovered that he had an inheritance from the founders. Now he faces murder charges."

"I'm not sure the police will charge him with murder," Charles said.

"Do you think someone else killed Gwen?" Carrie asked.

"It doesn't make sense to me. Brian acted like a kid pulling the poison pen letter prank with Hansen and then waving that gun around. Not the behavior of a cold-blooded killer."

"Are you suggesting the sister did it?"

"I don't know, but in my mind, she's the likely candidate."

"Have we eliminated Rachel?" Carrie asked.

"In the section I'm reading, Gwen states that she discovered that Rachel was a descendant of Dorchester and entitled to the country club lease payments. She comments that she thinks Henrietta will be pleased," Charles said. "She doesn't see this information as a threat."

"What about the Allwin children?" Carrie asked.

"Her report confirms Edwin's grandchildren are entitled to share in the Tri-City Building Corporation. Then she has a footnote with her concerns," Charles said. "I'll read it to you," Charles said as he adjusted his glasses.

The dilemma I face is the information concerning the Allwin heirs. I've received a letter from Edwin Allwin's grandchildren looking for a payout. I don't feel it's my decision to give them any information. They are not my clients. I feel duty-bound to provide this report to Henrietta Brighton-Stanford first and let her family decide on possible payments to the Allwin heirs. If they continue their demands, I will get additional help to solve the problem. I've made these notes in the event I can't personally deliver this report to Henrietta.

"Wow, that sounds like she had a real concern for her safety," Carrie said.

"Or if the heirs made a claim against her for withholding information, she had a document indicating her intent," Charles said.

Carrie wondered if Emily was the additional help or if it was the gun she had purchased. "Does she identify either heir by name?"

"No, and I'm not sure she will in this report. The way she phrased this section makes me think Gwen stored additional information somewhere," Charles said. "You have a photo of the handwritten document, but where's the original? And if she is worried about her safety, I'm sure she named her adversaries in another document we haven't found."

"I wonder where it could be. We've eliminated the locations we know about," Carrie added.

Before they completed their discussion, Charles's phone rang. "Detective Jenco, any developments?" Charles asked as he put his phone on speaker.

"I wish I were calling with better news, but we haven't found Brian. We checked all his known hangouts on and off campus, but he's still at large," Detective Jenco said. "Do you have any other suggestions about where he might be hiding?"

Based on his handling of the Barrington case, Jenco was not one of Carrie's favorite people. On the other hand, if she could help him find Brian, it would be worth her effort. "We know he has a sister," Carrie said.

"We knew that but don't know her name or if she's in the area. Do you have any additional information about her?" Jenco asked.

Carrie thought she heard a slight hint of anticipation in Jenco's voice even though his phrasing was that of the calm police officer.

"Not so far, but we're working on trying to find her," Charles said. "What about Hansen and Cindy? Did they have any suggestions?"

"Most of the places we checked were from them, along with names of other friends. No results so far," Jenco said.

"Are Cindy and Hansen at a safe place in case Brian tries to contact them?" Carrie asked.

"They're staying with Hansen's grandmother. She alerted her security company of the situation, and I have extra patrol cars in the area," Jenco said. "By the way, Brian's gun had blanks, no real bullets."

"I'm glad they're safe, and we'll let you know if we discover anything more about the sister," Charles said as he ended the call.

"No real bullets. That explains why we couldn't see what the bullet hit. It also confirms our theory that Brian didn't have murderous intent," Carrie added. "And is probably not our murderer."

The couple returned to work, and Carrie shifted her focus to the files they had downloaded from the historical society.

"These files trace the farm's history from Edwin's great, great grandparents to the present day," Carrie said. "Until Steven's children, all the previous relatives worked the farm until they died. The children's names were Lorna and Steven, jr."

"Perhaps we're going about this incorrectly," Charles said.

"What do you mean?"

"Instead of concentrating on the Allwin name, we should look at other names in the family. Brian changed his name to Amberson. Where did that come from?" Charles said.

"I understand what you mean. Was Brian using a family name or simply a name he created? We should start our search with that name," Carrie said. "And if Brian changed his name, his sister may have changed her name."

"Let's start with the aunt. I assume she was a sister of Steven's wife because we know Steven had no siblings." Charles swung his chair around and started typing on the computer. "The name Amberson shows in the Huntington area about 20 miles north of Allwin, but there is no specific information."

"Then it's time for another trip to the Village of Allwin," Carrie said. "Someone in Allwin must remember the children and their aunt."

36

As they started for the Village of Allwin the next morning, Charles suggested, "We should go by the Train Stop. We promised to keep Gloria informed."

Carrie was sure Charles's suggestion to go to the Train Stop included the desire for one of Gloria's Belgium waffles. They arrived between the breakfast crowd and the early lunch patrons at the restaurant. They had their pick of tables, and Gloria greeted them as soon as they sat down.

"I'm so glad to see you. I've wanted to get in touch with you, but we've been extra busy, and I'm short workers," Gloria said.

Charles looked around to see if Cindy was there, but he saw no signs of her. Hopefully, she was staying out of sight at Henrietta's home.

"Did you think of something additional to help us with your sister's case?" Carrie asked, remembering Charles's comment that some of Gwen's work may still be missing.

"The police returned Gwen's items to me, but they kept her gun," Gloria said. "That's the first I knew Gwen's gun was the murder weapon."

The couple didn't answer. Charles knew this confirmed what they suspected. The gun wasn't the murderer's. He knew they needed to provide Gloria with more answers to comfort her.

Gloria continued, "I've since found the paperwork for the gun purchase and several classes she took at the local gun range." Her eyes filled with tears. "Did you know about the gun?"

Carrie reached out and touched Gloria's arm.

"We knew the police found a gun at the scene, but we didn't know it belonged to Gwen until now."

"Had she only told me why she needed a weapon, maybe I could have..." Gloria stopped and picked up a napkin to wipe a tear. "No, I'm going to be strong. I can't dwell on what could have been."

"We've learned from our different cases you can't change the outcome. Even if Gwen told you she bought a gun, what would you have done differently?" Charles asked. "Instead, it's up to us to work together to find a solution and bring closure."

"I don't understand why she needed a gun," Gloria said. "We never had guns growing up." Then, as an afterthought, "Maybe she wanted a new experience like joining a country club."

This response seemed a little naïve. Charles had the impression Gwen did everything with a purpose, like hiding her research.

"We think she got it for protection. Let us tell you what we've learned so far," Charles said. "You start, Carrie."

"For Henrietta Brighton-Stanford's project, Gwen reviewed boxes of materials Henrietta had stored in her attic. We know she also visited the historical society for information and contacted the granddaughter of the original lawyer for Tri-City," Carrie said. "Multiple people told us Gwen had nearly finalized her report, but we can't find it."

"Isn't all of her research missing?" Gloria asked.

"That's been one of our frustrations. We had to start over and try to recreate what your sister discovered," Carrie said.

"And did you accomplish that?"

"We uncovered much of her original research with the discovery of a thumb drive in your sister's office," Charles said.

Gloria couldn't hide the excitement in her voice. "You did! Where was it?"

Charles told Gloria about receiving a hint in the letter from Gwen and then discovering a thumb drive taped to the back of a picture.

"Even though my sister gave you a hint, that was clever of you to figure it out," Gloria paused. "Any hints about her killer?"

"Nothing specific other than she mentioned that the Allwin grandkids, a brother and sister, wanted her research in hopes of getting a payout from the founders' descendants."

"Did you find them?" Gloria asked anxiously.

"We found Brian Amberson, the grandson. Does that name sound familiar to you?" Carrie asked.

"Brian Amberson... Amberson," Gloria repeated. "Wait, I remember. I met him at the memorial service," Gloria said. "Wasn't he Gwen's student helper or something like that?"

"Brian was her intern for the current semester. He harassed and pressured your sister to help him get money from the remaining founders," Carrie said.

Charles explained their encounter with Brian at the college while retrieving the thumb drive from the back of the photo and how Cindy and Hansen saved them from Brian's attack.

"I can't believe Cindy is involved in this."

"Cindy briefly dated Brian. Brian probably used her to get closer to Gwen and influence her to select him for the internship position," Carrie said. "Lately, she's been hanging out with Hansen Stanford."

"That explains why Cindy didn't come to work. I feel awful. As her aunt, not just her boss, I should have asked for more details about why she couldn't come to work," Gloria said, shaking her head. "I only worried about not having enough staff."

"Without having all the information, you reacted appropriately," Carrie said, offering some comfort.

"Is Cindy safe? Do you think Brian is going after Cindy? I need to have her here with me." She looked at Charles as her eyes reflected fear.

"Cindy is secure. She's staying with Hansen at his grandmother's home. The house has an updated security system, and the police have extra patrol cars checking her street," Charles said calmly.

"Does that mean Brian is the murderer?" Gloria asked.

"We won't know until the police catch and interrogate Brian," Carrie said.

The conversation stopped when one of Gloria's staff approached the table.

"Gloria, I'm sorry to interrupt, but the chef needs you in the kitchen for a minute."

Gloria excused herself, "I'll be right back. Don't leave." She headed to the kitchen.

"This is another example of why Jenco is not one of my favorite people. He or someone from the department should have kept Gloria informed of developments," Carrie said. "Suppose Brian came here looking for Cindy. Gloria wouldn't know the seriousness of the situation."

"You're right. The police shouldn't have left Gloria in the dark," Charles said. "I'll bet Brian is trying to get out of the area and not looking to contact Hansen or Cindy."

Gloria returned and asked, "Do we just sit and wait for the police to find Brian? How long must my cousin remain in hiding?"

"She's not in hiding. Staying with Hansen and his grandmother is a temporary precaution," Carrie said. "Brian doesn't have many options for escape, and I have no doubt the police are closing in."

"We wanted you to know what happened on the remote chance Brian contacted you."

Gloria nodded her head. "I appreciate your update," Gloria said. "What are you doing next?"

"We're trying to locate the sister. Both children lived with an aunt after leaving their grandfather's farm," Charles said. "Brian might try to reunite with his sister or seek help from this aunt."

"You said when you searched the historical society records, you couldn't find other relatives." Gloria sounded dejected.

"That's why we're going back to the Village of Allwin when we leave here," Carrie said."

"Why there?" Gloria asked.

"Someone in the village might know what happened to his sister or if the aunt is still alive," Charles said.

"As long as you're here, can I get you something to eat?"

Charles looked at Carrie briefly and then made a quick decision. "Thank you, but we only stopped by to update you. The sooner we get the Allwin, the quicker we find answers."

Gloria said, "Then I won't keep you any longer. I hope you find the answers to this case in Allwin."

37

Carrie and Charles left the Train Stop and headed to the Village of Allwin.

"I'm sorry you didn't get one of Gloria's Belgian waffles, but we can grab something at the general store," Carrie said.

"While I missed a chance for waffles, I felt our hanging around wouldn't help Gloria. She needs time to digest what she learned from us," Charles said.

"And she needed to know we're actively looking for Brian's sister and a solution to the case," Carrie added.

Because it was a weekday, traffic was light when the couple arrived on Allwin's main street. Charles got a parking space right in front of Phillips General Store.

Inside the nearly empty store, Charles walked to the counter, where a clerk decked out in a period costume greeted him.

"Welcome to Phillips General Store, the oldest continuously operating general store in the state. How may I assist you?"

Charles casually leaned on the counter. "Hi there. You display so many historical photos on the walls that I wondered if someone might know about the area's history."

The woman smiled, "You want to talk to Pops. He's a walking Allwin history book and can tell you about every photo on our walls."

"Pops," Charles repeated the name, unsure he heard it correctly.

"Sorry, everyone calls him Pops. He's Bobby Phillips, a descendant of the store's original owners and the current manager," she laughed. "He's out making deliveries but should be back shortly if you can wait."

"It's such a beautiful day, and I noticed your picnic tables outside the entrance. We'll get lunch. Hopefully, Pops will have returned by then," Carrie said.

They had finished their sandwiches when a man in his fifties approached their table. He was tall, lanky, spry, and dressed in jeans and a polo shirt with the store logo.

"Are you the folks asking about the history of the village?" he asked.

Charles stood up and extended his hand. "Yes, we're the Faradays. My wife, Carrie, and I'm Charles."

"Faraday, ...Faraday," he repeated. "I know that name. Faraday Press publishes the Tri-County Monthly. We carry the magazine here in the store, and our customers love it. Are you related?"

"That's my family's company," Charles said, adding, "Like you, I'm the current manager."

"I understand about carrying on the family business," Pops said.

Carrie didn't always realize how much the readers appreciated the Tri-County Monthly magazine, and Charles always downplayed his involvement in the family business. On the other hand, if the magazine got them an opening with Pops, it was a good thing.

"Please join us. We just finished a great sandwich," Charles said.

Mr. Philips sat at the table. "Looks like you had the pit beef. That's one of our specialties. The meat comes from a local butcher. Glad you enjoyed it,"

"Delicious. I'm taking some home for future sandwiches," Carrie said.

Pops smiled at Carrie's compliment. "I understand you have some questions about Allwin's history. How can I help?"

"My wife is working on a story for the upcoming anniversary of Tri-City's founding. Instead of going through the usual information about the ribbon cutting and the first buildings, we thought we would take a more human-interest approach and focus on the founding families. We've been in touch with Mrs. Brighton-Stanford and the remaining Dorchester heir, Rachel Pembrook, and now we'd like to get some input from the Allwin family.

"We understand that Steven had two children who are the only remaining descendants of Edwin Allwin. We hoped you could help us contact them or any other family members," Charles said.

"I'm afraid after the villages incorporated into the new city, the Allwin family wasn't as active as the other founders," Pops said.

"Why do you say that?" Charles asked.

Carrie thought Charles's method of asking Pops for information was perfect. He wanted to hear Pop's version of history without revealing what they knew. Also, they didn't want to mention that Brian was on the run and that they were trying to find his sister as a possible murderer.

"Edwin Allwin wasn't much of a businessman. He was a farmer. After the villages agreed to form Tri-City, Edwin retreated to his farm. When Dorchester and Brighton formed the building corporation to develop the area, Edwin refused to join," Pops said. "Many early village residents felt Edwin did them a disservice by not becoming more actively involved. We didn't get the development assistance that the other areas received."

Charles nodded, "We learned Edwin wasn't a member of the Tri-City Building Corporation, which constructed many of the buildings for the new city."

"That's correct. It's a shame there are no Allwins left in the area. Someone recently bought the old farm, and who knows what will happen to that land," Pops said.

Carrie made a mental note to call Henry. Once the permits were approved, Carrie thought it would be a good idea for Henry to hold a town meeting and inform the village about the plans.

While Pops talked with Carrie and Charles, he nodded and greeted customers as they entered the building.

"Will you be attending the community meeting, Pops?" a customer asked.

"You bet. Wouldn't miss it," Pops said. "We need to get our ducks in a row to work with the new owner of the Allwin farm."

When Pop refocused on the couple, Charles asked, "You said there are no longer any Allwins in the area. Are Steven's children still around?"

"I saw the photos on your walls but only found one picture of the Allwin children in a parade. Then we learned they both left to live with an aunt," Carrie said. "Was that aunt related to Stevens's side of the family?"

"Steven was an only child. But his wife was one of three sisters who grew up in Allwin. Steven's wife, Susan, who died of cancer, Nancy and Diane."

"And the children went to live with one of the sisters," Carrie said.

"They stayed with Nancy, the youngest of the girls," Pops said. "She lives in Huntington, about twenty miles away. Far enough for the kids to be out of sight of their grandfather."

"What is Nancy's last name?" Carrie asked.

"Amberson," Pops said.

There was the answer. Carrie knew Brian had selected the Amberson name from his aunt.

"Is Nancy Amberson still around?" Charles asked.

Pops looked at Charles with a twinkle in his eye. "Yes, she's still alive and active on the local council for economic development. She lives in her same house just up the road a piece."

Carrie hid her desire to laugh at the local jargon 'just up the road a piece.'

"How did Steven feel about his children moving away?" Charles asked.

"He didn't object. Steven felt that his father had lost a big financial opportunity for their family and future generations by not participating in the building corporation," Pops said as he rubbed his jaw remembering the details. "He wanted his children to have other options and not get trapped on the farm. Lorna went to live with the aunt after high school, and Brian joined them at the start of seventh grade."

"Did the children ever return home?" Charles asked as he drained the last of his iced tea.

"Not that I ever heard. Lorna was bright, and Nancy told me she had gone to university to further her education." Pops said. "And I believe Brian is now in college. I'm sure Nancy can tell you more details."

"Do you think you could introduce Nancy to us?" Carrie asked.

"Do you wanna go visit her now?"

"That would be great," Carrie said.

Pops pulled out his cell phone and called Nancy Amberson. Pops mentioned that Mr. Faraday owned and published the Tri-County Monthly magazine. When the call ended, Pops said, "Nancy can't wait to meet you."

Pops wrote instructions for the couple, and they drove to Nancy Amberson's home. They hoped this meeting would bring them one step closer to finding Brian and his sister.

38

With Pops's detailed instructions, the couple quickly found Nancy Amberson's home.

"What a lovely cottage," Carrie said. "It looks like something out of a storybook with a freshly painted white picket fence and the flowers along the edge of the stone house."

They had no sooner knocked when a woman in her late 60s, a little bit on the plump side with a pleasant face and a welcoming smile, answered the door.

"You must be the Faradays. Come in, come in."

Charles introduced them while holding the door for Carrie.

"I'm Nancy," she said.

They entered the living room with sturdy, well-used furniture that was clean and polished.

"I'm so glad to meet you. Mr. Faraday, I'm a big fan of your magazine and look forward to the latest issue each month," Nancy said.

"Thanks. We wouldn't be in business without loyal readers like you," Charles said, smiling warmly.

"We can sit here in the living room," Nancy said as she pointed to the overstuffed sofa and chairs, or we can meet in the kitchen. The kitchen is where my family has always shared stories."

"We love kitchen stories," Carrie said as they followed Nancy through a narrow hallway past the dining room and into the kitchen.

The couple took seats at a solid round wood table, slightly scuffed with six chairs and well-padded floral cushions that matched the tablecloth. The kitchen was spotless.

"I prepared coffee, but I can fix tea if you prefer," Nancy said,

"We never refuse a cup of coffee," Charles said.

Nancy poured the coffee while Charles eyed the plate of cookies and sweets she unwrapped.

"I always baked when my husband was alive and the children lived with us. You picked a good day to visit. I baked these items for the community meeting I'm attending later in Allwin."

"My husband is happy he came on a day for baked goods. He has a sweet tooth," Carrie said, staring at Charles and giving him a wifely glare not to go overboard.

Nancy missed Carrie's signal and held the plate for Charles to pick a treat and then set the plate in front of him.

"I understood from Pops that you're writing an article about Tri-City for the upcoming anniversary."

"We are. We wanted to concentrate on the founding families instead of the formation of the city, which our readers already know," Carrie said. "We've gathered information about the Brighton and Dorchester families but need to learn more about Edwin Allwin and his family."

"I'm not sure how much I can add," Nancy said. "In many ways, the Allwin story is sad and perhaps something you won't want to include."

"We appreciate anything you can tell us, and we will be discreet about what we print," Charles said.

"Here's the part of the story I can share. My sister, Susan, married Steven, the son of Edwin Allwin, one of the founders. It was a good marriage, and they were quite happy until my sister got cancer. It wasn't too long after her diagnosis before she passed," Nancy said as she took a handkerchief from her apron pocket and wiped a tear. "I'm sorry. I still miss her, and I'm still angry about her final days."

"We heard that Edwin Allwin didn't support her treatment," Charles said.

Nancy nodded. "The family had no health insurance, and the treatments were expensive. My husband and I couldn't help financially," she said softly. "But who knows if the treatments would have prolonged her life? Maybe it was her time."

"We understand that Steven and your sister had two children," Carrie said.

"Steven Junior was only three years old when she died, and his sister was nine. Those children suffered after my sister died," Nancy said.

"Why do you say that?" Charles asked, selecting a cookie from the plate. He knew what others had told them about the Allwin children, but he wanted to hear it from Nancy.

"Edwin Allwin was a cheapskate. Instead of hiring help to work the farm, he relied on Steven, one hired hand, and the children," Nancy said. "It could have been a thriving business. They had the acreage and a good crop most of the years." She took a cookie and passed the plate to Carrie.

"Did you keep in touch with the kids," Carrie asked.

"My husband and I weren't blessed with children. After my sister died, I would stop by the farm and bring the children little treats," Nancy said. "Then Edwin made it clear he didn't want me to visit."

"Did he give a reason?" Charles asked.

"He said it interrupted the children's routine. I stopped my visits, but I sent them birthday and holiday cards with some money," Nancy said.

"Do you think the children got the cards?"

"Oh yes, they always sent me thank you notes, and soon we corresponded regularly."

"I ran into a lady at the general store, and she said after high school, Lorna went to live with an aunt," Carrie said.

Before continuing, Nancy poured more coffee and moved the cookie plate back in front of Charles. Charles knew there was no greater compliment to a baker than someone enjoying the fruits of their labor, and Nancy's baking was delicious. He selected another cookie.

"Lorna sent me a note that she wanted to leave the farm. She was a smart kid and wanted to continue her education," Nancy said. "Her grandfather thought she had enough schooling, and now it was time to work on the farm."

"I'm surprised her father and grandfather agreed she could live with you," Carrie said.

"I contacted Steven, not Edwin. He felt it would be good for Lorna to leave the farm. His father used her as an unpaid laborer for all the household chores. If she didn't get a job somewhere else, she would be trapped, like him," Nancy said. "He felt it was one way he could help her as a father."

Charles knew he needed to ask direct questions to learn more about Lorna and how to contact her. After a sip of coffee, he continued, "Did Lorna receive any financial support from her father or grandfather?"

"Steven had no money of his own. Steven sent her a few dollars when he could, but he never came to visit," Nancy said. "Her grandfather disowned her and later her brother after he left."

Charles caught Carrie's eye, and she nodded. Nancy's statement explained why the state foreclosed the farm. The kids couldn't save it because they had no claim on it. No wonder they were bitter.

"That didn't bother Lorna. She was a go-getter. She got a job in one of the local factories here in town, worked hard, and saved until she could attend community college at night," Nancy said as she replenished their coffee for the third time. "After two years, she won a scholarship to finish her degree at the university. She graduated with honors and then earned her master's degree."

"When did Junior or Brian come to live with you?" Charles asked.

"Lorna kept in touch with her brother, and he begged her to ask me if he could live with us," Nancy said. "Edwin was ill and no longer able to manage the farm. Steven and his son didn't get along, probably because Edwin instigated fights between father and son. Junior was starting seventh grade when he came to live with us."

"Junior stayed with you through high school," Charles said.

"My husband was a good influence on Brian. They were both mechanically inclined, and Brian wanted to concentrate on computers," Nancy said. "Unfortunately, my husband died the summer after Brian graduated from high school. Money was tight. We scraped together enough that Brian could take a few computer courses at the community college while he worked as a waiter in the local diner."

A tear started to roll down Nancy's face, and she quickly wiped it away.

"Why did Brian change his name?" Charles asked, trying to help Nancy refocus.

"Throughout his childhood, they called him Junior because his father had the same name. I imagine he wanted to get away from that moniker. He reversed his middle and last name from Steven Brian to Brian Steven."

"And then changed his last name to Amberson," Charles prodded.

"Like his sister, he wanted nothing to do with his grandfather's name. He chose Amberson as a thank you to me and my husband." There was a flow of more tears. "Sorry, I still miss my husband and the children not being here. But I try to stay busy."

Carrie waited and then asked, "Did you hear anything from Steven in the later years?"

"Steven surprised us by coming to my husband's funeral. He looked drained. The economy wasn't good, and the farm became more challenging to manage," Nancy said. "I heard he had no interest in running the farm and produced only enough crops to sustain a meager existence."

"Are you aware the state foreclosed on the farm?" Carrie asked.

"Yes. That's why I'm going to the town meeting to discuss how we can influence the farm's development with the new owner," Nancy said. "We're waiting for the settlement records to see who bought it."

"Maybe I can get you more information," Charles offered.

"That would be helpful," Nancy said.

"Do you keep in touch with the children?" Carrie asked, returning the subject to the children.

"The children are both involved with school activities. I don't see them in person except during the summer and holidays, but we always exchange emails," Nancy said. "They seem quite happy except for financial worries."

"They're so young. What kind of financial worries?" Charles asked.

Charles was getting a different picture of the children from Nancy—not two young people involved in a murder.

"She has student loans and is trying to help Brian with his college expenses."

"You said they are both involved in school activities," Carrie said.

"Brian is taking classes, and his sister works for the university," Nancy said. She held up the coffee pot, but the couple shook their heads.

"Is Brian's sister a teacher?" Charles asked.

"Not yet, but that's one of her goals. Right now, she works for one of the professors."

Carrie could barely ask the next question. "Do you know the name of the professor?"

"Her name is Smith," Nancy laughed. "It's only because the name is Smith that I remembered it. I don't remember her first name."

Charles almost dropped the cookie in his hand. He couldn't believe what he heard. Here was the answer to their search—the connection to the university. But Charles needed to ask one more question to be sure. "Did Lorna also change her name?"

"Lorna was Edwin's mother's name, but like her brother, she wanted nothing to do with her grandfather," Nancy said. "She took the name Penny from Ben Franklin's saying, 'Watch the pennies, and the dollars will take care of themselves.' She thought it might bring her luck with her finances. And Stevens was after her father."

The proverbial other shoe dropped for Charles. Penny Stevens was Brian's sister and possibly Gwen's murderer. Charles wanted to jump up and say thank you very much, but we need to go. Instead, he and Carrie politely remained as Nancy told more stories about the children and what a blessing they were.

"Brian always made me laugh with his stories," Nancy said. "Brian never ran away from the farm but would go to the barn and hide to escape his grandfather. He called it a boy cave, where he often slept out in the barn with the animals."

Nancy looked at the clock, "Oh, my time flies. I've got to get to my meeting in Allwin. I've enjoyed our time together. I hope you come back again."

Charles felt sadness hearing Nancy's last comment. Knowing the children's future, Nancy wouldn't welcome the couple back to her home.

Once in the car, returning to Allwin, Charles said, "I can't believe we've been so close to the answer all this time. I never believed that Brian had the guts to murder."

"But you think Penny could be the murderer?" Carrie asked.

"Penny has a stronger personality than Brian, as we witnessed with her desire or, should I say, demand to continue Gwen's work," Charles answered. "What do you think?"

"I don't know, but we need to figure out our next steps."

"I want to look at the farm again," Charles said.

"Why? What are you thinking?"

"Even though Henry has put a fence around the house, nothing is around the barn. Brian may have returned there to his boy cave."

Carrie said, "There's only one way to find out. Let's see if Brian returned to the barn to avoid capture."

39

"We better call Jenco and let him know what we've learned. He can send out a police alert to bring in Penny Stevens," Charles said as he instructed the car phone to dial Jenco's number.

"Detective Jenco, it's Carrie Faraday."

"What can I do for you?" Jenco asked in his crisp, unfriendly tone.

"It's more what we can do for you," Carrie said. "We tracked down Nancy Amberson. The aunt the Allwin grandchildren lived with for several years."

"And what did you discover?" Jenco's voice now revealed the slightest hint of interest.

"Edwin Allwin's granddaughter is Penny Stevens. She was the administrative assistant to Gwen Smith," Carrie reminded Jenco.

"I know who she is," Jenco answered curtly. "I'll get an alert to have her brought in for questioning, assuming she's not fleeing with Brian."

"One more thing. Mrs. Amberson said whenever Brian had a problem at home, he hid out in the family barn," Carrie said. "Since we're out this way, we'll stop at the Allwin farm on our way home."

"Stop playing detective! We don't need another murder," Jenco said. "McCall and I are on our way to Allwin and will check out the farm."

There was no response.

"Did you hear what I said?" Jenco raised his voice.

As Carrie lowered her voice to a whisper, Charles looked at her, wondering what his wife was doing.

"Mrs. Faraday, did you hear me!" Jenco demanded.

"I'm losing the signal. What did you say?" Carrie's voice faded to silence.

This time, Jenco shouted, but Carrie disconnected the call.

Charles glanced at Carrie. "I take it we're ignoring Jenco's order not to visit the farm."

"You got it. We know Brian no longer has a gun," Carrie said. "I would like to hear his story before Jenco arrests him."

"He could have bought another gun," Charles suggested.

"He could have, but I don't think Brian is dangerous. He's not the murderer," Carrie said. "He's scared and probably hiding in the same place where he found comfort as a child."

When they reached the driveway of the Allwin farm, Charles pulled the car off the bumpy gravel onto the grass verge.

"The grass should muffle the sound of our car approaching the barn."

"Good idea," Carrie said.

Charles parallel-parked the vehicle in front of the barn's double doors. "If Brian drove here, I'm sure he would have parked his car inside. Our car will block any escape attempt."

"In case you didn't know, barns have back doors to let cattle, tractors, and farmers enter from the field," Carrie said, patting him on the arm. "Overall, it's a good idea."

They entered through the barn's smaller side door. Parked inside was a small, blue compact car.

Carrie called out, "Brian, Brian, are you here? It's Carrie and Charles Faraday."

Charles waited but heard nothing.

"Brian, the police told us your gun had only blanks. You weren't planning on shooting anyone. Nothing serious has happened," Charles said. "Come out and let us help you."

They heard a scuffle above them and watched remnants of hay and dirt fall from the rafters. Brian descended the loft steps. He looked like he hadn't slept. His clothes were messy, and his hands and face were dirty.

"Brian, do you have water? Have you eaten?" Carrie asked, remembering the pit beef and rolls she bought at the general store.

"I've got water upstairs. I'm okay, but I can't go with you," Brian said. "I'm waiting for ... I mean, the police won't understand. It's better if I disappear."

"Brian, you're a young man. You don't want to be on the run the rest of your life," Carrie said. "Are you waiting for your sister, Penny?"

Brian showed surprise. "You finally figured out Penny is my sister. Good for you." Charles noticed he sounded unphased by this news but started to move towards his car. Charles changed the subject to focus Brian on something other than escaping in his car. "We met your Aunt Nancy this afternoon. She's a lovely person."

It worked. Brian stood still. "Yeah, she was one of the best things that ever happened to us."

"You were about to tell us what transpired with Gwen," Carrie said softly, trying to calm Brian.

"When Gwen began working for Hansen's grandmother, she had no idea that Penny and I were related or that we were Edwin Allwin's grandkids," Brian said. He sat on the bottom loft step, and his shoulders slumped as if he couldn't handle anything else. "Penny learned that Gwen found an inheritance for Rachel Pembroke. We hoped she had found something to help us financially."

"Why didn't you ask Gwen this question instead of sneaking around behind her back?" Carrie asked.

"Penny thought about it, but Gwen had gotten jumpy and protective of her work."

"Why?" Charles asked.

"She had trouble with a couple of students who received poor grades. In retaliation, they accused her of stealing their Tri-City research for her project and giving them bad grades," Brian said. "They sent her anonymous notes threatening her."

Charles recognized this incident might have given Brian the idea for the poison pen letters he convinced Hansen to send to his grandmother.

"What did you and your sister do?" Charles asked.

"We backed off. Penny started independently researching our family at the historical society," Brian said. "Our grandfather cut us off. Penny learned he died without a will, so our father inherited the farm as his nearest relative."

"Did your father also die without a will?" Charles asked.

"He did, and we were his only heirs. The farm should have been ours," Brian said, wringing his hands and not making eye contact. "When we tried to claim the farm, we learned Dad owed thousands in back taxes."

"Did you try to arrange a loan?" Carrie asked.

"That was the second problem. The farmland had increased in value, and the tax bill was enormous," Brian said. "Even if a bank would lend us the money to pay the taxes, we couldn't afford the monthly payments. My school intern job doesn't pay, and Penny's salary wasn't enough."

"No other relatives in Aunt Nancy's extended family who could have helped?" Carrie asked.

"No, and we couldn't ask Aunt Nancy. She's a wonderful woman who helped us after we left the farm but struggled financially after her husband died."

With his business background, Charles knew that sources would be available if Brian and Penny had asked for help. Henry Brighton might have helped the kids with the property had he known the situation. Would this have stopped Gwen's murder?

Brian looked up, "When I confronted you in Gwen's office, you said we could claim shares from the original building corporation. Is this true? Do you have proof of this because Penny didn't find anything?"

"A copy of a handwritten note was on Gwen's thumb drive," Charles said. "It referenced a meeting where Brighton and

Dorchester put shares in the Tri-City Building Corporation aside for any heirs of your grandfather," Charles said.

"And Henry Stanford confirmed they still have the shares in trust. You and your sister are entitled to these," Carrie said.

"Did my grandfather or father know about this?"

"Brighton, Dorchester, and the other board members designed an agreement so the shares couldn't go to your grandfather or father. If future heirs came forward and inquired about the corporation's formation, they would grant the shares," Charles said.

"Why give shares if they weren't going to tell anyone?" Brian asked.

"Because the corporation's new board wanted no further dealings with your grandfather," Charles said. "While they recognized your grandfather's work on forming Tri-City, he caused such a commotion demanding free shares they decided to bypass him. And that left your father out, too."

"That sounds like my grandfather," Brian said.

"It's not too late to help you and your sister," Carrie said. "Tell us what happened the night you murdered Gwen."

"I didn't kill her," Brian screeched as he jumped to his feet.

Charles heard a sound from outside the barn. Neither Brian nor Carrie showed signs they heard anything. Perhaps Jenco and McCall had arrived.

"Tell us about what happened the night Gwen died," Carrie asked, trying to calm Brian.

"We learned the farm was about to go up for sale, and time was running out for us. Penny tried to find out if Gwen knew anything about the Allwin family. Penny read first drafts of Gwen's work, so she tried to make it sound like she was curious about other details," Brian said. "But Gwen got all high and mighty about sharing her report before she gave it to Hansen's grandmother. She blocked Penny's access to any of her work." Brian started to pace between the loft steps and his car.

"Why did Penny confront Gwen at my book signing?" Carrie asked.

"Penny kept Gwen's calendar. Penny saw she planned to go to the book signing and talk with you about her research," Brian said. "My sister didn't understand why she would talk to you, a stranger, and not her."

While Carrie kept Brian engaged, Charles tried to figure out how to get Brian to give up before Jenco appeared. If Brian jumped in his car, Charles wasn't sure how Jenco would respond.

"What happened when your sister confronted Gwen in the garden?" Carrie asked.

"I'm not exactly sure. I mean, I don't know," Brian said, sounding vague.

Charles suspected Brian knew what had happened, but he wanted to protect his sister.

"According to my sister, during their discussion, Gwen got spooked and started waving a gun around," Brian said almost in a whisper, "Suddenly, the gun fired."

"How did you get involved?" Carrie asked.

"Penny called me. She didn't know what to do," Brian said. "We went back in the middle of the night and moved the body to the yard where they held the book signing. This way, when they discovered the body, there would be lots more suspects."

Charles looked at Carrie. They finally knew what happened. Brian continued pacing back and forth.

"Penny didn't plan to kill Gwen. It was an accident," Brian said. He exhaled. "The police shouldn't charge her with murder. It's not fair."

Charles was so intent on listening to Brian and watching his movements that he didn't hear the barn door swing open.

"I got here just in time," said Penny, pointing a gun at the couple.

40

Carrie spun to face Penny. "We were wondering when Brian's sister would arrive?"

Penny looked surprised but recovered quickly. "You finally figured out who I am. Then, we better make this encounter brief. We have places to go," waving the gun at the couple.

"Oh, really, not another gun," Charles said.

"Why so many guns? Gwen had a gun, your brother had a gun, and now you have a gun," Carrie said, trying to sound calm.

"I'm surprised you two don't have a gun, considering how you get involved in everyone's business," Penny said. "You generate enough mayhem to need one."

"We have a gun, but we don't carry it around to point at people," Charles said firmly. "They have a nasty habit of going off, like when Brian got poked in the back with an umbrella."

Carrie saw Brian's reaction as he heard for the first time an umbrella and not another gun had ended the confrontation in Gwen's office.

"What about you, Penny? What happened between you and Gwen?" Charles asked. "Did the gun accidentally discharge? We know Gwen's gun was the murder weapon."

For a moment, Carrie caught a change in Penny's face as Penny tried to decide what to say next.

"I'm not discussing anything else with you. Brian, get your things," Penny said. "We're getting out of here."

"You won't get far," Carrie said.

"We'll get farther than you two. I've flattened your tires," Penny said. "Which reminds me, I'll take your phones." She held out her non-gun hand, confiscated the devices, and placed them on the loft steps next to her brother

Carrie didn't bother to remind Penny that their car also had phone capability.

"You can't keep running," Carrie said. "You have roots here. What about Aunt Nancy? She'll be devastated to learn what's happened and that you're on the run."

"We don't have a choice. No one will believe what happened," Penny said.

"Try us," Charles said. "Let us see if we can help you so you don't ruin your lives. What happened that night you confronted Gwen in the garden?"

"I admit I was upset, but I didn't go to the book signing to kill her," Penny raised her voice. "As you said, it was Gwen's gun that killed her."

"Why did you come to the book signing?" Carrie asked softly, trying to limit Penny's agitation.

"I told them you kept Gwen's calendar and planned on talking to Mrs. Faraday about the book," Brian said.

"Keep your mouth shut. Why would you tell these two any-thing?" Penny stared at Brian, "I came to the book signing to find out what she intended to tell you since she wouldn't talk to me."

"Why did talking to me bother you?" Carrie asked. "She planned on writing a book. I assumed she wanted to talk with someone who had published. Did you know Emily Hopkins gave Gwen my name?"

"I didn't know she got your name from Emily. As her assistant, I helped her with some of the research, but she kept other information from me," Penny said. "I wanted to know why."

Carrie started moving away from Charles, planning to split Penny's focus between them.

"No, you don't. Stand next to your husband," Penny said.

Carrie returned next to Charles as Penny waved the gun to herd her back into position.

"Did Gwen know you were an Allwin descendant?" Charles asked.

"Not at that time. Instead, I asked Gwen why she limited my access to her research," Penny said. "That's when I learned she wanted to turn the materials into a book."

Carrie nodded, but she didn't understand Gwen's reaction. Discussing research with Penny wouldn't limit her ability to publish unless...

"Could Gwen have thought you were trying to take the infor-mation and publish something before she finished her book?"

"I never thought of that. Gwen said she had information that would impact the city's founders and their families," Penny said. "After she said that, I wanted to know if there might be some financial help for us."

"What happened next?" Carrie asked.

"As Brian said, I saw the book signing on her calendar and decided to go. I parked on the side street by the garden," Penny said. "Gwen saw me enter through the gate and rushed to stop me."

"As I gave my talk in Joanne's living room, I could see a woman having an animated conversation with someone," Carrie said. "Later, I learned the woman was Gwen. I couldn't see you."

"Maybe Gwen became aware you saw us. She suggested we talk, but not in the garden," Penny said. "We saw a pathway and an open field behind the house. We agreed to meet along the path in ten minutes."

"Carrie and Joanne Quinn discovered the spot on the path behind the neighbor's house where you met," Charles said. "How did the murder take place?"

Penny shivered upon hearing the word murder but continued. "Gwen was on the path when I arrived. She started screaming at me to stop bothering her," Penny said. "Then she pulled out the gun."

Based on the people who knew her, Gwen going into a rage seemed out of character to Carrie. On the other hand, Gwen had bought and learned how to use a gun. Carrie looked at Brian, who said nothing but sat quietly while his sister talked.

"Gwen told me this was an important book for Tri-City, and she wasn't sharing her research until she published it," Penny said. "I admitted I was the Allwin descendant who sent her the letter, and all I wanted was to see if there was any financial help for me. That calmed her down."

Penny kept the gun pointed at the couple but relaxed a little as she leaned against the loft steps next to Brian. Carrie felt having her retell the story helped calm the situation.

Penny continued, "Gwen said there might be good news for me, but first, she needed to talk with Mrs. Brighton-Stanton about publishing."

"This all sounds friendly. How did Gwen get shot?" Carrie pushed to hear the whole story before Jenco arrived.

"It wasn't murder. When Gwen realized I wasn't a threat, she lowered her gun," Penny said. "Then she turned suddenly towards the hedge, and I realized it was an opportunity to take her gun away. We struggled for the gun, and then she slipped on the wet grass. The next thing I knew, we both fell and then the gun fired. It happened so quickly."

Penny's explanation of what happened seemed reasonable to Carrie. Carrie assumed Gwen had slipped when she turned to the hedge to retrieve her phone.

"I checked her pulse. Nothing. One minute, we're talking. The next minute, she's dead."

"Why didn't you get help? It was an accident," Charles said.

"I panicked. I had tried to take the gun away, so who would believe me? And I didn't know where the people were in the house we stood behind," Penny said, reliving the event.

"The people in the house were away. That's why they didn't respond to the gunshot," Carrie added.

Penny nodded. "I didn't know that. I only knew I needed to get away and have time to think at that moment."

"I take it you called Brian to help you move the body," Charles said.

"I couldn't leave Gwen lying on the ground. I was afraid no one would find her for days," Penny said. "That's where I made another mistake. I involved my brother."

Carrie saw a kinder Penny who didn't want to leave the body isolated on a path, not a murderer. Penny placed her hand on Brian's shoulder.

"Brian and I returned and moved the body back to the garden. If the body were in the yard of the party, the police would assume somebody from the book signing killed her," Penny said. "I wasn't on the guest list."

Carrie noticed a slight movement over Penny's shoulder and saw what she thought might be McCall or Jenco. With Penny still holding that gun, she hoped Jenco wouldn't come barreling through the front door.

"I should have handled this alone," Penny said, looking at her brother. "He's not involved. I need to get him away from all this."

Brian came to life. "It's okay, Sis, I'm here for you. Just because you're my big sister doesn't mean I can't help. We're in this together and will come up with a solution."

"The solution is to turn yourself over to the police. Based on what you said, this wasn't a premeditated murder," Charles said. "I'll pay for a good lawyer for you and Brian."

Penny dropped her hand at Charles's suggestion for help and pointed the gun toward the floor instead of the couple. Carrie momentarily entertained trying to take the gun away but decided that would be foolish with Jenco and McCall nearby. She didn't want another accidental shot that might kill one of them.

"My husband is correct. Penny, you're a bright woman. You must realize this is over," Carrie said. "We'll support what you told us."

Carrie wanted Penny to drop the gun before Jenco made his move. Unfortunately, that didn't happen. Jenco jumped out from behind one of the animal pens with his gun focused on the kids.

In a booming voice, Jenco said, "Drop the gun! We've got you covered."

Once Jenco spoke, McCall burst through the main barn door.

"Penny, don't make the situation any worse. Lay the gun on the ground," Charles said.

"Don't shoot!" Penny shouted. "I'm putting the gun down. It's not loaded."

Carrie had mixed emotions when she realized they experienced this ordeal with a weapon that wasn't loaded. But it was worth it because they finally had the entire story and a solution to the case.

Exhausted by the ordeal, Brian didn't move from the loft step. McCall rushed forward and placed him in handcuffs. Jenco cuffed Penny. Within moments, other officers escorted the brother and sister to the waiting patrol cars.

Penny yelled, "Charles, if your offer is still available, we could use a lawyer."

"I'll take care of it," Charles said.

Jenco faced the couple. "I asked you not to come to the farm because we would handle the situation." Anger showed in his voice.

"You should be glad we came," Carrie said. "You heard the confession that it was an accident. We were able to calm Penny and Brian, so they gave up without a further incident."

"Let's not jump to any conclusions. The prosecutor will decide the charges after we book the two of them," Jenco said. "Regardless, I need you to come to the station and make a statement."

Carrie retrieved their phones from the loft step where Penny placed them. She tapped her phone and shut off the record button.

"It will take some time to deal with your flat tires," Jenco said, almost pleased.

"Do you want me to call a tow truck?" McCall asked, sounding concerned.

"Thanks, but not necessary. I have a gadget in the car to inflate the tires. It won't take long," Charles said. "Then we'll drop by the station."

"Whatever," Jenco said. He seemed disappointed the couple wouldn't have to call a tow truck as he got in the car with McCall. They left Charles and Carrie with deflated tires.

"While I'm fixing the tires, why don't you call Hugh Simpson?" Charles asked. "Tell him the situation and see if he can get to the police station and help the kids."

"Good idea," Carrie said. "Simpson did a wonderful job as my lawyer defending me when Jenco charged me with Todd Barrington's murder."

41

The smell of roasted chickens filled the private dining room at the Train Stop. Charles found himself licking his lips in anticipation of a delicious dinner.

Gloria Smith had gathered the group together to thank the people who had helped solve her sister's death. While she no longer considered it a murder, she looked to this gathering to bring closure to the sad event.

Charles, Betty Canton, and Emily Hopkins wandered the room, looking at pictures of the early days of train travel in the Tri-City area. The photographs and paintings showed locomotives, the interiors of private cars, and the workers who kept the trains running. Gloria dedicated one section to her grandparents and the restaurant's early days. Charles thought about recent events and how history affected what happened.

Cindy, Hansen, and Rachel were in a corner talking about writing. Carrie was chatting with Henry Stanford and Henrietta.

"Okay, folks, we should take our places since we're about ready to serve the food," Gloria announced.

Carrie had helped Gloria put name tags on the long dinner table to make for friendly partners for the meal. Mrs. Brighton-Stanford sat between Emily and Betty at one end of the table. Rachel, Cindy, and Hansen sat at the opposite end. Gloria, Henry, Charles, and Carrie shared the middle of the table.

The guests took their seats while the chef brought in the roasted chickens and placed them on a sideboard to rest before cutting.

"Henry, I read a newspaper article in which you announced the development plans for Allwin. How did it go?" Charles asked.

"We met with the Allwin Community Association and any residents who wanted to attend. The community seemed pleased to have something positive happen with all that land," Henry said. "Most were happy we weren't building tract housing that would overcrowd the schools and cause other expansion problems."

"One of the residents told me they wanted something to revive the community," Carrie said. "The hotel will attract tourists and provide jobs that might give the young people a reason to stay in Allwin."

"Did you meet Pops Phillips?" Charles asked.

"I did. Pops has a lot of good ideas. We added him to our governing board to represent the businesses and find ways to work together to improve tourism," Henry said.

Gloria asked Hansen, "Are you planning on working at the new facility and helping your father?"

"Maybe, once construction starts in the fall. In the meantime, I have an internship at Faraday Press for the summer," Hansen said, nodding to Charles.

"Gloria, I love all the pictures on the wall depicting the history of the trains. There might be a story about the role trains played in Tri-City's development," Charles said.

"That's a great idea for a story," Hansen said.

"In that case, why don't you work on it? Start the research, and I'll assign an editor to work with you," Charles said.

In disbelief, Hansen looked at Charles and said, "You'll let me work on a story?"

"I'm not hiring you to run errands for others and get coffee for me. It'll be a sacrifice since I'll have to get my own coffee," Charles laughed.

Hansen screwed up his face at the thought of spending his summer running errands and getting coffee.

"He's kidding, Hansen. He always gets his coffee. Nobody, including me, fixes it how he likes it," Carrie said.

"I'll be glad to give background on the pictures," Gloria offered. "We can make copies of any of the photos you want to use."

"Speaking of writing. Rachel, I saw you had another short story published," Carrie said.

"I got writer's block working on my novel. I took some time and wrote a short story," Rachel said. "It worked. I got back on track with my novel and got paid for a published short story."

"Way to go," Hansen said in response to Rachel's news.

Charles watched and listened as the diners enjoyed each other's company. Life had returned to normal or, as he knew, a new normal after losing someone close. It was also apparent the guests avoided the elephant in the room that brought them to this event. Gloria must have sensed the same thing as she tapped on a glass and brought the room to attention.

"Before we enjoy this meal, I have an announcement. I've been clearing out my sister's things. One of the last places I checked was Gwen's locker, which she had at the restaurant," Gloria said as she held up a thick portfolio. "In the locker, I found her computer, the missing research, and the beginnings of a book. I wanted to turn this over to you, Henrietta."

"Henrietta, what will you do with these new documents from Gwen?" Betty asked

"Rachel and Hansen have volunteered to prepare all of Gwen's materials for publication. Charles said he would help us publish the final piece under Gwen's name," Henrietta said. "Now they'll have Gwen's book draft to guide them in how she wanted it prepared."

"Thank you for publishing under Gwen's name, but I want Hansen and Rachel listed as editors for their effort," Gloria said.

"I can't tell you how proud I am that these two young people are going to work together to finish the history," Henrietta said.

The chef raised his hand to get Gloria's attention.

"My chef indicates the food is ready, but I wanted to take a moment and say a few words. A series of unfortunate incidents caused my sister's death at the book signing." Gloria paused to control her emotions. "I want to thank each of you, especially the Faradays, for your dedication to finding the solution." Gloria said a short prayer and then said, "I hope you enjoy the meal and the company of good friends."

The group focused eagerly as the chef quartered the chickens, and the wait staff placed family-style bowls of vegetables and baskets of warm biscuits on the table. Charles couldn't wait to add honey and butter to the hot homemade biscuits.

Betty leaned over to Charles and quietly said, "I hear there won't be a trial."

"That's correct. On the advice of Hugh Simpson, her lawyer, Penny agreed to plead guilty to involuntary manslaughter and tampering with evidence at a crime scene," Charles responded.

"Will she go to jail?" Emily asked.

"The courts haven't scheduled sentencing, so we'll have to wait and see. I'm sure the judge will consider that she has no prior record," Carrie said.

"Based on the evidence, Penny gave an accurate account of how the gun discharged," Charles said. "It obviously was an accident."

"I still can't believe Gwen bought a gun," Emily said. "I don't know why she thought she needed a weapon to protect herself and her research," Emily said.

"As you told us, Emily, several students gave Gwen a hard time about her research and receiving bad grades," Carrie said. "They threatened her with anonymous notes. Those letters probably made Gwen feel her life was in danger."

Henrietta looked at Hansen, but he gave a shake of his head. It verified for Charles that Hansen had nothing to do with these threats.

"Another unfortunate incident," Betty added.

"You probably want to know my thoughts on punishment for Penny," Gloria said. "I'm satisfied with knowing what happened to Gwen. I have no desire to see Penny spend time in jail."

"What's going to happen to Brian?" Hansen asked.

"In her confession, Penny stated Brian had nothing to do with the mur…" Charles caught himself and changed the word 'murder' to death."

"What about the break-in at Gwen's condo, my office, and your home?" Henry asked.

"Penny said she did it all," Carrie said.

Charles saw Cindy give Hansen a poke. Like Charles, they knew Brian, not Penny, had the security system background and was at Henrietta's home and Henry's office.

"We're not pressing charges for our break-in," Charles said.

"We can do the same since we have no evidence of anything stolen," Henrietta said, looking at her son. He nodded.

"Such a sad situation. One life lost and two young people with their lives ruined," Betty said.

"What will happen to the Allwin money from the corporation shares? It seemed to be the root of all the problems," Emily said.

"That doesn't change. The money is in trust for Brian and Penny," Henry said. "Hugh Simpson has already contacted me about working out payments for the kids."

"That's the saddest part of all this. If Brian had told me the truth, I would have asked Dad to help him. Maybe we would have had a different outcome," Hansen said.

"None of us can change the past," Henrietta said. We can only learn from history and go forward, hoping to do better."

Charles agreed, recognizing the role history played in current events. Charles also felt satisfied that he and Carrie solved another case. Perhaps this would be the last time they needed to use their detective skills, but somehow, he doubted it.

BIO

Millie Mack is a pseudonym for the author who writes the Faraday Murder Series. She enjoys everything mysterious—stories, books, and videos. Even her cats can be very mysterious. Aside from writing the Faraday Murder Series featuring amateur sleuths Carrie and Charles Faraday, Millie is working on a new mystery series.

In addition to her mystery books, Millie also writes a blog all about mysteries at www.darkandstormynights.com. The blog features mystery authors, detectives, and techniques. And to challenge the reader's mystery knowledge, there is an assortment of word search and crossword puzzles.

Dear reader,
If you enjoyed this book, please consider
placing a review on Amazon.com or
Goodreads.com.

Thank You,
Millie